T0051074

CLAIMING
ALEXIS

DISCOVER OTHER TITLES BY SUSAN STOKER

This is a work of fiction. Names, characters, organizations, places, events, and incidents are either products of the author's imagination or are used fictitiously.

Text copyright © 2017 Susan Stoker
All rights reserved.

No part of this book may be reproduced, or stored in a retrieval system, or transmitted in any form or by any means electronic, mechanical, or by photocopying, recording, or otherwise, without express written permission of the publisher.

Published by Montlake Romance, Seattle

www.apub.com

Amazon, the Amazon logo, and Montlake Romance are trademarks of Amazon.com, Inc., or its affiliates.

ISBN-13: 9781477848630
ISBN-10: 1477848630

Cover design by Eileen Carey

Printed in the United States of America

CLAIMING ALEXIS

ACE SECURITY

BOOK 2

Susan Stoker

Beyond Reality Series

Outback Hearts

Flaming Hearts

Frozen Hearts

Stand-Alone Novels

The Guardian Mist

Writing as Annie George

Stepbrother Virgin (erotic novella)

SEAL of Protection Series

Chapter One

"So, what's your deal?"

Alexis Grant looked straight ahead into the darkness broken only by the bright headlights of the black Mustang as she and Blake barreled down the interstate toward Colorado Springs. They were going to the El Paso County Courthouse to provide security for a woman who was going through a nasty divorce and was scared of what her husband might to do her. Alexis brought the still-steaming cup of coffee up to her face, inhaling the sweet ambrosia, then sipped, buying herself some time before trying to answer the question.

"I mean, you've been working for Ace Security for almost three months, and I can't figure you out."

"What's there to figure out?" Alexis mumbled, closing her eyes and leaning back against the headrest.

"Can I be blunt?"

At the question, Alexis opened her eyes and turned to look at Blake Anderson, who was one of three brothers who ran Ace Security. She'd met him earlier that year when her brother, Bradford, had somehow found himself in the middle of an insane blackmail plot that involved two prominent members of the community, Walter and Margaret Mason, and some local gangbangers. Luckily, the plot had failed, and the Masons were now behind bars. Their daughter, Grace, had married the eldest Anderson brother, Logan, and was now pregnant with twins.

The triplets, Logan, Blake, and Nathan, had come back to Castle Rock to start a security company that specialized in helping victims of abuse. Alexis had volunteered to work with them to help find information that could be used against the Masons so their blackmail plot would fail and her family would be safe.

She never would've thought in a million years that she'd take one look at a man and fall head over heels in love with him, but that's exactly what happened the first time she laid her eyes on Blake. He was similar in looks to his brothers, but for her, at least, he stood head and shoulders above them.

He was deeply tanned, and the veins in his arms were well defined. Not bulging like they were going to burst forth from his skin, but they showcased the definition of his muscles and tendons. His arms in motion were the most amazing things she'd ever seen. Once he had helped Grace stand from her chair, causing the muscles in his arms to contract, and Alexis had nearly swooned. The man could've had a beer belly and a huge ass and she wouldn't have cared . . . his arms more than made up for any other flaw he might have. But so far she hadn't really seen any flaws that couldn't be overlooked.

He was a bit over six feet tall, with sandy-brown hair that he kept cut short and a strong jawline. His broad shoulders tapered down to a thin waist and well-developed thighs, making his body sleek and sexy like an Olympic swimmer's. Alexis had hoped what "they" said about the size of a man's feet was true, because Blake had really large . . . shoes.

She'd tried to tell herself there was no way she was in love with the man, but it was no use. The more time she spent around Blake, the harder she fell. Not only was he extremely attractive; he was a good brother, compassionate to the men and women they helped, and so excited to be an uncle that Alexis's ovaries almost exploded whenever she imagined him holding an infant against his shoulder. She definitely had it bad.

Her attraction to, and love for, Blake Anderson was completely inappropriate, irrational, and insane, given her background with men, but it was what it was.

And he had no idea. Not even an inkling, and it killed.

Killed.

Blake cleared his throat. "Lex?"

God. She loved the nickname he'd given her. She'd never had one before . . . other than "the rich chick," which was totally not the same thing at all, so it didn't count. "Yeah?" she mumbled distractedly, still thinking about Blake's arm flexing as if holding a baby, and what his arm muscles might look like if he was propped up next to her in bed.

He smiled, his teeth flashing white in the light from the dashboard. "It takes you forever to wake up."

Alexis tried to pretend she wasn't drooling over him. "It's four thirty in the morning, Blake. No normal person is up this early. Not to mention, you only gave me ten minutes of silence before you started yammering at me."

His grin widened, and his right hand punched her lightly in the shoulder in a "you're a good buddy" kind of gesture, which totally made her want to cry.

"If you're serious about doing this kind of thing for a living, you'd better get used to early mornings and late nights," Blake told her, smiling as if she'd said something hilarious rather than stating what most normal people would agree with wholeheartedly.

"Whatever." Alexis buried her head into the travel mug once again, inhaling the scent of vanilla. Blake had graciously had the drink waiting for her when he'd picked her up that morning. It was one more thing that killed her: that out of all the people in her life, he was the only one, other than the barista at the coffee bar down the street from her apartment, who could make her coffee exactly the way she liked it.

"So, can I?"

"Can you what?" Alexis asked, lost.

"Be blunt."

Oh yeah. He *had* asked that. "Sure. Knock yourself out." She should've braced, but she hadn't had enough caffeine yet and was still half-asleep.

"You're what . . . twenty-four?"

"Five," she corrected.

"Right. You're twenty-five, and from what you've said, you've had at least six jobs since you graduated. You're a hard worker. I haven't had to ask you to do anything twice since you've been working with Ace Security. You don't bitch about the work, even when it's boring, and you've had some really good ideas about advertising that Grace has already begun to implement on the website. You're old enough to have figured out what you want to do as a career and stop flitting from one job to another. Don't get me wrong, I'm happy to have you working for Ace Security, but I'm concerned that one day you're going to decide you don't want to do this job either, and you'll leave."

Ouch. She had no idea what she wanted to do with the rest of her life. Most everyone she knew had that figured out by the time they graduated from college. But not her. The disappointment that coursed through her was almost paralyzing. The fact that Blake thought she was bumming around, not starting on a career as most other people her age had, and was just killing time working for his company was as painful as if he'd told her she was hideously ugly and a loser.

Alexis took a deep breath and blinked back the tears that had sprung to her eyes. Glad for the darkness, she turned her head to look out her window. Unfortunately, all she saw was her reflection, as it was too dark to see the passing countryside.

She cleared her throat before she spoke, making sure that there would be no evidence of her tears in her voice. "Thanks for the first part. As for the jobs . . ." She paused to shrug. "I just haven't found anything to keep me interested for more than six months. But I promise not to just up and leave. I'll give you plenty of notice, if it comes to that."

"What'd you major in?"

"General studies."

At Blake's snort, Alexis turned to look at him. She could do so now that she'd gotten her stupid tears under control. "What?"

"General studies? What the hell kind of degree is that?"

Now she was pissed. "The kind that took me five and a half years to get because I kept changing my major. I couldn't decide what I wanted to do, and a counselor suggested general studies because otherwise I was going to be in school for another two years."

Alexis took another sip of her coffee and mumbled into it, "It doesn't matter anyway. All of the jobs I've had have only required a degree . . . not a specific major." She turned and asked Blake, "What's *your* degree in?"

"Got an associate's in computer science. Used tuition assistance from the army to get it while I was in."

"Have you ever wanted to get your four-year degree?"

Blake shrugged, shook his head, and kept his eyes on the road. "Not really. I learned the basics of programming, software design, systems, data management, and artificial intelligence in community college, and anything else I've needed since then I've learned from YouTube and other more nefarious sources on the net."

"Nefarious sources?" Alexis asked, leaning forward in her seat eagerly. She loved the sound of that.

He chuckled at her enthusiasm. "Yup. And no, I'm not going to share. Were the jobs you had boring? Is that why they didn't work out?"

Alexis reached over and put her travel mug in the cup holder. She ticked off each job on her fingers as she tried to explain. "My first job was the front desk receptionist at my parents' company. That got old really fast. I didn't report to them, but they still knew everything that I did. I love them, but that was a bit too much family time for me. I went from there to working as a waitress in a chain restaurant. I guess I didn't realize just how many assholes go out to eat."

She ignored Blake's choked laugh and went on. "I didn't mind being on my feet all day. I was friendly, and fast, but most of the time I only got, like, a ten percent tip. It was ridiculous. I quit the day I had a table with twenty people. We were down a waitress that day, and the asshole in charge of the group asked to see the manager and proceeded to bitch about the mandatory twenty percent tip that had been added to the bill. The manager, who, by the way, I'd refused to sleep with, was pissed at me, took off the tip, and let the guy put his own in. Do you know how much he gave me? And keep in mind there were three kids in the group, and they'd been there for three hours, and their bill came to over two hundred dollars."

"Uh—"

Alexis didn't give Blake time to guess before going on with her story. "Ten measly bucks. *Ten*. That's it. Oh, and he had the nerve to leave his phone number on the bill with the words 'Call me, baby' scribbled next to it. The guy was there with his wife and three kids. I'd had enough, so I quit."

"Can't blame you," Blake noted dryly. "That's taking asshole to a new level."

"Right? Anyway, after that I tried factory work. Wasn't for me. Then I thought maybe I could work in sales. So I became a pharmaceutical rep. The doctors I had to deal with were almost as bad as my boss at the restaurant . . . hitting on me, patting me on the head, and basically telling me they'd buy my drugs if I went out with them. Gross."

"Jesus, Lex," Blake bit out.

Alexis tried to ignore the shivers that raced up her spine from his tone. She liked his commiserating with her a bit too much. He almost sounded protective and pissed off for her. She hurried to finish up her sad employment history. "Then when I met you guys, I was working at the post office near my apartment."

"Working for the government is good," Blake noted. "I should know. You get benefits and the work is steady. Most people end up retiring from those kinds of jobs."

Alexis picked up her coffee again and took a long swallow. "Yeah. But it was boring."

"It was boring," Blake said in a tone Alexis couldn't interpret.

"Yeah, Blake, boring. Maybe if I got to deliver mail, it wouldn't have been so bad. I'd have been outside and seen people. But I had to sit in the back of the building, where there weren't any windows, and run the sorting machines. Then I had to distribute the mail into the boxes. It was horrible. Seriously. I was bored out of my skull. There's no way I could do that for the rest of my life."

"I guess I could see how it wouldn't be the most exciting job in the world. But it's a job, Lex. It's more than a lot of people have. Although I guess your family isn't exactly hurting for money. You can afford to try different things out to see what you want to do."

"Don't judge me," Alexis said harshly, glaring at him. She'd been half waiting for this subject to come up since she'd started working for Ace Security. "And don't you *ever* throw my family's money in my face again. You have no right to judge me. None. Yeah, I drive a Mercedes and have a kick-ass apartment, but you have no idea what it's like to be looked at as a money sign instead of a person with feelings, goals, and desires. From the moment my parents made their first multi-million-dollar deal, people have looked at and treated me differently. I *hate* that. I'm the same person I was before they made their money, but no one seems to see that, or care. Besides, it's not *my* money, it's my parents'."

"You're right, I'm sorry," Blake apologized immediately. His hand crossed the center console and rested on her thigh. Its weight heavy and comforting. "I was out of line and didn't mean to piss you off."

"It's fine," Alexis mumbled, looking down at the large hand covering her leg. Alexis could feel her skin tingling under the weight of his calloused hand. She wished she was wearing shorts rather than jeans; she wanted to feel his hand on her bare skin almost more than she wanted coffee in the mornings.

Her eyes roamed up from his hand to his forearm. The one she'd do anything to be able to snuggle up to at night, holding it between her breasts as they spooned. Without thought, Alexis's legs shifted apart, as if giving him room to slide his hand between her legs. The second she moved, he pulled his hand away and rested it back on the steering wheel. She mentally shook her head at herself; her attraction to him was hopeless. He was never going to see her as anything other than one of his employees. She was pathetic, wanting something she was never going to have.

Sometimes she felt like she was eight years old and desperate for everyone around her to like her . . . to be her friend. But she'd learned to hide that part of her deep inside. To outwardly portray herself as tough and gung ho about everything she did. Most people didn't seem to want to dig below her surface and get to the woman she really was rather than what she showed to the world.

Alexis wanted to get the conversation over with. "For the first time in my life, I enjoy what I'm doing here at Ace Security. Every day is different, and I feel like I'm making a difference."

"You're doing a good job, Lex," Blake said, the approval echoing loud and clear in the small cab of the car.

"Thank you for giving me a chance." Alexis was more than grateful for Blake and his brothers. They didn't have to give her a job, but she'd worked her butt off to be useful to them, and she'd finally gotten to the point where she thought she was actually pulling her own weight. A lot of times the technical aspects of the job went over her head, but she was getting really good at digging into social media and finding information on clients. Digital footprints were way vaster than most people knew or understood.

"So . . . no boyfriend?" Blake asked in a tone that he might've used to order a meal at a drive-through fast-food place. As if he couldn't care less what her answer might be.

Alexis could feel the coffee she'd drunk that morning threaten to come back up. After he'd touched her, she'd thought that maybe Blake was softening toward her. That *maybe* she had a chance to catch the gorgeous man's eye. Obviously, she was an idiot.

"Nope," Alexis said, exaggerating the last *p* in the word, trying to be funny. "Not at the moment. I've had my share, but no one's appealed in a while." It was a little white lie. She hadn't had that many boyfriends, but *he* didn't need to know that.

"Hmmm," Blake responded, keeping his eyes on the road.

What the hell did that mean? Alexis had no idea. Was he surprised because he thought she was good-looking? Did he think she simply wasn't interesting enough to keep the attention of a guy long-term? She had no idea. Just when she thought she would go insane trying to figure out what he was thinking, or burst into tears, Blake spoke up again.

"You're getting your sea legs."

Um what?

"What? My sea legs?"

"Yeah. You're like a new sailor trying to get used to walking on board a ship on the open ocean. At first it's hard to walk normally, but after a while, it gets easier and easier. When you get more comfortable in the job, and when you truly settle into doing something you enjoy, you'll be receptive to opening yourself up to dating again." He smiled over at her, the light in the morning sky just beginning to illuminate the world, including the inside of the car where they sat. "It's smart not to rush into a relationship right out of college. Good for you for not falling in love at first sight with the first guy to show you some attention. When the time is right, you'll find someone who is perfect for you."

Alexis bit her lip and turned her head to look out the side window again to hide the tears she couldn't hold back. If only he knew. She swallowed hard and mumbled, "I'm sure I will."

And she was sure. Because she'd already found him. It *was* love at first sight, but obviously only one-sided. Blake saw her as nothing more than a flighty college graduate who couldn't decide what she wanted to do with her life. There was no way she could stick around Ace Security and not be with Blake Anderson. She might be a virgin, but Alexis knew down to the marrow of her bones that Blake Anderson was the man who was meant for her.

But there was no way she'd be able to stand him dating, kissing, and possibly marrying another woman right under her nose. Her heart wouldn't be able to take it. She'd finish the job she started when her brother had been kidnapped, but after she gathered as much information as she could about the Inca Boyz gang and turned it over to the Denver Gang Task Force, she was going to forget about Ace Security and Blake Anderson and start over somewhere new.

Chapter Two

"So . . . want to stop and get some lunch?" Blake asked Alexis as he pulled away from the courthouse. It was eleven thirty, and the job had gone off with no issues. Not that he thought there would be any. The client's ex-husband hadn't showed up at the courthouse to make trouble for their client. Alexis's job was to stay near the entrance and notify Blake, via two-way radio, if he appeared. He hadn't, and they'd been able to leave Colorado Springs before noon.

He'd never thought hiring Alexis would work out. In fact, he'd been extremely reluctant to work with her. He was almost ashamed to admit it, but the fact that she was rich played a big part in his reticence. After seeing how Grace's very wealthy parents conducted themselves, and having more than his share of run-ins with women who had money, he hadn't wanted anything to do with someone who he assumed was probably spoiled rotten and used to getting her way. But Alexis had surprised him. She was down-to-earth and easy to be around. Most of the time he completely forgot she and her family had more money than he'd ever see in a lifetime.

Not only that, but she was actually an excellent employee. Willing to do whatever was asked of her without complaint. And, as a bonus, many times female clients were more comfortable with her than with him or either of his brothers. Lex was friendly and had a way of making their clients relax that he and his brothers weren't always able to do.

Some of it had to do with the fact that most of their clients were women who had been abused by men, but most of it was simply Lex.

When she first started working for Ace Security, Blake had thought she'd get bored within a week. He knew her work history, and the security business wasn't exactly glamorous. It was a lot of observation, research, and waiting around and watching for trouble. But Alexis had taken to it like a duck took to water.

He'd never spent as much time with a woman as he had with Alexis Grant. Most of the time she was quiet—so quiet that some days he forgot she was working in the office across from him. She didn't nag or bitch when things didn't go her way. She never threw her money in his face or flaunted it.

But she was also funny. She had a lightning-quick wit and wasn't afraid to stand up for herself or those around her. She tried to portray herself as an experienced woman who'd seen and done just about everything, but there were times when it just didn't ring true . . . and it was those times that fascinated and intrigued Blake the most. Made him want to needle her a bit more and get under the shield she seemed to keep up to hide from the world. In a lot of ways, she was a complete mystery, and lately he'd found himself more and more interested in Alexis Grant.

His conversation with her that morning had only piqued his interest. She'd tried to hide how hurt she was when he'd basically accused her of being nothing more than an airhead rich bitch, but he saw something different in her very expressive face that had been reflected in the window. He hadn't exactly meant for his words to sound the way they had, but her reaction proved that she wasn't a rich chick flitting around from job to job, but rather that she was still searching for something that fed the passion she obviously had inside her.

When he thought about how her former bosses and customers had hit on her, it made his blood boil. Yes, she'd had five or so jobs since she'd graduated, but he admired her for not putting up with any bullshit. Alexis Grant would never be anyone's doormat.

"I don't know," Alexis hedged. "Eating might take a while."

"Come on, you have to be hungry. We've been up for hours, and all you've had was that cup of coffee I brought you."

"It's not like I *need* to eat—I'm certainly not wasting away—but fine. Only if I pay."

Blake ignored the crack about her weight, not happy with Lex's perception of her curvy body. It seemed perfect to him, but he knew nothing he could say would sway her thinking. Like most women, her view of herself was skewed by the media's representation of what was "beautiful," and it would most likely take more than words to . . . but he wasn't going there. At least not yet. If nothing else, Blake knew he had to move slowly around the skittish woman. He had no idea what her experiences were with men, but she didn't exactly come off as experienced, no matter how hard she tried. "You are not paying," he told her firmly. "We've been over this. It's business." He thought he saw her flinch, but she quickly wiped any stray emotion off her face and shrugged.

"Business. Right. Then wherever you want to stop is fine."

Blake hated when her voice got flat. As if she couldn't care less about anything he said or did. They'd had the argument more than once about who would pay, and he'd found that the only way she'd relent was if he fell back on the "business" excuse. He didn't like making her think for even a second that it was the only reason he was asking her out, but he was trying to go slowly with her . . . for his own sake and hers. "There's a new seafood place that's supposed to be good," he said nonchalantly.

"Seriously?" Alexis asked with an eyebrow raised.

Blake nodded, smirking.

"You know I hate seafood," Alexis said grumpily. "But if that's what you're in the mood for, I'm sure I can find something."

"I *do* know it, Lex, and I much prefer when you're honest with me than when you go along just to be compliant. Where do *you* want to eat?"

Alexis turned to him and glared. "Whatever. I don't care."

"You *do* care," Blake insisted. "I have no problem with you speaking your mind. You usually don't hesitate to tell me, and anyone else who irritates you, exactly what you're thinking. So, where do you want to eat?" Choosing a restaurant wasn't exactly a life-or-death decision, but he wanted to take her someplace that she'd enjoy, not someplace that she'd just endure.

He *liked* it when Lex stood up to him. Even though he and his brothers were essentially born at the same time, he'd always identified himself as the "middle child." Logan was outgoing and aggressive; he'd protected both of his brothers from his mom's wrath growing up. Nathan tended to fade into the background, happy if everyone left him alone. But Blake was the peacekeeper. He tended to be more flexible than his brothers and more able to let things slide off his back. He found perverse pleasure in the fact that Lex wasn't like that. Most of the time she'd tell him if she disagreed with him and wouldn't agree for the sake of agreeing. It's why he pushed her now; he knew she was just going along with what he'd suggested.

"Fine. You're right. From now on I'll make sure you know exactly what I think about every little thing. You really shouldn't wear black socks with white tennis shoes. It's super weird, and you're not eighty, so that fashion statement isn't appropriate for you. If there's a Souper Salad around, I'd love to eat there."

His lips quirked up at her petulant tone, but he was happy to hear her picking at him, even if it was to make fun of his choice of clothing. "Sounds good." And it did. It might be a salad-and-soup place, but it was a buffet, and the food was awesome. Alexis might complain about her weight, but she didn't eat like the typical women he had dated. Blake enjoyed taking her out because she never seemed to worry about what *he* thought about what *she* was eating. She'd pile her plate high. And the woman had a serious sweet tooth. That was one of the first things he'd learned about her. She put so much vanilla flavoring in her coffee that it almost didn't even taste like coffee anymore . . . more like a liquid cupcake, which was disgusting and adorable at the same time. Frequently when they visited a restaurant with a buffet, she'd make more than one trip through the line as well. He loved that about her. Well, not loved . . . but . . .

"Is that okay? If it's not, we can eat anywhere. I really don't care."

Blake shook his head and turned his attention back to Alexis. "No, it's fine. Good choice."

They were silent the rest of the way to the restaurant. Blake parked and resisted the urge to walk around the car and open the door for Alexis. She wouldn't appreciate it, even though he'd tried to be a gentleman more than once. Every time, she'd shaken her head and told him she was perfectly capable of opening and shutting her own damn door.

She was an extremely hard woman to do anything for, almost going out of her way to do things for herself that most other women would consider polite. She made sure she got to the door first, so she could open it for him instead of the other way around. Insisted that he go in front of her in the buffet line, and always, *always*, tried to pay, no matter if it was already decided before they arrived that he'd be picking up the tab.

Today was no exception. She held the door open for him, but Blake grabbed the door above her head and held out his hand, gesturing for her to walk into the restaurant ahead of him. She got to the cashier first and ordered, but he was ready for her sneakiness and made sure to butt in and tell the woman that he'd be paying for both their meals. She even held out a tray for him when he shuffled in next to her.

Giving in, he took the tray but refused to start down the buffet line ahead of her. It was almost a game between them now. He followed behind her, smiling to himself as she once again piled her plate high with so much food that croutons spilled off the sides by the time they were at the end of the line.

After they chose a seat and a waiter took their drink order, Blake asked, "Have you found out anything more about the Inca Boyz?"

The Inca Boyz were a gang up in Denver that Alexis was looking into. A few months ago, Grace's mother had hired the gang to detain Logan so they could kidnap Grace and lure Bradford to a hotel and take lewd pictures of the two of them. Margaret had hired the gang via social media. It was ridiculously easy, and if Margaret Mason had been able to hire the gang to do her dirty work, the Anderson brothers and Alexis had wondered who else had hired the gang and for what.

Alexis finished chewing the bite and took a sip of her water before she spoke. "Actually, yeah. I was looking at their Facebook page the other day and saw a comment by a girl whose name sounded familiar. I didn't find anything with a Google search, but I *knew* I recognized her from somewhere. I didn't think it was from my college classes—let's face it, she didn't come off as all that bright in her comment—so I got out my old high school yearbook. Bingo."

"She went to your high school," Blake said.

"Yup. Actually, we were pretty close friends in middle school," she said, not looking at him but studying her food intently.

Something about the tone of Alexis's voice seemed off. "In middle school but not when you got older?" Blake asked.

Alexis shrugged and played with the salad on her plate and still wouldn't look at him as she answered. "Yeah. You know, people grow up, friendships change, and all that. I hadn't thought about her in years."

Blake wanted to know more about her growing up and changing friendships but didn't want to pry. It was more than obvious Lex didn't want to talk about it, but also that it was something that bothered her even ten years later. He let it go . . . for now. "True. Go on." She looked up at him then, and Blake knew she was more comfortable since he wasn't asking about her personal life.

"Right. And she'd commented on a post that Damian posted about his brother, Donovan, being in prison."

Blake chuckled. "What'd he say?"

"He posted something about how he visited Donovan that day and plans are in motion."

"Visited him in jail? Plans for what?" Blake asked, extremely interested now, leaning forward on his elbows. He didn't miss the way Lex's eyes flicked down to his forearms, then back up to his face. He'd noticed lately that she did that all the time. Anytime he shifted position or lifted anything, her eyes would be glued to his forearms. Curious, he'd begun to do childish things like flex his biceps to see if she had an arm fetish, but he'd barely gotten a glance. However, when he'd made a fist with his hand, and the muscles and tendons in his forearm had shifted, her eyes had dilated, and once he'd watched in disbelief as her nipples had gotten hard under the tight T-shirt she'd been wearing. She'd immediately turned away from him, hiding the evidence of her arousal, but that had been the moment he'd stopped seeing her as simply Bradford's little sister and more as an attractive woman whom he was extremely interested in getting to know better.

Her hair was neither short nor long. Blonde nor brown. She wasn't model gorgeous but was pleasing to the eye. She wore minimal makeup, just enough to enhance her face rather than overwhelm it. She wore high-priced quality clothes, but nothing that screamed money. She didn't freak if it was raining and she got wet. He'd seen her stand outside the courthouse in Denver in the pouring rain during one of their jobs, as if she didn't have a care in the world. While many women her size wore high heels to try to compensate, Alexis generally wore sneakers or one- to two-inch heels.

She was way shorter than he was; the top of her head barely came to his chin. He typically dated taller women, whom he didn't have to get a crick in his neck to kiss, but the more he thought about it, the more he realized that Lex would fit perfectly against him. He guesstimated that she was probably around five three or four. She'd once tripped over a curb; luckily he'd been walking next to her and had been able to reach out and catch her before she landed on her hands and knees. He'd hauled her into him, probably with more force than was necessarily. She'd turned in to him—her hands coming to rest on his chest, his crotch nestling against her soft stomach—and she'd looked up at him with wide, surprised eyes. Blake knew it made him a caveman, but it felt good to be so much bigger than her. He could wrap his arms all the way around her, pick her up, surround her with himself. Even the thought of how he might tuck her into his body as they slept, or after they made love, turned him as hard as stone.

And her body—Lord. There was nothing childlike about Alexis Grant. She was slender but had curves. She had a slight belly, with love handles that he could sometimes see when she wore low-cut jeans and tight shirts. Her legs were muscular but full. The thought of those thighs clutching at his hips as he lay over her was something he'd been fantasizing about more and more.

Lex liked to eat—he'd seen that firsthand—and the calories she consumed seemed to go to all the exact right places. Her breasts were full and soft as they'd pressed against him. The thought of her dieting and losing even an inch of her sexy curves made him crazy. The best thing about her body was that she wasn't so fragile that she wouldn't be able to take him when he wasn't in the mood to be gentle.

Blake realized in that short moment of holding her that all his life he'd been dating taller, modern women who were confident in bed and out, when what he really wanted was to find a woman who made him feel as though he could protect her. That he could stand between her and the world. Even if she was perfectly able to take care of herself, the sense of being responsible for someone else had always been missing in his life, probably because of the fucked-up way he'd been raised. And he craved that now. All it had taken was a split second of holding Alexis Grant in his arms to realize it.

The fact that she apparently had a thing for his forearms wasn't lost on him, and he'd started wearing more short-sleeve T-shirts than long, simply so he could enjoy her eyes glaze over as she looked at him.

Blake turned his attention back to what Lex was saying about the gang.

". . . sure what plans he was talking about, but Kelly obviously knew. She posted, and I quote, 'Good you went their'—t-h-e-i-r—'and saw you're'—y-o-u-apostrophe-r-e—'brother. Next time tell him I said hi and I can't wait to see him.'"

"What did Damian say to that?" Blake asked, bringing himself fully back into their conversation and trying not to think about what Alexis would look like lying naked and waiting for him on his sheets.

"Nothing," Alexis said shrugging. "They actually don't do a lot of posting on their Facebook page, which is weirdly smart for them. They seem to use it more as a means of communication with people outside their inner circle, and to brag in code about some of the things they've done."

"Code?" Blake asked.

"Yeah, code," Alexis confirmed. "I've been taking notes on the things they say and that other gangs talk about on their own Facebook pages. They think they're really smart and will talk about just about any-thing, but they use alternate words. Like a gun has been called a 'biscuit' or 'clickety,' bullets are 'electricity' or maybe 'food.' Money is usually something like 'bread.' So, a conversation between two gang members might start with someone saying they need bread for a clickety, and that they need electricity so later they can 'dump it on.'"

"Dump it on?" Blake questioned.

"Shoot someone," Alexis told him without missing a beat. "It's actually fascinating and ridiculous how much they openly chat online about this kind of thing. They really must think people are idiots and can't figure out what they're saying." She shrugged then, stuck a large bite of food in her mouth, and swallowed before telling him, "I'm assuming they delete some posts from people asking about them, and they probably message back and forth privately as well as post on the public page."

"Do you think Kelly is dating Donovan?" Blake was impressed with Alexis's efforts.

"It sounds like it, but since they didn't exactly chat about their personal lives, it's hard to be sure," Alexis told him.

"What have you found out about the people who have 'liked' the Facebook page?" Blake asked.

"Not much. Most of the names seem to be fake. It's so easy to make new accounts. The only ones who seem to be real are the people higher up in the gang. Donovan, Damian, maybe two others, and now Kelly."

"Hmmm."

"So, anyway, I thought that since I knew Kelly, maybe I would message her and say that I want to reconnect with her. Maybe I can find out more information about the Inca Boyz that way. If she *is* as close to Donovan as she seems to be by her comment, maybe we can find out more information."

"No." Blake's denial was immediate and firm.

"What? Why?" Alexis demanded, her brow furrowing in confusion.

"I don't want you anywhere near Donovan," he said, leaning back in his chair and crossing his arms across his chest.

"But I'm not going near him. He's in jail."

Blake leaned forward suddenly and reached across the table. He put his palm on her arm and said earnestly, "Lex, if Kelly is Donovan's girlfriend, then he'll find out about you suddenly being buddy-buddy with her. You know as well as I do that just because someone is in jail doesn't mean they don't have contacts—dangerous contacts—outside of it. Do you think he's gonna like that his girlfriend is suddenly talking to the sister of the man they were hired to blackmail? No fucking way."

"But, Blake—"

He cut her off. "Besides that—you said it yourself—you and Kelly weren't close in high school. It's going to look really suspicious if you message her out of the blue and want to be buds. And what are you going to say? That you saw her comment on the Inca Boyz page? Yeah, right."

"I'm not that stupid," Alexis growled, sitting back in her chair, successfully breaking contact with him, crossing her arms over her chest, mirroring his body language from a moment ago. "I know I can't say that. I haven't figured out exactly *how* I was going to make contact with her, but I was hoping you might help me figure it out. I thought about something along the lines of finding where she lived, watching her, seeing where she shopped, and 'accidentally' running into her." Alexis shook her head and dropped her arms, looking down at her hands in her lap, her brows furrowed. "I know you think I have no idea what I'm doing and that I'm a loser for having so many jobs, but I'm not."

"I'm sorry," Blake apologized, willing her to look up at him.

It took a minute, but she finally raised her eyes to his, working her bottom lip with her teeth before telling him. "I thought I'd run it by you. You're the security expert. But if I act like I did in high school, she'd most likely think I had no idea of her connection to what happened to my brother."

So many thoughts ran through Blake's head, but he settled for asking, "How did you act in high school?"

"Oh, well, you know." Her eyes dropped as she refused to meet his eyes. "Everyone knew my family was rich, so I acted like they thought I should act." Continuing to avoid eye contact with him, she picked up her fork and put a bite of salad in her mouth as if the conversation was over.

Blake waited until she'd finished chewing before asking patiently, "And how was that?"

Alexis waved a hand in the air, trying to be nonchalant. "Surely you remember high school, Blake. The rich kids act like the only thing they care about is their clothes and themselves, and ignore anything negative that might be happening around them."

"And you think this Kelly person will buy that?" Blake was skeptical. Now that he'd gotten to know Lex, the real Lex, there was no way he'd ever think she was only concerned about herself. She was one of the least self-absorbed people he knew.

Alexis nodded. "Oh yeah. She'll buy it."

She sounded one hundred percent sure of herself. "Why?" Blake asked skeptically.

"Why will she buy it?" Alexis asked, her head tilted in confusion.

Blake nodded.

"Because."

Blake stared at Alexis hard. "I need more than that if you want me to talk over this plan of yours with my brothers and to agree to it. For the record, I think it could be a good idea, *if* what you say is true. And that's a big if, Lex. If Kelly has *any* inkling that you're snooping for information, you could be in danger. The last thing I want is the Inca Boyz putting a target on your back. Talk to me."

Alexis pushed her salad plate to the side and leaned forward on her elbows, mimicking his body language. Blake had no idea if she was purposely doing it or if it was an unconscious thing, her brain trying to connect with him in some way . . . but he liked it.

"Kelly and I were friends in middle school, I told you that. She lived in a bad part of Denver, but we were close anyway. We did everything together. When my parents first got rich, they went a little crazy, buying me and Bradford all sorts of new clothes. Fancy shit. I was twelve. I thought it was awesome. But it wasn't long before the kids at school started noticing and found out that my parents were loaded. It changed all of my relationships. Girls who hadn't talked to me before, the 'popular' ones, started wanting to hang out with me and be my friend. I ate it up. But I didn't drop my friends I had before, if that's what you're thinking."

Blake shook his head in denial. "I wasn't thinking that, Lex. I couldn't see you doing that."

"Whatever." Alexis's eyes roamed around the restaurant, once again not meeting his eyes. "Anyway, Kelly cornered me one day, accusing me of being a stuck-up rich girl now that I had money. She told me she wanted nothing to do with me anymore. I tried to tell her that I didn't care about the money, but she wouldn't listen. I tried for the rest of the year to get her friendship back, but it didn't work."

Something in Alexis's voice made Blake pause. "What did she do?"

She looked at him then. "What do you mean?" Alexis tried to sound airy, but Blake heard the pain beneath her words.

"I can tell she did something. What was it? Why'd you try for the rest of the year? If she told you she didn't want to be your friend, you would've dropped it. What happened, Lex?"

She sighed and grimaced. "Why do you have to be so darn observant?"

He chuckled, but the sound wasn't exactly a humorous one. "It comes in handy in my line of work."

"Yeah, I'm sure it does." Alexis took a deep breath, then let it out slowly. "Fine. We were in eighth grade. Middle school is a weird time for girls. We have all these new hormones coursing through our bodies, and what other people think about us means more than anything else, even our pride or self-preservation."

"What'd she do?" Blake's words were harsh, no sign of amusement anywhere on his face now.

"It's not a big deal," Alexis said, her tone unknowingly contradicting her words. "She would invite me out with her and her friends . . . bowling, for hamburgers, ice cream, whatever, and somehow I'd end up paying for everyone. At first I wanted to, money didn't mean anything to me, and I really wanted everyone to keep being my friend. I used it to try to buy my way into friendships. Kelly would tell me stories about how she and her friends were so broke that their parents couldn't afford food until their food stamps kicked in at the end of the month. Stuff like that. I had no problem paying because I had lots of money and knew what it was like to be poor."

"What a bitch," Blake breathed.

Alexis shook her head. "No, it wasn't her fault. She didn't know how to deal with the change in our status, and I was the one happily going along with it."

"No, Lex. She knew exactly what she was doing. She was using you. Using the friendship you had to get what she wanted. What happened at the end of the year?"

Alexis wouldn't meet his eyes again, and Blake knew she was going to downplay whatever it was that happened, as was typical for her. "She told me that when we got to high school the next year that she didn't want to be my friend anymore. I didn't understand why. I didn't understand yet the friends I should have wanted were the ones who wanted to be around me because they liked *me*, not because I had money. Kelly eventually told me that if I ever talked to her again, she'd make sure I regretted it."

"Oh, Lex. I'm sorry." Blake's heart hurt for the teenager Alexis had been back then. It was obvious she'd lost her way and allowed the wrong kinds of girls to get close to her . . . but all they'd wanted was her money. Not an actual friendship.

"It's fine, Blake. Whatever. It was a long time ago." Alexis waved her hand in the air as if she was shooing away a pesky fly.

Blake could tell it *wasn't* fine, and that she wasn't okay with what had happened to her in high school. He was going to drop it but had one more question before he did. "And did you talk to Kelly again?"

"Once."

Blake was silent, but his raised eyebrows asked the question for him.

"It was around Thanksgiving of ninth grade. I saw her in the hall. I forgot and said hi."

When Alexis didn't elaborate, Blake asked, "And?" It was like pulling teeth to get information out of her.

"And the next week I got jumped between classes. Three upperclassmen guys got me into the boys' dressing room and beat the shit out of me. Not my face, but they shoved me on the ground in the shower and kicked me until I was black-and-blue. I think they cracked a few ribs. I never told anyone about it. But I also never said a word to Kelly again. Not one."

"Jesus, Lex," Blake breathed.

"Again, it was a long time ago. I was fine. I learned my lesson. I knew my place."

"Fuck, I hate teenagers," Blake said in a flat tone. "Tell me this then. And I'm truly not saying this to be a dick. If Kelly didn't want to talk to you back then, what makes you think she'll want to talk to you now? What if she does the same thing? Gets some of her Inca Boyz friends to rough you up for talking to her?"

"Blake. We're adults now," Alexis protested.

"And?"

"Look. I know how people like her think. Back then she was all about looking tough. I've learned a lot since then. Now she just thinks she's tough. She's going to want to manipulate me all over again. She's gonna get off on it. I just have to play my part. Long-lost friend . . . who has money. I'll act nervous around her, like I'm still scared of her. I'll tentatively ask her out for lunch or something, offer to pay. I'll give her a business card that lists my address. She'll know it's in a nice part of town and that I've still got money. She'll take me up on my offer. I'll pay for lunch, extend another invitation. She won't be able to resist using me for my money. I'll talk about how miserable I am without a man, she'll brag about *her* man, and eventually she'll lower her guard because she'll think she's so much smarter than I am."

Blake eyed Alexis closely. On the surface it was a good plan, except for the address part. There was no way he was going to let her hand over her real address to anyone associated with the Inca Boyz. If he was being honest with himself, if it was anyone but *Alexis* who had the plan, he wouldn't have had an issue with it. But it *was* Lex. And when Kelly was fourteen fucking years old, she'd had her friends beat the shit out of Alexis for simply saying hello in the hallway. They could've done a lot more.

If Kelly ever found out that Lex was playing her now, he had no doubt the bitch would use her gang connections to kill her former friend, and that was *after* the gang members used her body however they wanted. Of that he had no doubt. They wouldn't stop with only beating on her like the boys back in high school had.

"We'll need to run it by Logan and Nathan and figure out every single thing that could go wrong and what you should do if any of them do happen. But if we *do* follow through with this, I want you wired every time you meet with her. That's not negotiable." Blake was practically growling, his eyes narrowed and piercing.

"Done," Alexis agreed immediately, not breaking the eye contact this time.

"And you won't go anywhere with her that isn't in public."

"Agreed."

"And you'll tell me when and where you'll be meeting with her, and I'll be your backup."

"Blake, I don't think—"

"Those are my stipulations, Lex," Blake interrupted. "Again, I'm not saying yes right now, only that on the surface it looks like it could work, but until we talk it over with my brothers, it's not going to happen. But I don't like you being around her by yourself. She's got deadly friends. If she has any inclination that you're using her for information, she won't hesitate to use those connections to hurt you. I can't in good conscience let you do this without backup."

They looked at each other for a long moment. Blake would've paid anything to know what she was thinking. Finally, she nodded, and he noticed an excited spark in her eyes that he hadn't seen before.

"Wired, public, and you don't meet with her unless I'm there watching your back. I'm serious about this. If you screw any of that up, you're done at Ace Security. Got it?" His voice was hard. Blake knew he should've let it go at her nod, but he pushed anyway.

"Got it. Absolutely," she agreed immediately, her voice just as unemotional and flat as his. "I like working at Ace, Blake. It feels good to be able to help people. I feel like I'm making a difference . . . contributing positively to the world rather than interacting on the shallow level I've done for so long. I know I've done idiotic things in my past, but I am *not* an idiot. You done?"

She hadn't eaten but half of the food on her plate, which wasn't like her, but Blake knew she'd shut down. He couldn't take back what he'd said, as he meant every word. She'd misconstrued it as being concern about the business rather than her personally, but that was as far from the truth as it could get.

He'd allow her to be pissed at him, for now. But deep down, Blake knew their discussion had changed everything. He understood her a lot better now. She might be pissed at him, but she'd let a lot of things about herself slip. Things that helped explain why she was the way she was and why she'd been so eager to work at Ace Security.

Alexis Grant was no longer simply Bradford's sister or a temporary employee. Blake wanted to know everything about her. Wanted to know more about what made her tick, what was going on behind her very expressive brown eyes. Wanted to be one of the privileged few to get under the superficial shell she showed the world.

He wanted to know the real Alexis Grant. Because Blake had a feeling that woman was going to be the most precious thing he'd ever found in his entire life . . . if he could keep her safe from herself.

Chapter Three

Blake dropped Alexis off at her Mercedes at the Hampton Inn. She'd taken to staying at the hotel the night before they had an early job. It made sense, as she still lived up in Denver, but she refused to let Ace Security pay for it, even though Blake had tried to convince her. It annoyed him, but he didn't fight her on it. He knew he needed to choose his battles with her wisely.

After he watched Alexis head north toward her apartment in Denver, he drove to downtown Castle Rock, noticing with pleasure the Italian restaurant Scarpetti's had finally opened in the space Mason Architectural Firm used to occupy. For Grace and Logan's sake he was thrilled to no longer have to see Grace's parents' business every day when he went to work. He parked his Mustang and walked toward Ace Security. When he entered the office, his brother, Nathan, was in front of the computer where he spent most of his time.

"Hey, Nathan. What's up?"

"Hey," his brother answered absently.

"Where's Logan?"

"Grace was getting another sonogram today," Nathan said.

Blake nodded. If Grace was going to the doctor, there was no way Logan was going to be anywhere but by her side. "Is he coming back here afterward?"

Nathan nodded, still not looking up from the computer screen. "Yeah. As long as all is well with the babies. He said he'd check in when they were done."

"Good."

Nathan finally looked up. Something in Blake's voice must've caught his attention. "Did everything go okay this morning?"

"Yeah, why?"

"You sound off."

Blake eyed his brother. While Nathan might look like a stereotypical computer geek, he was not a weak man. Blake had no doubt Nathan could hold his own in a fight. He might lose in a battle of brute strength, but he was smart enough to not let any confrontation get that far.

As a teenager, Logan had always been their protector, standing between them and their crazy mother when she was on one of her rampages. But apparently growing up with an abusive mother and not being strong enough to protect himself had made Nathan eager to figure out how to get out of a situation before it escalated to throwing punches.

Blake had seen his brother's talents the first time he'd been on a security job with him. Logan had been busy, and they'd had no choice but for Nathan to work the field. They'd escorted a man to his ex-girlfriend's house so he could safely gather his belongings, and the ex had lost her shit. She'd rushed her ex and had started throwing punches at him. Blake had stepped forward to carefully restrain the woman, and Nathan had immediately started talking the woman down from her crazy. If he hadn't been standing there watching, Blake wouldn't have believed it, would've said nothing could get through to the woman. But within moments, the woman was sobbing and apologizing, and they'd been able to end the potentially volatile situation relatively peacefully.

And while most people underestimated Nathan because of his looks and demeanor, Blake had learned that not only could his brother protect himself and others around him without any kind of weapon other than thinking fast on his feet and reading people accurately, he also had an uncanny way of reading between the lines. He was sensitive and seemed to be able to figure out what people were feeling even when they didn't say a word. Like now.

"The job went fine," Blake tried to reassure Nathan.

Nathan waved his hand in the air as if to dismiss his brother's words. "So, what's up then? Is it Alexis? Something happen? Does she need to be dismissed?"

"No!" Blake answered heatedly. "She's fine. She's great for the business." He looked around the cluttered office—anywhere but into his brother's eyes. "I just needed to talk to Logan about something else."

Nathan didn't take his eyes from his brother.

Blake finally brought his gaze back to Nathan's. Neither said a word.

Finally, Nathan nodded and turned his attention back to his keyboard. "If you need my help, you know you got it." And that was that.

Blake inwardly sighed in relief. He knew his brother figured something was up, but Nathan wouldn't pry. He also wouldn't get bent out of shape if Blake spoke to Logan about something and left him out. It wasn't Nathan's way, and Blake appreciated it more at this moment than he ever had in the past. "I do know that. Thanks."

Blake wanted to talk to Logan about Alexis's plan. It wasn't that he didn't trust Nathan, but Logan was directly involved with the Inca Boyz because of what happened to Grace. Lex's plan seemed like a good one, but it made him extremely nervous at the same time. He wanted to talk it through with Logan and get his take on it. It was possible he was too close to the issue . . . cared too much for Lex to see any holes in her logic.

The Andersons had seen firsthand the depravity of the Inca Boyz, and Blake didn't want Alexis anywhere near them. Yes, he wanted the gang taken down, but having Lex go undercover didn't seem like an ideal way to reach that goal. And not only because the thugs were dangerous but because of the lost and hurt look in Lex's eyes when she talked about her disastrous relationship with Kelly. He didn't particularly want Alexis to have to deal with her again and maybe bring up emotions and pain she'd finally worked through. What the girl had done made his stomach turn.

An hour and a half later, when Logan finally arrived at the office, Blake told him everything he'd learned from Alexis that morning and what she wanted to do.

"What's different now from a few months ago when she first brought up helping us find information on the gang?" Logan asked. He sat across from his brother, one ankle resting on his knee. He looked relaxed, but Blake knew his brother well enough to know that any discussion about the Inca Boyz meant that Logan was anything but.

Blake knew exactly what was different now but wasn't ready to admit it out loud . . . yet. The first person who was going to hear about his intentions would be Alexis.

Somehow that morning had made him realize that while he enjoyed having Alexis as a friend, his feelings had grown. She was fun to be around, worked hard, and liked his brothers, and not once in all the time he'd spent with her had Blake been bored or wished he was with someone else. Not only that, but he hadn't once had the desire to date anyone. She'd slipped under his radar so sneakily that he would've been wary of her intentions if he didn't know for a fact that she wasn't purposely trying to catch his attention, she just had.

"Does it matter? She wants to try to befriend this Kelly chick to get in closer to the gang. That doesn't exactly sound safe," Blake told his brother.

"It definitely doesn't. But she's right. We haven't gotten very far stalking them on social media. We've found out some good information, but it's always after the fact and nothing we can definitely prove. We'll never get enough information to pass along to the task force, so they can take them down before they do something, unless we change tactics. They'll just continue to hire themselves out to beat people up, to intimidate them, or, God forbid, as contract killers. If Alexis wears a wire and gets good enough information, it could be enough for an arrest warrant."

"Is it worth making her an enemy of the gang for life? If they find out what she's doing, she could be in danger for years. You know they won't let it go. They'll have to make an example out of her for anyone else in the future who would even think about being a snitch or working with the cops."

"Then she needs to be extra careful and not get caught." Logan's words were matter-of-fact.

"Do you even care?" Blake bit out, unnerved by his brother's seeming lack of concern toward the danger Alexis could be putting herself in.

Logan dropped his foot and leaned forward, piercing Blake with his intense gaze. "My first responsibility is to my wife and my unborn children. Grace's parents are behind bars, but I want every single one of those assholes in that gang wiped off the face of this earth. If I can't do that, then I'll have to be content with them being behind bars. I'll do whatever it takes to get them there."

Blake sat back but didn't break eye contact with his brother. "Even at the expense at another woman's life?"

Logan took a deep breath and slowly sat back in his chair, his eyes boring into his brothers'. "I don't know Alexis that well. You and Nathan are the ones who work with her the most. I believe you said it yourself. When she gets bored, she'll move on to something else. If she's not going to stick around, I'm not going to bother getting to know her. I don't know why *you* care so much. She's just one of what is mostly likely going to be a long line of Ace Security interns coming through here. It's not like you're dating her. If she's willing to get chummy with a girl she knew when she was younger, and it will bring us one step closer to eliminating the Inca Boyz . . . why not?"

Blake wanted to lash out at his brother for being so coldhearted, but for once, he was right: Logan *hadn't* spent time with Alexis. He didn't know her. Blake got where his brother was coming from—he did. But he couldn't let the diss to Alexis go unchallenged.

"I honestly can't believe you'd be okay if those assholes found out what Lex was doing and killed her. That's not the kind of man you are. I'm more than okay with Grace and your sons being your first concern, but they shouldn't be your *only* concern."

The two brothers stared at each other from across the room for a beat before Logan blew out a breath, his cheeks puffing up as he let it out. "You're right. I'm sorry. It's just . . . seeing my sons kicking and moving in Grace's belly today, hearing their heartbeats . . . it made me realize just how close I came to not having *any* of them in my life. I'm feeling extra protective. They're my life. I'd do anything to protect them, even if that means putting someone else at risk."

Blake nodded but didn't speak.

"As far as Alexis's plan goes, you're right, it's risky, but I also think it could work. However, we'd need to make some tweaks to it. I agree that there's no way she should give those assholes her address, no matter if it'll make them salivate because she lives in a good part of the city. There's a possibility, based on what you've told me, that this Kelly chick could blow Alexis off, but there's just as good of a chance that she'd go for it. As long as Alexis plays it cool, doesn't seem too eager, it might actually work. Lord knows we have dick on the gang right now. We can't even prove the Inca Boyz were behind my accident, even though we both know they were. But my question is, Why would Alexis *want* to put herself in the line of fire like this? What's in it for her?"

"I'm not a hundred percent sure," Blake answered. "I've thought about that too. I think it has to do partly with the way she was treated in high school. People were her friends because she had money, not because of who she was, and she contributed to that by throwing more money at them. She told me today that she wants to make a positive contribution to the world, and that working with us was helping her feel as if she was doing that. Giving her a purpose. Not only that, but I'm assuming her brother is also a motivational factor too. He was also victimized by the Inca Boyz. She knows what it's like being a victim and wants to prevent it from happening to anyone else."

"She knows what it's like being a victim?" Logan asked, his eyes narrowing in concern as he looked at his brother.

He didn't want to share anything that he'd been told in confidence. Even though Alexis hadn't asked him not to tell his brothers, it felt like something he shouldn't share without her express permission. "Yeah. Her teen years were tough" was all he said. The more he thought about the position Alexis was willingly putting herself in, the more he was amazed. The bravery she was showing in her desire to help take down the gang, despite the risk to herself, was both crazy and admirable.

"Okay, you asked for my thoughts," Logan said. "Is it dangerous? Yes. Are there risks? We both know there are. Could she pull it off? You'd know that better than I would, but I'm thinking it's likely. Would it be helpful? Yes. But you were absolutely right in that she shouldn't do *anything* without your knowledge—without *our* knowledge. This is dangerous as shit, and she'd be an idiot to try to go undercover on her own. And, if for some reason you can't be on her when she meets with Kelly, you know me or Nathan would gladly do it. You have her back, and we'll have yours. Period."

Blake breathed out a sigh of relief. That's what he wanted to hear. "Thanks, Bro. I appreciate that."

"Never doubt it, Blake. The Grant family might not be high on my list of people I want to be best friends with, but I know they got swept up into Grace's parents' plan and were just as shocked and horrified about what happened to Grace as I was. And, more importantly, I trust *you*. If you tell me that Alexis is on the up-and-up and can handle this, then she can."

"Again, thank you."

"You're welcome."

"Did you get pictures of my nephews today?" Blake asked, breaking the tension.

"Is the pope Catholic?" Logan asked, reaching into his back pocket for his wallet.

Chapter Four

Two weeks later, Alexis was sitting in a car outside a Walmart in northeast Denver . . . right in the middle of Inca Boyz territory. She'd spent a week stalking Kelly, first online, monitoring Twitter for hashtags related to gangs and searching for keywords on Google, then as Kelly went about her business in the rough part of Denver the gang was known to frequent. She learned which stores the woman liked to shop in and came up with somewhat of a schedule. Kelly was extremely predictable, going to Walmart almost every afternoon.

Alexis had no idea what in the world the woman had to buy every day but figured she was probably buying things for the gang . . . alcohol, cigarettes, ammunition, and who knew what else. Gross and disturbing visions of ropes, shovels, duct tape, and condoms also came to mind.

"Whatever you do, don't fiddle with the wire," Blake lectured for the millionth time. "I know it's uncomfortable, but she'll clock it a mile away if you can't keep your hands off it or if you fidget. If you can approach her, do it, but if it doesn't look like it's going to work, back off and we'll make the approach another day."

"I *know*, Blake. Jeez. Back off already," Alexis scowled at him. "I might not like having this shit taped between my tits, but I'm not going to play with myself in the middle of Walmart. Give me some credit here."

At least he looked a little contrite when he said, "Right. Go on then. Let's get this done. I'll be listening out here. If anything goes wrong, just say the code word, and I'll be there in less than a minute."

Alexis nodded. "I will. Don't worry, I'm not going to try to be a superhero. I'll leave that to you and your brothers." And she would. Even though it'd been years ago, she remembered every second of lying on the disgusting floor of the boys' locker room when she was fourteen and being kicked over and over. She knew no one was going to burst into the locker room to help her back then. She'd been on her own. Even though she was technically on her own once she got out of Blake's car . . . she wasn't really. All she had to say was "I gotta go," and Blake would come running.

She was wearing a brand-new, expensive outfit. One that screamed "I have money. Lots of it." The blouse was silk, a dark-maroon color, and had a scoop neck in the front and back. She was wearing the two-carat diamond studs her mom had given her for a graduation present. They were too big and ostentatious for her taste, so she'd only worn them once, but her mom had meant well. Alexis paired the shirt with a gray pencil skirt with ruffles at the bottom that brushed her knees. It was sexy, but not overly so. For the first time in years she'd worn a pair of heels double the height of her usual two-inch ones. They were Christian Louboutins, and she'd balked at purchasing them. They were ridiculously expensive, but Blake had argued that Kelly would most likely know what they were at a glance, which would only help their cause.

Alexis wouldn't admit it, but she felt really sexy in the outfit . . . even if it was only for show. The heels accentuated the muscles in her calves and although she wasn't super skinny, the clothes highlighted her good points and camouflaged her bad ones. She'd had her hair done that morning into a fancy updo, with wisps of hair brushing the sides of her face, and had gone heavy on her makeup.

When Blake had first laid eyes on her when he arrived at her apartment to pick her up, he'd stared at her for a long moment, his eyes going from her hair to her face, pausing slightly at her chest and hips, then continuing down her legs to her feet. She swore she could almost feel his eyes physically caressing her as she stood in front of him, letting him look his fill. She thought she'd seen lust in his eyes, but whatever she thought she'd seen was replaced by a look of casual friendship moments later. He'd merely nodded hello and turned his attention to the street in front of him as he'd started the car and taken off toward Walmart. Darn it.

"Be smart in there, Lex," Blake warned in a low tone, reaching over and placing his palm on her upper back as she prepared to get out of his Mustang.

Alexis could feel the warmth from his hand seep into her skin and caught herself before she leaned into him. How embarrassing would it be if she did and he pulled away with a look of horror on his face?

She looked over at him and barely glanced at his forearm before bringing her eyes up to his face. "I will," she said quickly. "I'll be back in a jiffy." She nodded at him and opened the door, breaking their physical contact, and climbed out before she said something sappy that she'd definitely regret. What she really wanted to do was tell him how nervous and scared she was, but if she did, she had a feeling Blake would call the whole thing off. He'd told her several times if she wanted to back out of the meeting with Kelly he wouldn't think less of her. That he and his brothers would find a way to get the information about the Inca Boyz without having to put her in harm's way.

Over the past couple of weeks, ever since the job down in Colorado Springs, when she'd opened up to Blake about her motivations behind working at Ace Security, she'd sensed that Blake was treating her differently, but she'd convinced herself that it was nothing more than wishful thinking. He seemed more protective, asking her to text him when she got home and to drive safe. He'd even called and chatted on the phone a few times, and almost every conversation ended with them talking about nothing in particular, and nothing that had to do with Ace Security and the job. It was weird and wonderful at the same time.

Alexis had no idea what to do with a man like Blake. She'd kept men in general at arm's length for so long she probably wouldn't even realize if someone wanted more than just a roll in the sheets. Between her diminutive size and average looks, men tended to treat her like their little sister or a buddy more than anything else, unless they were trying to get in her pants. Her jovial mannerisms and tough demeanor didn't help. And up until Blake, that had been just fine with her.

But for the first time in her life, Alexis wished she knew what to say or what to do to encourage a man to want her. And not just any man, but Blake Anderson. She wanted him to look at her as more than just the friendly chick he worked with. She longed for it.

Trying to block the morose thoughts swirling through her brain, Alexis took a deep breath. Now wasn't the time to lust over Blake or to wish for something she had no idea how to get. She needed to concentrate on the task at hand. Without looking back at the car, or Blake, and ignoring the way the tape pulled on the microphone against the sensitive skin between her breasts with every step, Alexis walked quickly toward the entrance of the store. She had an idea about how to casually approach Kelly, but timing was everything.

Blake watched Lex walk toward the store, and he ground his teeth together in frustration. She looked sexy as fuck, and it was all he could do to keep his hands to himself when she'd folded herself into the seat next to him. Her legs looked miles longer than usual in the heels she was wearing, and the silky material of her shirt made his palms itch to run his hands up her sides to cup her breasts. Not to mention the glimpse he'd gotten of her shapely thigh as she'd eased herself into the seat of the Mustang. He'd never seen her as dolled up as she was this morning. Even though it seemed like a costume, and she bore little resemblance to the real woman he'd gotten to know, Blake couldn't lie and tell himself he didn't like the way she looked. Her outfit screamed money and class, but to him, it only made him want to hike her up against the nearest wall and muss her up. The dichotomy of the woman he knew, the one who had no problem letting him know when he was being overbearing and obnoxious, and the way she looked sitting prim and proper next to him made his cock spring to attention faster than it had ever done in his life.

It was getting harder and harder to keep his feelings to himself. Most of his life he'd had women throw themselves at him. He hadn't had to pursue a woman in so long he'd almost forgotten how. No, that wasn't true. He'd forgotten the feelings of anticipation, frustration, and excitement that being the aggressor in a relationship made him feel. Too many women thought nothing of pressing their phone number into his hand, leaning into him, pressing their tits against his arm, and even playing with the hair at the nape of his neck without his approval or encouragement.

They took flirting to an obnoxious level to let him know they would approve of, and accept, his advances. And in the past, he'd taken advantage of their actions. He'd had a couple of one-night stands and had met a few of his girlfriends because they'd made the first move. But after he got out of the army and moved back to Castle Rock, the games had gotten old. He wanted to be the pursuer, not the pursued. And for the first time in a fuck of a long time, he'd found a woman he wanted to pursue.

But the hell of it was that Lex wasn't giving him any cues that she'd be receptive of his advances. She didn't flirt. It was as if she didn't even know *how*. And that was intriguing as all get-out. No matter how many times he oh-so-casually touched her, she never seemed to reciprocate. Didn't lean into him, didn't seem to even notice he was touching her. At least outwardly. But she couldn't hide her unconscious physical reactions: The tightening of her nipples when he did touch her. The way her eyes followed his arms when he moved. The look of longing in her beautiful brown eyes.

For the first time in his life, Blake was unsure how to proceed. He wanted Alexis Grant and was fairly confident that she wanted him back. But he was kind of her boss, and now he was putting her smack-dab in the middle of a volatile situation, and she was relying on him for backup. It wasn't exactly conducive to starting, or continuing, a relationship.

But watching Lex walk into the store, and listening through the headphones to her quicker-than-normal breathing as she looked for Kelly, Blake realized that he was done playing games. He didn't want another day to go by without telling Lex that she meant something to him. That he wanted to go on a date with her. That he wanted to see if the chemistry he felt around her was returned. Alexis's bravery was almost as attractive to him as her outward appearance. Whatever it was about her, Blake wasn't willing to let one more hour go by without her knowing what he felt.

"Found her."

The husky whispered voice came through the earpiece loud and clear and almost made Blake jump. He was so into his head about what he wanted to say to Alexis he'd almost lost track of what he was there for.

Knowing she couldn't hear him, he mumbled, "Good girl," anyway.

For twenty minutes he heard nothing but Alexis's deep breathing as she followed Kelly around the store. Blake knew she was pretending to shop as she tried to find a way to approach the other woman.

Another agonizing five minutes went by before he finally heard Lex speak again.

"Kelly? Kelly White? Is that you?"

"Who wants to know?" Kelly's voice was rough, as if she smoked a pack and a half of cigarettes a day. And she sounded pissed off.

"It *is* you!" Lex said in a chirpy voice that Blake had never heard come from her before. It was weird and made her sound years younger. "It's me! Alexis Grant! You remember me, right? We went to middle and high school together."

"Oh yeah, sure, I remember you. You still loaded?" Kelly sneered rudely.

Jesus, Blake hated the woman, and she hadn't said more than a dozen words yet.

Lex giggled, another odd sound he hadn't heard from her before.

"Yeah. Well, my parents are at least. You still live around here?"

"Yup. Wouldn't be shopping at this fucking Walmart if I didn't," Kelly retorted acidly.

"Right, silly me," Lex replied, sounding like an airhead and not at all put out by the chilly reception Kelly was giving her. "We had some fun times in middle school, didn't we? Remember when we used to go to the mall? You were always so forgetful. I can't even remember how many times you forgot your purse and I had to pay. It was so funny."

Subtle, she wasn't, but Blake knew immediately what Lex was doing. They'd discussed the best way to approach Kelly. They'd decided not to beat around the bush but to get right to the point. Alexis was doing exactly as they'd talked about. He held his breath as she continued.

"It always used to bug me, you know," Alexis said in what he assumed was supposed to be a nostalgic tone, "that my parents could easily afford things for me that my friends couldn't. The world is definitely not a fair place. I'm sorry we didn't get to hang out more in high school. I missed our friendship. It looks like you're doing well for yourself now. I love that blouse."

Kelly snorted and simply said, "Yeah."

Lex continued on as if she wasn't hearing the ice in the other woman's voice. "My parents still give me a monthly allowance, if you can believe that. It's crazy. I don't even have to work, but I found an easy part-time job. I get bored laying around the house or shopping all day."

"You don't live around here, do you?" Kelly asked.

"Here? Oh no!" Lex said, sounding appalled. "I live downtown in one of those remodeled apartment buildings. You know, the kind with the pool on the roof, the security desk when you go in, and the elevator that takes a key card to get to the correct floor."

"What are you doing here then?"

Blake tensed. Kelly sounded intrigued and skeptical all at the same time. He wasn't sure their cover story would hold.

Lex giggled again before saying airily, "Oh, there's a bar near here that I like to go to. My parents don't like it when I go to establishments that are 'beneath our station.'" Blake could just imagine Lex using air quotes when she said that last bit. She continued. "Sometimes I get the hankering for something more exciting than a martini, if you know what I mean."

Blake held his breath. Would Kelly take the bait?

"Really? You like to hang out in bars in *this* neighborhood?"

"Well, yeah. They're exciting. The men are just so much more . . . manly, if you know what I mean. I find a guy sexy who doesn't give a crap about what other people think about him. I'm not a violent person, but there's just something about a man who pulls out a knife or a gun if someone says something rude to him. I mean, who wouldn't want to be with a man who can protect you? The last guy I dated was from around here and had all sorts of crazy tattoos and insisted on only wearing certain colors." Alexis's ditzy giggle sounded loud in Blake's ear through the microphone. He wondered if she was overdoing it, but she continued. "But wait . . . is there something wrong with the bars around here? Are they dangerous?" Alexis whispered the last word as if it was something dirty that she shouldn't be saying in public.

"No. Not at all," Kelly said in a tone slightly warmer than the polar-ice-cap tone she'd been using earlier. It was a good sign. "They're great. And I agree with you about the kind of men here. I had no idea you were into that sort of thing. I had you pegged as someone who would be dating a lawyer or maybe one of those fancy architects who work for your parents. Maybe we should get together sometime. I could introduce you to some of my friends."

Hook. Line. And freaking sinker. Blake should've felt better about it, but he didn't. The last thing he wanted was to prolong this entire situation. He'd agreed to involving Alexis, but now that it looked like the plan was working and things would progress, he hated it. To sit outside of some seedy gangbanger-infested bar and listen, helpless to do anything if Lex got in trouble, was not something he wanted to do in this lifetime, especially considering the epiphany he'd had about Alexis as she'd walked away from his car. Suddenly he wanted nothing more than to lock Lex inside her expensive, but safe, apartment and never let her out again.

"Awesome! I'd love that!" Lex said in a voice that mimicked the chirpiest, happiest teenybopper on the planet. "We could catch up! I'd love to meet your friends. I could buy a round for old times' sake." And cue the ridiculous fake giggle again.

Blake heard a muffled voice through the mic but couldn't understand what was said. Then he heard Kelly say in a fake tone, "Oh shit, I can't find my credit card."

Then Alexis said in the perky voice he was quickly becoming to hate, "Really? Wow, it's just like when we were in middle school. No problem, Kelly! Let me pay for your stuff. It would suck for you to have to leave it now when it's all bagged up. I'm so happy I ran into you. What a coincidence."

"Yeah, me too," Kelly drawled.

"I can't wait to meet your friends. Should we exchange numbers then? So we can make plans to get together?" Alexis asked.

Blake heard more scratching against the mic as Alexis pulled the burner phone they'd bought a few days ago out of her pocket for just this purpose.

"Sure, although I don't have mine with me. Why don't you just give me your number, and I'll text you."

"Great!"

Red flags were popping up all over for Blake, but he wasn't surprised. Kelly was obviously street savvy and wasn't going to hand over her phone number to Alexis.

There was more scratching over the microphone as Alexis dug for a business card, complete with hearts and flowers on it. She handed it over to her new "friend" Kelly and said, "Here's my card with my cell number, e-mail, and Facebook page. Make sure you friend! I can't wait to hear from you! Have a good day, Kelly!"

"Later," the other woman mumbled.

Blake listened to Lex chirp to the checkout girl about nothing in particular as he watched the entrance of the store. He clocked Kelly the instant she exited the automatic doors. She looked exactly like Lex had described. Long, thin blonde hair that was dyed purple on the ends. Skinny. Unhealthy-looking. Tall, wearing high heels, a short denim skirt, and a T-shirt tight enough to belong to a child rather than an adult. At least it looked like she was wearing a bra today. Lex had said when she'd seen her during her last surveillance, her boobs were practically falling out of the crop top she'd been wearing.

The second Kelly cleared the automatic doors, she pulled a phone out of the large bag on her shoulder. Blake would've given anything to hear what she was saying, but he could imagine. She was probably calling someone from her posse, reporting that she'd just talked to a "long-lost friend" and they'd all be drinking, if not more, for free very soon.

Kelly didn't wait around. As soon as she'd loaded her purchases that she didn't have to pay for, thanks to Lex, into the backseat of her piece-of-shit Saturn, she peeled out of the parking lot, the phone still stuck to her ear.

Blake heard Lex thanking the cashier, and moments later she said softly, "I'm coming out . . . I hope the coast is clear."

It was. They'd made arrangements that if Kelly was still in the parking lot, he'd move the car to let her know. Alexis would then pretend to have "lost" her car and would go back inside. But since Kelly was long gone, Blake stayed right where he was, watching as Lex walked back to him.

Not back to the car. Back to *him*.

That's how it felt. That she'd gone up against the devil and had come through to the other side unscathed. To him.

Blake stayed seated but popped the trunk so Lex could put whatever crap she'd bought as a decoy away. He watched in the rearview mirror as she put the couple of plastic bags inside and slammed the trunk shut. Then she walked around the car, opened the passenger door, and sat, turning to smile at him.

It was open and friendly. A bit triumphant. And exuberant.

Lex's smile was the last straw. Between his feelings of lust from the second he'd picked her up, to his anxiety about the situation she was putting herself in, to his relief when it had actually worked, back to lust when he'd seen her skirt ride up her thigh as she once again sat in his car, it was all too much.

Blake reached for Lex the second the door closed behind her, putting one hand behind her neck to pull her into him and turning her shoulder to face him with the other.

His mouth crashed onto hers and she gasped at his actions. He took advantage and surged inside her mouth like a man possessed. Blake knew he wasn't acting rationally, but he couldn't stop himself. He needed to show her how much she meant to him. That she was his.

He ate at Lex's mouth, relieved when he felt her tongue come out to tangle with his own. She was hesitant, and it was obvious she was acting more on instinct than actual experience, but she was with him, not pushing against him or freezing in his arms. It was all the encouragement he needed to continue.

Moving his hand from her shoulder to the other side of her neck, Blake used both hands to turn her head to just the right angle for his mouth. As he devoured her, he felt Lex's hands come up and grip his forearms, digging her slight fingernails into his skin as he continued their kiss. He hoped she was leaving marks on his skin. He wanted her to claim him right back.

She made little noises as he wrapped his tongue around hers and sucked. When he drew back only far enough to nip her bottom lip, she groaned, which in turn made him growl low in his throat and thrust into her mouth again. What sounds would she make when he pushed inside her? When she came? He couldn't wait to find out. In the meantime, Blake couldn't get enough of her. She tasted like the mint she'd popped in her mouth before she'd gone into the store. Mint and Lex. It was a lethal combination.

Knowing he had to pull back, before he moved them both into the miniscule back seat and threw their backs out or, more likely, got them arrested, Blake eased away, thrilled beyond belief when Lex whimpered in protest when she lost his mouth. She leaned toward him, and he rested his forehead on hers, keeping his hands where they were so as not to give in to the temptation to explore.

He saw Lex close her eyes and felt the heat of her embarrassment rise up her neck under his palms, until it bloomed on her face. For several seconds neither of them said a word. Finally, Blake said softly, "Fuck, you taste good, Lex."

"Um . . . thanks?"

He smiled. Damn she was cute. He pulled his head back but didn't remove his hands from both sides of her neck.

Her eyes finally opened, and he almost lost control again at the desire and suspicion he saw in her eyes. He hated that she doubted him, whatever she doubted him for, for one second.

"I've been wanting to do that for a while now," he told her honestly.

"Do what?"

"Kiss you."

"Oh."

He liked this befuddled Alexis.

"Why didn't you?" she asked, shyly.

"Because I wasn't sure you wanted me to."

"But you are now?" She sounded completely confused.

"I wasn't one hundred percent sure before I actually kissed you, no."

"Then why did you? Because you were happy with what happened with Kelly?"

"Hell no. Because you walked toward me in those heels, looking like you did, smiling. Happy because your plan worked out. I heard you breathing through the mic in my ear, and I decided I was done fighting my attraction to you anymore. I wanted to hear you out of breath, panting in my ear for real."

"Did you shut off the tape?"

Blake nodded. "As soon as Kelly left the store. Anything we do together stays between the two of us. You don't have to worry about that. Ever. In case you haven't noticed, Lex . . . I like you."

"Oh. Wow. Um, well, I'm glad. I . . . like you too."

"Why didn't you tell me? We've wasted a lot of time. Time we could've had together."

"Well . . . because. You seemed to be the kind of guy who likes to do the chasing. And we work together. And you're . . . you." She waved her hand then, as if she were encompassing everything he was with the gesture.

"What does that mean?" Blake was honestly confused.

"Women throw themselves at you. Beautiful women. And you haven't shown one lick of interest. I figured if *they* didn't interest you, there was no way *I* would."

"First of all, you're beautiful, Lex." At her obvious look of disbelief, he hurried on. "I'm not saying you'll ever be a model . . . you're too short, for one thing." He smiled at her to let her know he was teasing before continuing. "I could list all the things that make you attractive, but I don't think you'd believe me. I'll show you exactly what it is about you that makes you beautiful in my eyes. I haven't even noticed any other women in months. Not since I finally saw what was right in front of my eyes . . . you.

"And Lex, you're right. I like making the first move. But from here on out, all you have to do is ask, and I'll give you anything you want. Yeah?"

Blake expected her to look coy and say something like "Anything?" but all she did was blush again, and nod. Her eyes looked over his shoulder, then down at the front of his shirt . . . anywhere but at him.

He kinda liked this uncertain Lex. He'd gotten so used to her saying whatever she thought that the fact that she was shy and not sure how to act in his arms made him realize how much of her personality was bravado. Her shyness communicated that she wasn't all that experienced, and he liked that. A fuck of a lot.

Her thumbs were softly brushing back and forth over the skin on the inside of his arm. He didn't think she had any idea she was doing that. Wishing he could take her fully into his arms, Blake reluctantly let her go, sitting back into the driver's seat and unabashedly adjusting his rock-hard cock as he did, showing her without words how much she turned him on.

She sat back as well, blushing anew when she saw him squirming uncomfortably in his seat and touching himself. She licked her lips, then bit the bottom one nervously. "So . . . that seemed to go well," Alexis commented, obviously trying to put things back on a professional level.

Blake nodded and reached for the key in the ignition. "It did. You were wonderful. You had her eating out of your hand almost from the second she laid eyes on you. You did good, Lex. Although, if you ever speak to me in that high-pitched, rich-bitch tone, I'll have to fire you." He smiled as he said it, so she knew he was kidding.

She laughed, as he meant for her to. A real laugh, not the fake one she'd been using with Kelly. The sexual tension from earlier broken, and Alexis obviously feeling more like her old self, she said, "I thought I might have a chance to get to her if I kinda cornered her in line. If I approached her in the store somewhere, she could've stormed off. But she was stuck once she had all her stuff on the conveyer belt. And can I say . . . the thought of why she needed to be buying three boxes of condoms, two bottles of lube, a carton of cigarettes, and a twenty-four pack of beer . . . skeeves me out. But anyway, I figured she probably hadn't changed much, and if I could remind her how she used to get me to pay for everything when we were kids, she might try again."

"And of course you bragging about your apartment didn't hurt."

"Nope. She really did look kinda skanky . . . don't you think?" Alexis tilted her head as she asked the question.

Blake didn't know if Lex was fishing for compliments or not. He didn't think so—it wasn't really her style to do something like that—but he had no problems reassuring her nevertheless. "Yeah. You outclass her by a mile."

Lex wrinkled her nose. "I wasn't comparing myself to her, Blake. I would hope even at my worst, sitting at home in my sweats and T-shirt, I wouldn't look like her."

"I'm sure you don't."

"I definitely don't. Shit, I'm surprised she didn't get propositioned right there in the store. But I swear someone should tell her that smoking really is gonna kill her someday."

"I think smoking is probably the least of her worries with the kind of life she's leading," Blake said with a small head shake as he pulled out of the parking lot and headed for Lex's apartment.

"I guess you're right. But man, I'm thinking she did me a favor back then by deciding not to be my friend anymore."

"Yeah, Lex. She totally did. Although I doubt you would've put up with her mooching off you throughout high school."

"Maybe." But she didn't sound very sure of herself at all. "I wasn't very strong back then."

Blake rested his arm on the console, palm up. "Give me your hand, Lex."

She did, without a word. Lacing her fingers with his and letting the weight of her arm lie against his. It felt good. Really good.

They held hands the rest of the way to her apartment complex in downtown Denver. Blake pulled up in front of the valet station and waved the man off who came up to take care of the car.

He walked around to the passenger side, happy, for once, that Lex let him open her door and help her out. He didn't back away when she stood up, keeping her trapped with the door next to her, and him in front of her.

Looking down, Blake thought again how well they fit together. He put his arms around her, happy when Lex laid her head on his chest and snuggled into the hug. He kept it short and pulled back, holding on to her biceps.

"I'll have Logan and Nathan listen to the tape tonight. We'll figure out how to cover you when Kelly invites you out."

"You really think she will?"

"Lex, she was on her phone the second she cleared the store. She's gonna want to take as much advantage of you as she can. I think she and her friends will be on their best behavior for as long as they can use you. That's the only reason I'm even *considering* letting you meet up with her." He was glad she didn't take offense to his somewhat controlling comment.

"Yeah, that's what I think too. If I'm being honest, it's the only reason *I'm* considering meeting up with her. Because I figure she wants to keep the gravy train going. She won't want to scare me away."

"You know today changes things between us," Blake told her, leaning in a bit to make his point. "I'm not content being only your friend anymore."

Alexis smirked and said somewhat snarkily, "Really? I hadn't noticed. All my bosses kiss the stuffing out of me when we're on a job. It's a good thing that I want to be more than friends too."

"You wanna go on a date with me, Alexis Grant?"

She grinned. "Yes. Please."

"You gonna let me pay without giving me the third degree over it?" he asked playfully, running his index finger down the tip of her nose.

Her lips curled up, but she said semiseriously, "On our first official date, yes, you can pay. I'm kinda old-fashioned in that it seems like the right thing to do. But if we go on another, all bets are off. I'm not the kind of woman who expects the man to always pony up the cash."

"I'm well aware of that, Lex. And I'll tell you right now, there *will* be more dates after the first. Count on it."

"You might not like me in that way once you really get to know me," Alexis warned. "I tend to say what I'm thinking and don't really get into the normal date stuff."

"What do you consider normal date stuff?" Blake asked, genuinely curious.

"Oh, you know . . . eating out, watching movies, walks in the park . . . that sort of thing."

"Good to know. What kind of dates *do* you like?"

The confidence that she'd been showing in their banter disappeared from her eyes, but she gamely tried to continue anyway. She shrugged. "Whatever you like."

"Don't. You haven't been afraid to speak your mind to me in the past. Don't start now," Blake told her, raising a hand and smoothing a lock of hair behind her ear, using his fingertips to caress the side of her neck when he was done.

She shivered in his grasp and said, "I like hiking. And finding cool antique stores. I love to window-shop. I don't buy a lot, but it's fun to look. And eating. There are some awesome food trucks downtown."

"Then that's what we'll do."

"Really?"

"Really."

"Cool."

Blake grinned then. Huge. He liked making her happy. "How about a kiss to seal the deal?"

Instead of answering verbally, Alexis stood up on her tiptoes and leaned into him, trusting him to keep her from falling over in her heels, and lifted her chin.

Taking what she offered, Blake covered her mouth with his own, loving how she immediately opened for him to take what he wanted. She wasn't an experienced kisser, but she more than made up for it with her enthusiasm.

When he finally pulled away, she murmured, "I hate being short."

"I like it."

"What? Why?"

Blake ran his hand through her hair, feeling the shiver that ran through her from his actions. He put his lips next to her ear and whispered, "Because all I can think about is how much I'm gonna like turning you this way and that in my bed . . . when we get there."

She gasped and blushed, then protested, "Blake. I can't believe you said that."

He chuckled and stepped back, giving her room to sidestep away from the car so he could shut the door. "Believe it, Lex. I've been on my best behavior, but honestly? I am one hundred percent sure you'll be worth the wait. Everything you do, you do with enthusiasm. I can't wait to see that energy and passion in my bed. Call me if you hear from Kelly tonight, yeah?"

"I will. You'll . . ." She paused as if unsure.

"What? Remember what I told you earlier? Say whatever you want."

"You'll text me to let me know you got home all right?"

She constantly surprised him. "I'll get home all right," he told her in a soft but firm voice.

"But you'll let me know?" she pressed.

It felt good to be worried about. It had been a long time since he'd been in a relationship where a woman worried about him, rather than expecting him to only worry about *her.* "Yeah, Lex. I'll let you know."

She smiled then and backed up, almost tripping over the curb because of the unfamiliar heels on her feet. She held out a hand to fend him off when he made a move toward her to catch her. "Ha, sorry. I'm good. Just clumsy. The longer you hang around me, the more you'll get used to it. I'll see you tomorrow."

"Good job today, Lex. I mean it."

"Thanks. I'll see you later."

"Later, Lex."

Blake waited until she happily greeted the doorman, Osman, then disappeared through the revolving door. When he couldn't see her through the glass anymore, he climbed back into his Mustang and headed back toward the interstate, smiling all the way home.

Chapter Five

Alexis swallowed hard before pushing open the door to Ace Security the next day. The meeting with Kelly couldn't have gone better, but what happened later with Blake had her tossing and turning all night.

She'd been in love with the man for what seemed like forever, and it seemed unreal that he returned her interest. But she had no illusions about them having a long-term relationship—she was a novelty—and after spending almost every day together for the last few months, he probably just wanted to get her into bed, to have what had been in front of his face for so long. In her experience that was how men were wired.

After Blake screwed her, he'd most likely move on to someone else. She didn't have what it took to keep his attention long-term. Especially when he found out exactly how inexperienced she was. Being a twenty-five-year-old virgin was embarrassing. The best she could hope for was a few weeks or months of good sex. She'd have to be content with that, even if it would break her heart when Blake tired of her. And she had no doubt he would.

"Hey, Alexis," Nathan said distractedly as she entered the office. The Ace Security building had a front reception area that included a door that led into the back office area. There were several desks, one for each brother as well as herself, and in the rear of the office space there were a couple of smaller desks and a large table they used for meetings. There were windows on one side that let in some natural light.

"Good morning, Nathan," Alexis returned as she made her way to her desk. It was sitting perpendicular to Blake's, and most days she forced herself to ignore his presence for her own sanity, but today wasn't one of those days.

"Hey, Blake." He was looking right at her. She'd seen him the second she'd entered, and his eyes had been intense as they followed her across the room. She was wearing her normal attire today—jeans, sneakers, and a T-shirt from the University of Denver—not the sex kitten outfit she'd had on yesterday, but the look in his eyes was amazingly the same as it had been the day before.

She tried to walk normally, to not put more sway into her hips than usual, but it was tough with the way he was devouring her with his eyes and how much she enjoyed the look on his face.

"Lex."

Even the one word oozed testosterone. It was all she could do not to melt into a puddle right there at her desk.

"Sleep well?" he asked.

If sleeping well meant she'd tossed and turned and had finally had to get herself off with her trusty vibrator before falling into a fitful sleep where she'd dreamed about him all night . . . then yes, she'd slept well. "Yeah. You?"

He smiled as if he could read her mind. "Not really."

His answer surprised her, as they'd had this conversation many times over the last few months, and every time his answer had been a simple affirmative.

"Really? Everything all right?"

Blake's voice dropped but was still conversational in volume. "I couldn't stop thinking about you."

Alexis blushed furiously and glanced over at the other two men in the room. Nathan seemed oblivious, typing away at his keyboard, but Logan was smirking as he looked down at the paper he was reading in his hands. Deciding she needed to change the topic before she self-combusted with embarrassment, Alexis asked loudly, "Did everyone listen to the tape yet?"

Logan answered, "Yeah, we did that first thing this morning. You did a good job, Alexis. You didn't beat around the bush, got right to it, and she fell right into your trap."

Hearing Logan praise her felt good. But then he continued, letting the other shoe drop.

"I'm not sure it's exactly smart to jump right into the lion's den, though. Meeting Kelly on Inca Boyz territory isn't the best idea. We had discussed someplace neutral. The bar they hang out in isn't exactly neutral territory. If something happened, we might not be able to get to you in time. They could haul you off, or hurt you, before Blake, or any of us, could step in. Has Kelly contacted you yet?"

If Alexis was being honest with herself, she wasn't exactly keen on going by herself to any of the seedy bars on the northeast side of the city either. Not when simply driving through the area made her uneasy. It didn't matter that Blake would be outside listening. She shook her head in response to Logan's question. "No, nothing yet."

"What if you tried to do what you originally thought?" Blake spoke up. "When she contacts you, see if she wants to go to lunch. If we can think of somewhere upscale, that would be expensive for you, but where she wouldn't feel so out of place, it might be a good icebreaker."

"Yeah, that would make me feel better," Alexis agreed. "I'm not saying I'm not willing to go to a bar, but only if it's a last resort."

Blake nodded approvingly, which made goose bumps rise on her arms. Jeez, she had it bad if a simple nod turned her on.

"It's a moot point until she calls or texts," Nathan observed from his desk. Even though it looked like the man wasn't paying attention, he never had any issues keeping up with conversations.

"True," Logan agreed. "She could contact you today or a week from now or not at all. All we can do is wait. In the meantime, Blake can bring you up to speed on our other upcoming cases."

And she certainly liked what she was looking at as well. He was wearing another short-sleeve T-shirt today. Black. Alexis hardly noticed the design on the front—her eyes were drawn to his arms—his forearms garnered her attention, as usual.

Blake held out one arm and gestured to the space next to him at his desk. "Pull your chair over here, and we'll go over the schedule for the week."

Alexis took a deep breath. What she'd give to have him wrap that huge arm around her. She'd dreamed about standing in front of him and looking down to see that muscular forearm wrapped across her chest as he pulled her into his body.

She forced her silly fantasies from her mind and tried to concentrate on work.

A couple of hours later, her burner phone vibrated. She'd gone back to her own computer after sitting next to Blake reviewing the schedule for thirty minutes. He'd smelled delicious that morning, and she would've sworn he was purposely torturing her by twirling a pen in his fingers, making the tendons and muscles in his forearm dance right in front of her eyes. She'd gotten wet, not able to pull her eyes from his arm for several moments.

Alexis had been following up on Google alerts for the Inca Boyz and several other cases when the phone vibrated. Her eyes immediately went to Blake's for some reason. Reassurance? Comfort? Help?

"It's okay, Alexis. We've gone over what you're gonna say. Go ahead and answer it. Put it on speaker," Blake said in a calm tone, pushing back from his chair to walk over to her. He put one hand on her upper back and gently rubbed, showing her that he was there and was supporting her. It was all she needed.

Nodding, Alexis took a deep breath. She could do this. She closed her eyes for a moment, as if channeling the rich-bitch Alexis, then opened them, reaching for the phone.

"Hello, this is Alexis," she chirped happily into the speaker.

"Yo, this is Kelly," the voice on the other end of the line said, her raspy voice echoing into the large room.

Blake's hand pressed harder against her back, showing her his support. Nathan hadn't moved, but he was looking over at her from his spot behind his desk.

"Hi! I was hoping I'd hear from you," Alexis told her, wiping her sweaty hands on her jean-clad thighs.

"I talked to my friends, and they're looking forward to meeting you," Kelly told her without much enthusiasm.

"Goodie," Alexis exclaimed. "Although something came up this weekend. My mom and dad are having some fancy party that I can't get out of, so I can't get to the bars. But I'm free for lunch. Wanna go somewhere and get something to eat? You're welcome to bring one of your friends if you want. My treat."

There was silence on the other end of the line for a beat, and Alexis hoped she hadn't blown it. She'd done exactly what they'd all discussed, but for some reason it felt like the entire operation was all on her shoulders.

Until Blake shifted behind her, bending over and wrapping one arm around her chest and put his head next to hers, rubbing his rough cheek against her own. He'd never touched her in front of his brothers before. The kiss they'd shared last night was seared into her brain, and Alexis turned her head to look at the sexy man standing behind her chair, completely in her space, and shivered.

"I guess so," Kelly whined. "Although I thought we were gonna drink together."

"We will," Alexis confirmed happily. "There's nothing I like more than throwing back some shots and letting loose." Her voice dropped to a sickly sweet, disappointed tone, "But not this weekend, darn it. But I'm happy to meet you for lunch. Where do you want to go?"

"You coming over here?"

Knowing Kelly meant her side of town, Alexis was quick to reassure her. "If you need me to."

"The bar we like to go to serves lunch. We could do it there next week."

Alexis swallowed hard. She'd thought Kelly would suggest a restaurant of some sort. She wasn't sure how to answer.

Blake turned his head so his lips were at her ear as he whispered. The warm air of his breath tickled her ear, and goose bumps zipped down her arm as she once more grew wet between her legs at the delicious sensation. "Tell her that's fine. There will be a lot less people around for lunch at a bar. You can give her an excuse about why you need to leave after an hour or so. I'll keep you safe, Lex. Trust me."

Without looking up at Blake, Alexis nodded. She was nervous to go to a bar in gang territory with Kelly, but going in the light of day would be easier than showing up at night, when it was sure to be more dangerous.

"Great idea," Alexis gushed to Kelly. "I love bar food. When and what time?"

"How about next Tuesday? Eleven?"

It was soon, but the more Alexis thought about it, the better she'd feel to get it over with. Having to wait a week would be torture, but it was better than going the next day. It would give them time to scope out the bar and the area and come up with a contingency plan just in case. It would also give the guys a chance to tell her what the hell she should be doing to stay safe. This so wasn't in her comfort zone, but if she could have a hand in taking down the Inca Boyz, she'd do it. She looked up at Blake and raised her eyebrows in question. He, in turn, looked over at Logan. Alexis didn't take her eyes off Blake, knowing Kelly was waiting for a response.

Blake got the okay from Logan, and his eyes came back to hers and he nodded.

Alexis licked her lips, liking the way Blake's eyes dilated at her unconsciously sexy actions, and swallowed hard before answering Kelly. "Awesome! I wasn't sure you'd be able to get together so soon. I can't wait to hear all about what you've been doing since we graduated. I know it's been a while, but I've missed hanging out with you, Kel. I want to hear about everything you've been up to and if you have kids and if you're dating or married. It'll be so fun."

"Yeah, right. So, next week. Snake's Bar. You know it?"

Once again, Alexis looked to Blake. He shrugged and his eyes went to Nathan this time. Alexis followed his gaze to see the other man typing quickly on the keyboard in front of him. He nodded and gave them a thumbs-up.

"I'm sure I can find it," Alexis told Kelly. "This is so great. I'm so happy I ran into you." It was getting harder to keep up the chirpy, happy voice, but she did her best.

"Later," Kelly said decisively, and disconnected.

"Bye," Alexis told the other woman unnecessarily, as she'd already hung up, and clicked the "Off" button on the phone.

"Snake's is on Thirty-Fifth and Wabash," Nathan told them. "It's smack-dab in the middle of Inca Boyz territory, but at eleven on a Tuesday not too much will be going on."

"Right. She probably did that on purpose. They want to check Alexis out before getting their club too involved. Want to see if what Kelly says about her is true or not," Logan guessed, heading back to his desk.

"You did good," Blake told her, standing up but keeping his hand on her back. He'd propped himself up with his other hand on the desk top in front of her. "You okay?"

"Yeah. Why wouldn't I be?" Alexis asked, her eyes glued to Blake's arm right next to her. She could feel the warmth of his hand against her back, and she wanted to close her eyes and lean into his touch, but with Logan and Nathan there, she didn't dare.

"You're tense. Your fist is clenched and you're gripping your thigh with your other hand. I know this is new to you, and you've got some bad memories when it comes to Kelly. You don't have to do this, you know. We can stop it now, before this goes any further. It'll be easy for you to tell her something came up and you can't make it. Just say the word."

Alexis looked up at Blake. She could see the sincerity in his eyes. There was no judgment in his face, just concern, which made her relax. He'd make sure nothing happened to her when she met with Kelly. "I'm good, Blake. Promise. I want to take them down as much as you guys do."

"You have a history with the Inca Boyz other than that thing with your brother?" Logan asked severely from his desk.

Stiffening at his tone, Blake stood and put himself between his brother and Alexis and answered his question. "With the bitch, Kelly."

Logan looked at Blake and then at Alexis with his eyebrows raised.

Alexis kept her lips shut. It was one thing to share with Blake her pathetic attempts to win friends when she was younger; it was another altogether to share with his brothers.

"Not your business, Bro. It's nothing that will hinder our investigation," Blake answered for her, keeping his eyes on his brother's, not backing down.

"It better not. It goes against all my better judgment letting you get involved, Alexis," Logan stated firmly. "I'm a hard son of a bitch sometimes, but because you're important to Blake, you're important to me. I certainly don't want you getting hurt."

"She's not going to get hurt. Lex is one of the most competent people I've worked with. You have nothing to worry about, Logan."

Blake's compliment wound its way around her heart, but she couldn't help but be confused. It seemed that somehow her status at Ace Security had changed at warp speed from merely being an employee to being "important to Blake." It felt good, but since the relationship would certainly be temporary, it didn't make much sense either.

Logan nodded at his brother and put down the paper he'd been reading before Kelly had called. "Looks like we got some shit to talk about then. Let's figure out how this lunch will go down. We can scope the area out and get the lay of the land before you have to meet. Alexis, Grace and I would be happy if you joined us sometime for a meal. I should've asked before since you've been an employee of Ace Security, but now it seems especially important that we get to know you better. We all"—Logan motioned to Nathan and Blake, then continued—"try to get together at least once a week outside of work."

The invitation surprised her. She'd been working there for months, and as much as she wanted to get to know Grace better, she hadn't wanted to push herself somewhere that she wasn't wanted. Grace probably had to work through what had happened with Bradford and her family, so she hadn't pushed. "Oh, um . . . I don't want to intrude."

"You wouldn't be. If nothing else, it'll be a good time to talk about what we find out about the bar, and if it's after you meet with them, we can talk about that too."

Alexis nodded. "All right then, I'd love to. Thank you."

Blake's hand moved from her back to the nape of her neck. He massaged the tight muscles there.

Alexis blushed in mortification because she could feel the damn goose bumps that rose way too easily every time Blake touched her with his palm. And if she could feel them, he had to as well. But he didn't mention them. He only said, "We might talk business, but that's not why my brother asked you to eat with us."

Alexis waited for more; when he didn't say anything else, she tilted her head back, looking up at him, trapping his hand against her skin. "It's not?"

The heat in Blake's eyes was intense, and she felt his thumb caressing her nape as he stared down at her. It wasn't Blake who answered, but Nathan.

"No. It's because we made a deal that if we are seriously interested in a woman, we'd make sure to include her in our lives so everyone could get to know her and approve."

Alexis swallowed hard. Jesus. That felt good. She wanted to get to know Blake's family outside the office. It was fast, but she certainly wasn't going to complain. Not at all.

"The Anderson brothers don't fuck around when we want something," Blake said quietly, his face close to hers. "Nathan and I learned that from Logan. It took him ten years to come back to town and claim Grace, and it was almost too late. We aren't gonna make that mistake."

Alexis couldn't think. Her mind was completely blank. All she could think of was how much she *wanted* to be claimed by Blake Anderson. It wasn't very modern of her, but for the first time in forever, she didn't feel as if she had to buy someone's friendship. She knew without a doubt that Blake couldn't give a shit how much money she had. He'd made it more than clear in the many times she'd tried to pay when they were on jobs. In fact, he probably hated the fact that she was loaded . . . which was something she'd never dealt with. Ever.

The hand at her nape tightened, and Blake leaned down into her space once more. She felt his lips brush against hers, felt his hot breath as his words brushed against her as he spoke. "It took me months to see what was in front of my face, but mark my words . . . I see you now, Lex." Then he moved the scant millimeters it took to touch his lips to hers. It wasn't a short kiss, but it wasn't long either. His tongue swiped along the seam of her lips, and Alexis opened to him immediately. He swept inside her mouth, and she tasted the coffee he'd been drinking before her phone had rung.

He was delicious, and he pulled away too soon for her liking. Alexis opened her eyes slowly as if she'd been drugged and blinked up at Blake.

For once, she had no comeback, but luckily he didn't seem to care. He moved his hand from her nape to the side of her face and gently swiped his thumb along her bottom lip, wiping the moisture from their kiss away.

Nathan's voice broke the spell between them. "Who do you think Kelly is going to invite? Do we have any ideas about how this should go down?"

Alexis watched as Blake backed away from her and strode back to his own desk a few feet away. She took a deep breath and cracked her knuckles, trying to get her mind back to the task at hand and how nice Blake's lips felt against her own. She needed to figure out what she was going to ask Kelly and how the lunch next week would go. She'd worry about hanging out with the Anderson family after she made it through lunch with Kelly and her friends who were most likely members of the Inca Boyz gang.

But she couldn't keep the butterflies in her stomach from whirling. Blake had kissed her . . . in front of his brothers. Had made it more than clear he was interested in her. As nervous as that made her, it also made her deliriously happy.

She, Alexis Grant, virgin extraordinaire, had apparently managed to catch the attention of one of the sexiest men in Castle Rock.

Oh shit.

Chapter Six

A week later, after they'd gone over every possible scenario and driven around the area where Snake's Bar was located, Alexis still wasn't sure she was ready.

Logan, Blake, and Nathan had done their best to give her a crash course in what to look for and how to protect herself. She'd tried not to freak out as they instructed her how to knee a man in the balls and stick her fingers in his eyes before running like hell, how to tell when the situation was going to get out of hand or to make sure she didn't drink anything that she didn't see poured, with her own eyes—but it wasn't easy. The scenarios they'd discussed made her almost physically ill: from shoving her in the trunk of a car, locking her in a room before bringing in more of the gang to subdue and hurt her in ways no woman ever wanted to be hurt, to smacking her around just to see how she'd react. With each and every scenario, Alexis had wanted to call the whole thing off, but she couldn't.

She needed this. Needed to feel as if she was making a difference. And backing out now wouldn't make her feel that way . . . not at all. The other reason she didn't say anything was because it was obvious that all three men weren't all fired up to be putting her in danger. That alone made her feel better, because it meant they cared about her. They weren't using her. She realized that all three Andersons were doing everything they could to make sure she was protected.

She was by no means an expert after their lengthy prep session, but she felt a lot more confident about handling whatever might come up . . . and if she couldn't, she knew how to look for an escape and get the hell out of there. It was enough to give her the confidence she needed to get through the lunch meeting.

Alexis stood at the entrance to Snake's Bar. She resisted the urge to turn around and run back to her Mercedes. Blake had met her at her apartment earlier in the morning with not only the wireless transmitter, but also a small video camera. It was well hidden in a gaudy pendant she wore around her neck. It wasn't something she'd normally wear, but it looked expensive, and that was all Kelly and her friends would care about.

Knowing Blake, and ultimately his brothers, would see and hear every single thing that happened was both soothing and disconcerting. She didn't want to screw anything up, especially not after all their patient instructions and training. She wanted to get more information on the gang, but she was also scared something would go wrong. The last thing she wanted was to be caught. Alexis wasn't an idiot. She knew exactly what would happen if they figured out what she was doing. But this needed to be done. The people in the gang were assholes. They needed to be stopped. And at the moment, she was one of the few people in a good position to try to do something about it.

The plan had been for Blake to arrive at the business across the street first. He was using Nathan's piece-of-crap car, so it would blend into the surroundings better than his Mustang. Blake would monitor every second of her lunch with Kelly, and if things got out of control and if for some reason Alexis wasn't able to put into practice what she'd been taught, he would intervene. The gang most likely knew who Logan was because of the media coverage of the Masons' and Donovan's trials, but the brothers were pretty confident that Nathan and Blake were still relatively unknown to them.

Blake had assured her that he didn't give a shit if they did know exactly who he was. He wouldn't hesitate to intercede if it looked like things were going south, which was all the reassurance Alexis needed. Between her newfound self-defense knowledge and knowing he was nearby, she was as ready as she was going to be. Blake wore a pair of jeans that were molded to his legs and a plain black T-shirt. He'd fit into the surroundings of the bar and, if needed, would pretend to be Alexis's jealous boyfriend in order to get her out of there. It wasn't ideal, but in a pinch it could work . . . especially in the middle of the day when hopefully the bar wouldn't be full of people who either supported the gang or would look the other way when violence occurred.

Over the last couple of days, she and Blake hadn't spent a lot of alone time together. Besides the training with his brothers, they'd worked two security jobs, one in Denver and one in Pueblo. They were easy escort jobs, making sure their clients weren't harassed when they moved their belongings out of the house and apartment, respectively, they'd shared with their ex-spouses.

She and Blake had talked a lot about what might happen at the lunch. Who might be there, what they'd say, what they'd want from her. He still touched her often, and he kissed her briefly when they met and when they parted, but there hadn't been any of the deep, drugging kisses they'd shared before and no more talk of a date. Alexis would've been worried that Blake had changed his mind if it wasn't for the way he continued to look at her . . . as if he wanted nothing more than to throw her to the ground and have his way with her.

As frustrating and confusing as it was, Alexis let Blake set the speed of their relationship. He'd said he liked being the one to chase, so she'd let him. But her patience was wearing thin. She'd been trying not to push him, but she was getting increasingly more frustrated and wanted him to take things to another level. If he didn't hurry up and do something, she'd have to let him know of her displeasure. She smiled at the thought. Blake seemed to like it when she spoke her mind. It was one of ten thousand and twenty-three things she loved about him . . . what others considered annoying, he found amusing.

Alexis had paired a dark-green designer blouse that was high in front and dipped low in back with a pair of black slacks. She wanted to be sexy but not show off so much cleavage, because of the microphone. It was taped between her breasts, but with all her other concerns about what could happen, she barely even noticed it.

She'd gone heavy on her makeup once again, keeping it classy but obvious, and put large, dangly emerald earrings on to match her shirt—and of course the gaudy necklace with the fake stone and tiny camera. She'd also put on her high school class ring her mom insisted on buying for her—the first time she'd worn the stupid thing—and three other rings with large expensive stones. She'd then finished off her flashy jewelry with a diamond tennis bracelet and a charm bracelet, again with several diamonds, emeralds, rubies, and aquamarines embedded in the various charms.

She felt like she had a sign on her forehead that screamed, "Rob me! I'm a stupid rich chick!" There was no way she'd be dumb enough to wear any of that jewelry in this part of town if she hadn't had Blake at her back and if she wasn't purposely trying to look like a rich airhead.

Blake hadn't said much when he'd come to pick her up at her apartment, which had worried Alexis. She was afraid he'd come to his senses and would refuse to let her make the meet with Kelly. But after she'd put on the wire under her clothes and she'd come out of her room ready to go, he'd taken one look at her and moved toward her.

"Fuck me," he'd murmured as he quickly strode to her. Her hands had come up automatically and landed on his chest as his own hands had taken hold of her face. Blake had leaned down and taken her lips as if he were a starving man and she were a four-course meal. She hadn't realized how much she needed this before going into the lion's den. They'd barely touched except for her hands on his chest and his on her face—and of course their lips—but it was more intimate than anything Alexis had ever experienced before, even their first kiss in his car.

She'd shifted in his arms as their tongues entangled, pressing her thighs together to try to assuage the ache between them. Alexis had felt her panties get damp as their teeth had knocked in their attempt to get more of each other. When Blake had bitten down on her lower lip and sucked on it at the same time, Alexis moaned.

The sound had broken whatever spell they'd weaved between them, and Blake had pulled back, reluctantly.

Alexis had breathed heavily, as if she'd just run a mile, and stared up at Blake. She'd licked her lips, tasting Blake on them. His eyes had followed the movement of her tongue, and he'd grimaced as if in pain. But he'd leaned down and kissed her forehead before dropping his hands and taking a step back.

"You'd better go touch up your lipstick before we go."

His words had made her eyes go to his lips, where her lipstick was smeared. Alexis had blushed thinking about what her own lips looked like. She'd swallowed and nodded, saying softly before she turned to go, "I've got tissues in my living room, so you can clean up. As much as I like my mark on you, it's probably not the image we want to portray if you have to come inside the bar."

He'd smiled broadly. "Always thought it disgusting to be covered in a woman's lipstick. But now that I've got *yours* on me . . . I'm not that eager to get rid of it."

She'd smiled at him and paused halfway through her turn to go clean up. She hadn't wanted to go meet Kelly. She'd wanted to find out, though, what all the fuss about men was. Why women through the ages would gladly give up everything they were and everything they owned to be with the men they loved. She liked seeing her lipstick on him. Liked knowing how it got there.

She'd had no idea what Blake was thinking, but if the glint in his eyes and the tent in his pants were any indication, his thoughts were similar. Just when she'd thought he was going to say the fuck with the meeting and take her into his arms once more, he'd spoken.

"Go on, Lex. We need to get going. I'll meet you by the door."

She'd nodded and tore her eyes from his. Damn she had it bad. Without another look at him, she had gone into her bedroom to fix her lipstick.

Now she was standing at the door to Snake's Bar trying not to bite her lips and remove any more of the lipstick she'd reapplied earlier. She had a part to play, and it was time she got to it.

Alexis pushed open the door and let her eyes adjust to the dark, smoky bar. It was bigger than she expected. To the left there was a large raised platform with three pool tables. Only one was currently in use. There were several tall tables around the pool tables, allowing the players to put their drinks down while they played. Scattered around the area in front of the pool tables, and on the main floor, were square tables haphazardly strewn about. There were wooden chairs, some pushed in, some not, around each table. The tables were wooden, and many had graffiti carved or written on them.

There was a four- or five-foot path from the entrance that led straight to the mahogany bar in the back of the room. A large mirror was centered behind the bar, making the room look twice as big as it was. Alcohol lined shelves on either side of the mirror, in no particular order that Alexis could see. There was a bottle of top-shelf tequila next to a bottle of Royal Gate vodka. A large keg sat on a stand behind the bar, with a tap dripping beer onto the floor. Stools that had seen better days were scattered around the place. They were missing spindles, and one didn't even have a back to it.

To the right of the mahogany bar was a hallway with a sign that proclaimed the restrooms were to the right. Another sign read **BATHROOMS ARE FOR SHITTING & PISSING, NOT FUCKING. KINDLY KEEP FORNICATING TO THE HALLWAY OR MAIN BAR AREA.**

She had no idea if it was someone's idea of a joke or not but made a mental note to give the hallway a wide berth, just in case.

"Yo! Over here!" Alexis heard.

She turned her head to the left and saw Kelly waving from a table near the pool table platform. Alexis put on a wide, fake smile and headed over to the table, not surprised to find that Kelly was sitting with two rough-looking men. One was wearing a red bandanna on his head, tied in the front with a knot. He had tattoos up and down his arms, mostly of naked women—easily seen because of the short-sleeved shirt he was wearing—and he scowled at her as she came toward the table. He was Hispanic, and his brown eyes and dark skin blended in with the low light of the bar.

The other man was white, and the smirk he aimed her way scared Alexis almost as much as the scowl on the other man's face. His teeth were crooked and brown. He was wearing a long-sleeved shirt, but she could see tattoos on his knuckles and, when she got close enough, saw three teardrops tattooed near his eye. She'd done enough research to know that they probably represented the number of men he'd killed. *Fuck.*

Alexis kept her smile in place and made sure to keep her body centered on the table, to try to give the camera the best view of the occupants. She stopped near the empty chair, which unfortunately had its back to the room, which meant *her* back would be to the room, and chirped, "Kelly! It's so good to see you. I hope I'm not late."

"Nope, right on time," she mumbled.

"I can't wait to meet your friends," Alexis continued, ignoring the surly tone of the woman. She turned to the white man and stuck out her hand in greeting. "I'm Alexis. It's so great to meet you. It's been forever since I've seen Kelly, but any friend of hers is a friend of mine." She hoped she wasn't overdoing it, and somehow managed to keep the silly smile on her face as the man took her hand in his.

She got an immediate feeling of claustrophobia as his large hand engulfed her smaller one. He squeezed a bit too hard, but Alexis didn't flinch.

"A-lex-is," he drawled her name out, making it sound as if she had a stripper name rather than a perfectly normal one. "Pretty name for a pretty girl. And I think you have it wrong. Any friend of Kelly's is a friend of *ours*."

She noted that the man didn't tell her his name, but she ignored it for now, dipping her head as if embarrassed. The man held her hand for a beat longer than was socially acceptable, but Alexis didn't let the smile fall from her face for even a moment. He finally dropped her hand, and she turned to the other guy at the table and stuck out the same hand. She really wanted to rub her palm on her pants to wipe off the feeling of slime the first man had somehow left on her skin, but gamely pushed onward.

The Hispanic man didn't say anything and ignored her outstretched hand. He only lifted his head in greeting and grunted. *Okay then.*

Trying to stay in her role of a ditzy socialite who was slumming, Alexis pulled out the chair at the table and sat. Making a big deal out of putting her leather Coach bag over the back of her chair before turning around and putting her elbows on the table in front of her and leaning in.

"So . . . it's so great to meet you guys," Alexis repeated, giggling. "I haven't heard of Snake's, and I've been coming to bars in this area for ages and ages. Kelly, what've you been up to all these years since high school? Do you have a boyfriend? What do you do for a living?"

Feeling the strain of being the only one saying anything, Alexis really wanted to get Kelly talking.

The other woman looked at both men for a beat before saying, "Oh, you know, this and that. I've got a man. Of course I do. The economy sucks, so I do what I can to keep my head above water. What is it you do again?"

It was a completely vague answer that said nothing, but Alexis went with it and launched into the cover story she and Blake and his brothers had come up with. "Oh, I know what you mean. I've had so many jobs since college it isn't even funny. I've waitressed, been a secretary, been in sales, and generally had to deal with all sorts of rich assholes. So annoying!" She rolled her eyes to emphasize her point. "And I know *I'm* rich, but I sure hope I don't act like some of the jerks I come in contact with. It's partly why I like to hang out in bars on this side of the city. I get to meet real men, rather than the metrosexuals who slick back their hair and think they're God's gift to women. I decided that working full time just wasn't worth it. Why do something I hate all day when I don't need to? It's not like I really need to work; I've got the money, and it's more fun to hang out and party."

"Where, woman? Jesus, just spit it out. Fuck!" the Hispanic man growled harshly.

He brought his hand up in the air in Alexis's direction so swiftly she instinctively flinched away from him. Laughing, he didn't take his eyes from hers as he bit out loudly, "A round, Bear!"

Realizing he *hadn't* been about to hit her but was signaling the huge bartender, whose name was apparently Bear, Alexis giggled nervously, not faking it this time.

"Sorry! I work at a boutique downtown. Just chatting with the women who come in and helping them find clothes and accessories. It's boring as hell, but I don't have to do anything hard, and, as I said, I don't really need the money. I do get discounts, which is nice. I can get as many designer purses and clothes as I want. And the best part is that I only have to go in in the afternoons, so I've got time to get over any hangovers I might have from the night before."

A woman appeared at their table as soon as Alexis stopped talking. She was wearing a short miniskirt that barely covered her crotch and was so tight it looked painted on. Her halter top looked more like a push-up bra than an actual shirt, and Alexis couldn't help but think about how uncomfortable it had to be for the woman, with her boobs in her face all day, but if it was, she didn't show it. She leaned over the table, practically spilling out of her top, and slowly placed four shot glasses on the table, one at a time.

The Hispanic guy—she still didn't know his name—put his hand on the back of the waitress's thigh and moved it upward as she was bent over. The woman didn't squeal and slap him as Alexis would've done if someone had tried that with her, but instead she coyly turned her head, smiled, and widened her stance. Alexis pretended not to notice that the man was feeling her up right there at the table and instead exclaimed, while clapping her hands and bouncing in her seat ridiculously, "Shots! Awesome!"

She really didn't want to drink any kind of alcohol, but it wasn't like she could refuse. She'd talked with Blake and his brothers about the possibility of having to drink to fit in, and they'd suggested she just go with the flow. If she could, they told her to choose a mixed drink that had relatively little alcohol in it, but it didn't look like she was going to get a choice in the matter.

"You like shots?" Kelly drawled, her eyebrows shooting upward.

"Oh yeah. Sex on the beach, blow job, lemon drop, and blue Hawaiians are some of my favorites."

"Pussy drinks," the Hispanic man snarled. "You want to drink at Snake's, you start with tequila and go from there."

Damn, damn, damn. Alexis hadn't ever done a shot of tequila, or really *any* straight alcohol, and knew it was way out of her comfort zone, but she wasn't being asked, she was being ordered.

So she said, "Sounds good to me," as if it was the best idea she'd heard in ages.

The waitress cracked open the new bottle of tequila and poured four generous shots of the dark-brown liquid into the glasses on the table.

The men and Kelly each picked up a shot glass and looked at her expectantly. Alexis reached out and grabbed the last one and held it as if she were toasting. "To old friends . . . and new!"

No one said anything, and Alexis saw Kelly roll her eyes, but pretended she didn't. Then they all threw back the drinks. Saying a quick prayer, Alexis copied their movements, bringing the glass to her lips and swallowing the vile alcohol in one gulp. She smiled, then immediately started coughing as the alcohol burned its way down her throat and threatened to come back up.

The white guy laughed and patted her way too hard on the back, the Hispanic man eyeballed her with narrowed eyes, and Kelly grinned evilly at her discomfort.

When she felt as if she could speak, Alexis croaked out, "Strong."

"The more expensive the liquor, the easier it goes down," the white guy drawled, with his hand still on her back. He was caressing her now, much like Blake did, which made Alexis's skin crawl. Blake's touch she craved; this man's, not so much. But she could see where he was going with his comment. It looked like she'd have to prove herself sooner rather than later.

Without a word, she twisted in her seat, luckily dislodging the white guy's hand from her back in the process, and pulled out her wallet from her bag. She made a production of opening it on the table, so everyone could see the contents, and took out four one-hundred-dollar bills. "Well for God's sake, I think we need the most expensive stuff this place has. The easier it goes down, the happier I'll be." It wasn't exactly a lie.

The waitress, who hadn't moved from her spot next to the Hispanic guy, maybe because of the way his hand was moving under her skirt and the obvious enjoyment she was getting out of it, or maybe because she wanted to see Alexis's humiliation, snatched the money from her hand and drawled, "I'll be back with the best shit we've got."

"Can I get a salad too?" Alexis asked quickly. She wasn't sure she could get anything down, but since she was there supposedly to eat lunch, she needed to play the part. Not to mention anything in her stomach that would soak up the alcohol had to be a good thing. "Oh, and a bottle of water too. Gotta rinse the taste of that cheap stuff out of my mouth," she ad-libbed.

The Hispanic guy's lips finally moved up a fraction at that. "I think we're gonna get along just fine, *chica*," he drawled, putting the index finger that had been busy under the waitress's skirt into his mouth and sucking it.

Alexis shuddered. Gross. Jesus, this was a nightmare. These men were rude and crude, and she wanted nothing to do with them. What the hell had she gotten herself into? She wasn't a PI. She was in way over her head. As if a bad omen, a shiver ran down her spine.

"We had some good times, didn't we, Alexis?" Kelly said in a tone that actually sounded like she was reminiscing.

It was the first time Alexis had seen any trace of the girl she'd once been best friends with. "We did." This time the smile Kelly aimed at Alexis seemed genuine.

Quicker than she would've thought possible, the waitress was back. This time she had two bottles of some sort of dark alcohol as well as a tiny bottle of water for Alexis that was no more than a shot itself. She was relieved that it was actually a bottle, though, because after all the stories she'd heard from Logan about what happened to women who accepted drinks without seeing them being made, she wasn't going to take a chance and drink anything anyone in this bar gave her that wasn't sealed from the get-go.

The waitress then placed the two bottles of liquor down, one in front of each of the men.

"Tequila Tapatio. Best shit we've got. Enjoy."

Without a word, the Hispanic man opened the bottle in front of him—the safety seal crinkling loudly in the quiet bar—and quickly poured a generous shot into each of the glasses on the table, not caring when it overflowed and spilled onto the carved-up wooden tabletop. He picked up his glass, sloshing it over his hand in the process, and turned to Alexis. "To a pretty *puta* I can't wait to get to know better."

Alexis smiled gamely, pretending not to know he'd just called her a bitch, and picked up her own glass. *Fucking shit.* She'd never been a big drinker, much preferring the sweet mixed cocktails she'd mentioned earlier. She glanced at her watch. It was only ten minutes after eleven. *Damn.* She needed to stay as long as possible to get as much information about the gang as she could, but she was going to be completely shitfaced in no time if the men kept pouring the shots as fast as they were.

No matter how drunk she got, she knew without a doubt that Blake would take care of her. He'd make sure she got home safely. All she had to do was play her part until she could safely escape. And it looked like she'd be making that exit sooner than she'd planned if things continued as they were.

Bringing her glass up, Alexis said, "Running into Kelly at the store was the best thing that's happened to me lately."

"Us too, Alexis Grant. Us too," the white guy said grinning.

The use of her last name when she hadn't given it to either man was the last real clear memory she had of lunch. She did shot after shot, smiling and laughing with Kelly and the two men as they continued to drink. Her salad came, and Alexis remembered eating as much of it as she could between the shots the men were pressing on her.

The room was spinning, and Alexis knew if she drank one more glass of liquor she most likely wouldn't be able to walk. She'd lost count of how many shots she'd done, but one bottle was empty, and they'd made quite a dent in the other one.

The white guy—his name was Chuck, which she thought was more of a nickname than a real name—had gotten more and more handsy with her as lunch had continued. He'd pulled his chair closer to hers and had his hand resting on her leg. His fingers brushed against her inner thigh, and Alexis knew she really would throw up if he tried to feel her up. Thank God she was wearing pants. She was pretty sure that if she'd been in a skirt he would've had his hands up it.

Even the Hispanic guy, who turned out to be *the* Damian, Donovan's brother, had seemed to ease off her a bit as the lunch went on. He asked lots of questions, which Alexis hoped she'd answered correctly. It was getting tougher and tougher to keep her mind on what she was supposed to be doing. And Kelly seemed to totally relax. They'd laughed over things they'd done as preteens and reminisced about their friendship before the seventh grade.

Alexis finally called a halt to the lunch. "What time is it? Twelve fifteen? Oh shit, I gotta go."

"Don't go yet. We're just starting to party," Chuck drawled, clamping his fingers together roughly on her leg when she tried to stand.

Holding back the whimper at the pain his hard grip was causing, Alexis giggled like the airhead she was trying to be and pushed at his wrist playfully. "Some of us gotta work, ya know!"

"But you said you don't *have* to work," Damian drawled. "Stay here with us, *chica*."

"I don't really, but I'm supposed to be there today," Alexis told him, smiling. "Don't worry, I'd love to hang out with you guys again. You're fun. If you wouldn't mind?"

"We wouldn't mind," Chuck answered immediately.

He ignored the scowl Kelly threw his way.

"Did I pay for the shots already?" Alexis asked, trying to sound confused.

"No, you said you'd run a tab," Kelly was quick to say.

"Oh shit. Okay, I've got cash, I can pay. How much was it, do you think?" Alexis could hear her voice slurring, and she wasn't even acting now.

"How much you got?" Damian asked, leaning forward.

How they could've drunk as much as she did and not even look tipsy in the least was beyond Alexis.

She fumbled in her bag and once more brought out her wallet. She made a production of looking in the compartment that held her cash. She wrinkled her nose. "It's dark in here. I can't see. How much do I have?" She held out her wallet to Damian. He did as she wanted and took it from her, rifling through it.

He pulled out some bills—Alexis had no idea how many—and handed her wallet back. "This ought to do it."

"Thank you so much," Alexis trilled at him, smiling. "Jeez, I need to build up my tolerance," she giggled.

She stood, dislodging Chuck's grip once and for all off her leg. She held her hand up to her face, using her pinkie and thumb to mimic talking into a phone, and turned to Kelly. "Call me, Kel. I can't wait to do this again."

"I'll be in touch. Don't worry. Later."

"See ya, doll," Chuck said, leering at her, his rotten teeth making her look away so she wouldn't throw up in his lap.

Damian just lifted his chin at her once again and poured himself another shot of the top-shelf alcohol she'd just paid for . . . twice.

No one at the table, or even in the bar for that matter, said one word about calling her a cab as she stumbled drunkenly to the door, obviously completely shitfaced. They didn't give a damn if she drove drunk; they'd gotten what they'd wanted out of her: money.

Alexis pushed open the door, wincing at the bright light that assaulted her eyes. She turned back once more to the dark room and waved in the direction of the table she'd been sitting at for the last hour or so even though she couldn't see a thing.

"Bye, Kelly! Bye, Chuck and Damian! It was great meeting you guys and seeing you again! Till next time!"

No one answered, so she turned back toward the fresh air, tripping over the jamb on her way out. The door slammed behind her and Alexis stood in front of it, trying not to fall over, squinting to try to see where she'd left her car. She vaguely remembered parking on the side and to the back, out of the way of the front door of the bar.

She took a deep breath of the fresh air, but it only made her dizzier. She took a step toward her Mercedes. Then another. She had no idea how in the hell she was going to drive out of there, but she'd do it . . . if only far enough to park in the nearest parking lot away from prying eyes. Her thoughts were muddled. She knew she absolutely shouldn't be driving anywhere, but she had to get her car out of the lot; it stood out like a sore thumb.

She somehow reached her Mercedes at the far side of the lot and took her keys out to put in the lock, when a hand closed around hers and a large body pressed her hard into the side of her car.

Chapter Seven

"Get in the car, Lex."

"Blake," she breathed out in relief.

He didn't respond but clicked open the lock and opened the door for her. He watched, furious as Alexis clumsily crawled over the driver's seat on her hands and knees and into the passenger side. Her ass in his face should've turned him on, but he was so pissed off at what had happened in the bar, at what Alexis had been made to do, all he could think of was getting out of there and back to her apartment.

"What about Nathan's car?" Alexis slurred as Blake started up her Mercedes.

"That piece of shit will blend right in here. No one will touch it."

"I could've left mine here."

"Lex," Blake said in exasperation. "You know we can't leave your Mercedes here. It'd be stripped before nightfall. Trust me, Nathan's piece of shit won't be noticed."

"Oh. Yeah." She furrowed her brow in confusion. "Okay."

Blake clenched his teeth together. The second that asshole Damian ordered the first shots of tequila, he knew lunch wasn't exactly going to go as planned. He'd had to sit and watch and listen as Lex downed way too fucking many shots for her slight frame. It'd be a miracle if she remembered anything. He was impressed she was still upright at the moment.

But even though he was pissed, he was as proud of Lex as he could be. Not once did she break her cover. She gamely got as much information out of Kelly and the men as she could, all the while choking down the alcohol.

Because of Alexis, they'd learned that Damian was visiting his brother every week, and Donovan was still very much in charge of his gang. He gave Damian orders to be carried out, and Damian seemed more than happy to do so. He didn't tell Lex specifics but insinuated enough for them to know Donovan was just as dangerous behind bars as he was free. They'd also found out that Kelly was Donovan's girlfriend, as they'd suspected, but if the tone of the other woman's voice when she'd talked about a mysterious ex-girlfriend was any indication, she wasn't too happy that Donovan still kept tabs on his ex. Chuck seemed to be the gang's main enforcer. He was a mean motherfucker, who not only seemed to screw any chick he felt like, whether she wanted the attention or not, but he had no problem using the pistol he kept in a holster on his leg, which he happily showed to Alexis when she expressed interest in seeing it.

All in all, Alexis getting drunk had seemed to loosen the trio's lips—probably because they rightly assumed she wouldn't remember anything they'd talked about. Luckily, Ace Security had both the audio and video of the lunch.

As he'd done the first time, Blake had stopped the recordings as soon as Alexis left the bar and right before he made his way to her. He knew she'd be embarrassed to be on tape while drunk, and anything she said or did after leaving the bar was no one's business but theirs.

"I'm drunk," Alexis announced unnecessarily as Blake drove away from Snake's Bar toward the interstate to head back to Denver and her apartment.

"I know, Lex," Blake said patiently.

"No, Blake. I'm *drunk*," she insisted.

"Alexis, I *know*," Blake repeated. "I fucking sat there and watched you do all those shots."

"They were gross," she stated, still slurring.

His lips twitched at that. Not quite ready to smile, but he couldn't help it. The assholes she was with, especially Chuck, could've easily taken advantage of her drunken state. Blake had been on the verge of getting her out of the bar several times over the last hour. The men could've taken her to a back room, or even spirited her out the back door. Yes, he and Logan had told her what to do if they'd tried it, but they hadn't taken her being completely trashed into account. She would've been completely vulnerable . . . not able to defend herself in any way against them. The thought scared the shit out of him.

"I don't even like the taste of alcohol. I can drink sweet wine and froufrou drinks, but not that." She shuddered. "Tequila. Yucko."

"I'm afraid you're going to be in quite a bit of hurt later," Blake told her honestly.

Alexis laid her head back on the leather headrest and nodded. "I figured. But you'll take care of me." She sounded completely certain, and Blake was touched. Now that he'd gotten her out of the bar, he was getting less pissed off, but her flat out saying she knew he'd have her back went a long way toward making him relax. He had her now. Safe and sound.

"I was scared," she continued, drunk. "I didn't know what else to do." She swiveled her head in his direction. "But I knew you were listening and watching me. You'd protect me in case they did something. It's the only reason I kept drinking. Blake?"

"Yeah, sweetheart?"

"I don't like them. At all. Not even a little."

God, she was killing him. "I know, Lex. Neither do I."

"But I like *you*."

Damn.

She went on, the alcohol loosening her tongue, making her say exactly what she was thinking. "I used to think tattoos were sexy. But not anymore. I'm so glad you don't have any. Wait, do you? I haven't seen you naked, so I don't know for sure."

"I don't have any tattoos, Lex," he reassured her.

"Good. Although, I know yours would be cool. No teardrops. 'Kay?"

As if. "I need to get you some water," Blake noted, talking more to himself than to her.

"I tried to drink some between shots, but the skank waitress wouldn't bring me another bottle."

"I know, I saw, remember?"

"Oh yeah. You probably saw her boobs hanging out too. My boobs aren't that big." Alexis bought her hands up to her chest and lifted her breasts to show him. The alcohol had done its job well enough to lower her inhibitions to the point she obviously wasn't even thinking about what she was doing. "Do guys only like big boobs like that? Did you see Damian stick his fingers up that skank's skirt?"

He ignored her question about boobs. As far as he was concerned, her tits were perfect, but now wasn't the time or place to discuss it. "Yeah, Lex. I saw what he did."

"I about *died.* It wasn't sexy. Not in the least." She closed her eyes for a second; then they popped open again as she suddenly remembered something else. "And Chuck's hand on my leg *hurt.* Not like when you touch me."

"He touched you?" Blake's hands tightened on the steering wheel in his agitation. "I didn't see *that.*"

"Yeah. And it hurt. Kelly was acting so nice at the end. Do you think she's gonna invite me out again?"

Her changes in conversation were abrupt but easy to follow. He wanted to talk more about that asshole Chuck touching her, but he'd get a look at her leg soon and make sure she was okay. "Yeah, I'm sure she will. She's gonna want to meet up with you again. Hell, Lex, you gave them almost a thousand bucks. It's probably the easiest money they've made in a long time. They're gonna want more of that."

She was quiet for a long time. Blake thought she'd finally passed out until she spoke again. Quiet. And her words were clear, with no slurring, as if what she was saying was important enough for her to be clear and concise.

"People have only wanted to be my friend because of my money. I know it was my fault and I made it happen, but it's how it's always been and probably how it always will be. Those men scare me, Blake. Sitting there, knowing they were being nice only because of my money and all it would take was one wrong word on my part for them to turn on me reminded me of when I was thirteen, and I knew those boys were stronger than me and could do whatever they wanted."

Blake couldn't keep his hands to himself anymore. He wanted to take Alexis into his arms, but he had to wait until he got her back to her apartment. He pressed down on the gas, needing to get there as soon as possible. He moved his right hand from the steering wheel and wrapped it around the back of her neck as he usually did. His thumb stroked the skin right under her ear. "You're done, Lex. You don't ever have to see them again."

Her head fell against his arm as if it were too heavy to keep upright. "I do have to." Her voice was slurring again. "They want more money. So I will. As long as I know you'll be there to keep me safe, I can do it."

Fuck, she was seriously killing him. "Lex—"

She didn't let him say what he wanted to say. "I'm scared, but you won't let them hurt me. If you were around back then, you'd have taken all those boys on for me. I know it."

"Damn straight. I would've protected you back then, and I sure as hell will make sure nothing happens to you now, sweetheart."

Alexis lifted her head and turned in her seat, dislodging his hand from her neck, bending one leg at the knee, and facing him awkwardly with the seat belt holding her immobile. She caught his hand as he was pulling it back to the steering wheel and placed it on her knee.

Then she ran both her hands up his forearm, past his elbow, until her fingertips disappeared under the fabric of his T-shirt. Then she reversed her actions, running her hands over him until she reached his wrist. She did this several times, seemingly mesmerized by the feel of his arm under her.

When Blake didn't think he'd be able to stand it anymore, she finally spoke. "I love your arms. They're so strong. Not crazy mus-cu-lar, but they're so hot. I've dreamed about them."

Blake felt his cock hardening under his jeans. Damn, she was so sensual, even when plastered. He should stop her—she'd be embarrassed that she'd been so candid with him—but he couldn't seem to make himself do it. Her hands on his skin felt too good.

"What do you dream, Lex?"

She raised her eyes and met his then, and Blake had to swallow at the lust he saw there. She was way past drunk, which made her bolder. Made her say exactly what she was thinking.

"Your arms around me. Holding me still as you take me from behind. Slicked up in the shower. Shit, Blake, all you have to do is flex, pick up something, and I'm so wet for you I have to change my panties."

Unbelievably, he was getting embarrassed. He'd known she liked his arms—had guessed—but hearing her straight up admit it made the times he saw her nipples get hard and her breathing increase all that more potent. Because she'd done it a lot. Practically since the first day they'd worked together. Knowing she'd been turned on by him since the beginning was hot. "Lex, I don't think—"

But she was on a roll. "I don't know why your arms do it for me so much." She wrinkled her forehead, deep in thought. Her head tilted as if she was thinking hard, and she bit her lip before she spoke again. "I don't look at Logan's that way. And he's muscular too. Nathan's arms do nothing for me. Not that he's bad looking, but he's not you. I wasn't such an arm whore until I met you." She ran her fingertips over the veins in his forearm as she looked down at it. "Arm porn—that's what your arms are for me."

Before Blake could respond to her sexy-as-fuck statement, she leaned over and ran her tongue up a prominent vein on the outside of his arm. He jerked in reaction. Luckily he'd just pulled up in front of her apartment; otherwise he probably would've wrecked her car. He felt her hot, wet tongue as if she'd licked his cock rather than his arm.

He pulled his arm out of her grasp and slammed the car into park. Without a word, he exited the vehicle and walked around to the other side and opened her door.

Alexis hadn't moved. She was still facing the driver's side and had her seat belt around her. Her head was resting on the seat, and she looked like a twisted pretzel as she sat there, trying to keep him in her eyesight merely by moving her head but not changing position in the seat. Blake leaned across her and clicked her seat belt open, then easily turned her and took hold of her hand, helping her to stand.

She sighed and looked down at where he was holding her up for a moment, then met his eyes. "See? It's so damn sexy."

Blake couldn't respond; he was on the edge. Wanting her more than anything, but knowing there was no way he'd *ever* take advantage of her when she was so drunk. But damn, Alexis pushed all his buttons.

"Come on, Lex. Let's get you upstairs."

"Are you coming too?"

"Yeah." But not for what she was probably hoping if her puckered nipples and dilated eyes were any indication.

"Good," Alexis told him, wrapping her arms around him and laying her head on his chest trustingly.

Blake gave her car keys to the valet and ushered her to the door. He was carrying her more than she was walking, but at least they were moving.

The doorman spoke quietly in his Indonesian accent as Blake approached. "Is Miss Grant all right?"

"She's good, Osman. Just had a bit too much to drink at lunch," Blake reassured him.

"That's not like her."

"It's not," Blake agreed. "But I've got her. She's safe." He met the smaller man's eyes. Whatever Osman saw seemed to reassure him as he nodded and held open the door.

Blake and Alexis were quiet in the elevator as they made their way up to her apartment. He held on to her as he helped her weave her way down the hall to her door. Within seconds they were inside, and Blake led her straight to her bedroom.

"Can you get changed on your own, or do you need my help?"

Alexis looked up at him with huge eyes. "Change?" She went to look at the watch on her wrist but gave up trying to read it, looking up at him instead. "But it's early . . . isn't it? It's still light outside."

"Trust me, Lex. In a few hours you're gonna feel like you're gonna die. You'll fare better if you put on a pair of sweats and a T-shirt."

She looked confused but nodded anyway. "Okay."

"So? You need me to help you? Can you get the wire off by yourself?"

"I can do it."

Blake wasn't sure she could but gave her the benefit of the doubt. "Okay, sweetheart. I'm going to get you some water and maybe make you some toast. You think you could eat that?"

"I'm not hungry," she told him, looking befuddled.

"I know, but it might help . . . later."

She shrugged. "Okay, Blake. Whatever you think."

Blake couldn't help himself; he leaned over and kissed her on the forehead and took her into his arms. "Whatever happens later, Lex, don't be embarrassed, okay?"

She looked up at him, eyebrows furrowed, frowning. "Is it gonna be embarrassing?"

Ignoring her question, he said instead, "I'm so fucking proud of you, Lex. Just remember that."

"'Kay. I'm proud of you too."

He smiled at that. "Change," he ordered, stepping back, keeping a hand out to make sure she was steady on her feet before taking another step toward her bedroom door. "Put the necklace and the mic on the dresser. I'll be right back."

She nodded then but didn't take her eyes off him as he walked backward to her doorway, then disappeared into the hallway.

Fuck. He'd liked Lex before, but a drunk, turned-on Lex, saying whatever popped into her brain, was cute as all get-out and almost impossible to resist. But he would. He'd never do anything to her without her full and sober consent. He didn't even want to pump her for information about how she felt about him, not that he'd needed to in the first place. She was more than eager to tell him. Prying for information while she was drunk felt wrong somehow. He needed to distract her; maybe they could watch a movie or something until she passed out or fell asleep.

Blake had no doubt that she'd be throwing up later. He didn't think she could drink as much as she did and *not* throw up. Hell, most men he knew wouldn't be able to. He'd stay until she was over the worst of it, then get back to Castle Rock with the audio and video tapes. He'd discuss with Logan and Nathan their next steps. He'd do all he could to keep Alexis out of it, but he was afraid that wouldn't be possible anymore. She was neck-deep in the middle of the op, and now that it'd started, they needed to see it play out.

He'd told her she was done out of sheer frustration and because he was scared for her. Hopefully, she'd only need to meet with the gang one more time to get information about upcoming jobs and how they were contacted to do them. That should be enough ammunition for the task force to start making arrests. If luck was on their side, the gang members wouldn't have any idea that it was Alexis who had been their downfall.

When Blake came back to her room after getting her some water and food, she was lying on her bed, wearing a pair of black sleep shorts and a tank top. She sat up, and he took a deep breath at the vision in front of him. The tank was tight, outlining her curves clearly. He could see her nipples straining against the front of the material and her slight love handles. It was sexy as hell on her. He wanted nothing more than to strip the tank up and off her so he could see, and touch, her exquisite body.

She moved to sit cross-legged on the mattress, and Blake almost swallowed his tongue. She was covered . . . barely. The shorts pulled up her thighs with her movement and, if he was a different kind of man, gave easy access to her sex. All it would take was pushing the scrap of fabric to one side, and he'd see all of her. His mouth almost watered at the thought of her pink pussy. Blake knew she had absolutely no idea how sexy she was or how much willpower it was taking for him to keep his hands to himself.

He put the glass of water, the pills he'd found in a cabinet in her guest bathroom, and the two pieces of toast on her bedside table. "You feel okay?" Blake asked softly, not able to completely keep from touching her. He put one large hand on her knee, running his thumb over her smooth skin, and the other he used to brush a light-brown lock of hair away from her face.

"Dizzy," Alexis responded, her eyes closed, leaning into his hand. "But okay."

"Good. Here, drink as much of this as you can, and take the pills too." He leaned over, snagged the glass of water, and held it out to her.

Opening her eyes and gazing at him trustingly, she took the glass from his hand, the warmth of her fingers brushing against his, making his cock jump in his pants. She drank half the water before stopping to breathe. She threw the pills into her mouth without even asking what they were, trusting him enough to do whatever he asked, and washed them down with another long swallow.

Blake handed her a piece of toast, and she nibbled on it without saying a word, her eyes having shifted from his face to his forearm as she ate. After she'd eaten the first piece, he tried to get her to eat the second, but she shook her head, then washed down what she'd eaten with the rest of the water from the glass.

She lay down then, curling on her side, bringing her eyes back up to his.

"Tired?" Blake asked.

"A little," she said, softly. "Will you stay in here with me?"

She sounded a little better, although he knew she was still very drunk. "Until you fall asleep."

"Will you be here when I wake up?" she asked.

"Yes. We need to talk about what happened."

She wrinkled her nose, and Blake thought she looked exactly like a little kid who was just told there was no Santa Claus. "I drank too much—that's what happened," she declared.

"No, Lex. They made you drink too much. There's a difference."

"They didn't hold a gun to my head, Blake. They didn't *make* me. I could've said no."

"Would you have gotten shitfaced at eleven in the morning if you weren't there undercover trying to get information about the gang?" Blake asked bluntly.

She scrunched up her face and shook her head. "No, but—"

"Do you think they would've opened up if you hadn't done those shots with them?"

"Probably not, but I could've—"

"They made you drink too much, Lex. Period."

"Whatever," Alexis said in a huff, sounding very put out.

Blake couldn't help it. She sounded exactly like she did when she was completely sober and irritated with him. He chuckled.

Her face softened, and she reached out a hand and ran it up his arm, which was bracing himself up next to her. "I like it when you smile at me. You don't do it enough."

She was right; he didn't. Ever since he was a teenager, he didn't like putting his emotions on display or letting go of the control he'd always kept around his feelings. But it was getting harder to maintain that control around her, especially since they'd kissed. "I'll try to be better at that."

Alexis licked her lips and looked up at him with wide eyes. "Good. Are you going to make love to me?"

"What?" Blake asked, sitting up in shock.

"You said I'd be embarrassed later. You said you wanted me, and I figured you realized I hadn't done it before, so I'd be embarrassed later when you got naked with me. No one's seen me naked before, so . . ." Her voice trailed off.

"Fuck me," Blake breathed. How in the world had the beautiful woman lying on the bed in front of him never had sex before? He'd known she was inexperienced—it wasn't something she'd hidden very well—but he had no idea that she'd never had sex before. "You're a virgin?"

She rolled her eyes, and he loved seeing some of her innate sass come out, even when she was drunk as a skunk. How in the hell she'd hidden this part of her personality from Kelly, Damian, and that asshole Chuck, he had no idea. "I hate that word. It's stupid. *Virgin.* It makes me feel like we're back in the stone ages. I haven't had a real dick inside me, no, but I've seen videos. I know how it works."

With every word out of her mouth, Blake came closer and closer to saying fuck it, and taking her as he longed to. "A *real* dick?" It wasn't what he wanted to ask, but the question popped out anyway.

"Yeah. I have vibrators . . . dildos . . ." She gestured to the night table, and it was all Blake could do not to pounce on the handle and jerk it open to see exactly what kind of toys Alexis Grant used on herself when she was alone and horny. "I don't think I have a . . . what's it called? That thing in romance books guys always have to push through and it makes the girl bleed?"

"Uh . . . a hymen?" Blake asked, completely flummoxed by the conversation.

"Yeah!" she exclaimed happily, propping herself up on an elbow, making her tits move and bounce under the tank top she was wearing. "That's it! I don't think I have one anymore because it doesn't hurt when I push my dildo all the way inside me . . . but I hope it doesn't feel like a real dick, because the one I have is really hard and is kinda painful. The first time I put it in, it hurt really bad. I didn't use it again that way for another year . . . so I don't do it all that much. I like my vibrator on my clit more. *That* feels good. It sucks guys don't have a clit. You don't know what you're missing."

"Okay, I think we're done with this conversation," Blake said in strangled voice, shifting his hips away from Alexis, not wanting her to see what her not-so-innocent words were doing to his body.

"Good." And with that she sat up and brought both hands to the bottom of her tank top and went to pull it up and over her head. "Don't laugh at me, okay? I'm kinda fat, and it would suck if you laughed."

Blake quickly caught her hands, but not before he got a glimpse of her soft belly and the underside of her tits. Jesus, he wanted his hands on her. Bad. "You are most certainly not fat. Why don't we just lay here together for a while first?" he suggested.

"Oh. You need more foreplay. 'Kay. Will you lay behind me with your arm between my boobs? I've dreamed about that too."

Blake took another deep, fortifying breath. She had no idea how much strength it was taking for him not to come in his pants. Every word out of her mouth went straight to his dick. He almost felt dizzy with the blood loss from his brain.

"Sure, Lex. Turn over."

She immediately lay on her back and shifted over to her side. Blake glanced down at her long legs and saw for the first time a bruise forming on her upper thigh. He'd been so distracted by her shorty shorts earlier he'd missed it. He stopped her from rolling with a hand at her waist. He brushed his fingertips lightly over the mark. "What's this from?"

Alexis lifted her head from her pillow and braced herself on her elbows, looking down at herself. She scrunched up her nose in concentration, then said, "I don't . . . oh wait . . . maybe from Chuck?"

"Chuck?" Blake bit out.

"Yeah. He was really handsy. That must've happened when I went to leave. I told you he touched me. He grabbed me and it hurt."

"Mother*fucker*," Blake swore, then hurried to soothe Alexis when she flinched. "I'm not mad at you, sweetheart. I'm pissed at him."

"Oh, okay." She didn't quite look convinced.

"Turn over," he ordered, trying to make his voice sound normal, wanting to get the sight of her bruised flesh out of his vision as quickly as possible.

She did as he asked, and Blake settled himself onto the bed behind her. He tried to keep some distance between then, but she wasn't having any of that. Alexis squirmed her hips back against him, snuggling into him until his cock was pressed up against her ass. She sighed and pulled his arm around her chest.

"Put it between my boobs" she ordered, wiggling her chest and shoulders until his arm was where she wanted it. "Yeah, like that."

Blake closed his eyes against the exquisite feeling of the heat of her breasts cradling his arm. His hand ended up resting against the side of her neck, and Alexis signed in contentment.

She grabbed hold of his forearm with both of her hands and ducked her chin into his wrist. "This," she murmured. "*This* is what I've dreamed about."

Blake had to admit it was amazing. He hadn't felt this close to a woman in . . . ever. No one had grabbed hold of him and held on as if he was the only thing keeping her from shattering into a million pieces the way Lex was right this moment. She was small enough that he completely surrounded her small body, engulfing it with his own. The way she cradled his arm and hand was both erotic and sweet. It was as if she was using his arm as a security blanket.

"We'll get naked later," she told him softly.

"Yeah, Lex. We will," Blake confirmed, although his definition of later and hers probably differed. He knew she would be in no condition to even think about making love in a few hours.

He lay in the bed behind Alexis until she fell asleep, or passed out; he wasn't sure which. He counted her breaths, reassuring himself that she was breathing normally. He could feel her heartbeat under his arm, and it made him realize for the first time in his life he wanted to do nothing but lie in bed, in the middle of the day, and cuddle with a woman, just as he was doing right this moment. And not any woman. *Alexis.*

As she lay snoring lightly in his arms, Blake vowed that she'd be his. He'd be the only man to see her naked. The only man to get inside her. The only man she'd dream about. She was his.

Chapter Eight

Alexis woke up with an urgent need to barf. She tried to throw off her blankets to get to the bathroom but couldn't. Panicking, she struggled against whatever was holding her down, and within seconds she was free. Feeling the vomit at the back of her throat, she quickly stumbled to the bathroom and barely got the lid of the toilet up before she was puking.

And puking.

And puking.

And puking.

Her stomach heaved trying to rid itself of the poison she'd consumed however many hours ago.

She moaned as she clutched the side of the toilet as her bile swelled up from her stomach again; she was completely miserable and wished she would die. Anything would be better than experiencing the hell she was in at this moment. When she couldn't bring up any more liquid, her body continued to rebel against her, leaving her dry heaving and gagging over the toilet bowl.

Just when she didn't think things could get worse, Alexis felt a pair of hands gently pull back the hair that was falling in her face as she leaned over the commode. She couldn't talk but tried to push whoever it was away. It was as if she was pushing against a brick wall.

"Shhhh, Lex. I got you."

Oh Lord. She was dead. This had to be hell.

If she wasn't mistaken, Blake Anderson was squatting behind her, holding back her hair as she puked her guts out.

Slamming her eyes shut, Alexis tried to control the overwhelming urge to purge every single molecule in her stomach. She vowed never to drink again. *Never.* Not even to find out more information about the Inca Boyz. Not even if Blake begged her to do it. Although she knew without a doubt he'd never do that to her.

"Here, sweetheart. Take this. A towel."

Without opening her eyes, Alexis felt the soft cotton material pressed against her hand. She gripped it as if it was a lifeline and brought it to her face. She wiped the vomit from her nose as best she could, then her mouth. Finally, she sat back on her heels, feeling Blake ease back from behind her, giving her some room.

"You okay?"

"Don't know," Alexis mumbled into the towel, not ready to look up at the man who had no idea how much she loved him. She did *not* want him to be there. To see her this way. She was completely mortified.

"Don't try to move yet. Just stay here. I'll be back."

Alexis nodded, not caring where Blake was going, just that he was *going. She* surely wasn't going anywhere.

She tried to breathe deeply, but that made her stomach roll again. After a minute or so, she turned, stretched her legs out, and rested her head on the cold tile floor of her bathroom. She should've been grossed out but couldn't get herself to care at that moment.

How long she was lying there, she had no idea, but she hoped it was enough for Blake to have seen himself out. But she wasn't so lucky. She heard him step into the bathroom again and settle himself on the floor in front of her bathtub.

"You don't have to stay," Alexis felt compelled to say.

"I know," was his calm answer.

Fuck.

"I don't want you here," she tried again.

"I know that too."

"Then why are you still here?" she moaned, still keeping her eyes closed.

"Because you need me."

Alexis sighed and pushed herself up until she was sitting. The room spun, and it took her a moment to breathe through her mouth, pushing the need to puke again down. When she felt she could talk without wanting to barf, she said, "I don't need you. People wake up with hangovers every day of the year. I'll be fine . . . eventually."

She glanced over at Blake. He was sitting with his back against her tub, one leg stretched out straight and the other bent. One arm was propped up on the bent knee, and he was looking at her with an intense stare that she'd seen from him before but still wasn't sure what it meant.

"I'm not leaving, Lex."

"Can you please at least leave the bathroom then?" she begged.

"Nope."

"Dammit, Blake. I don't need—" Alexis swallowed hard and closed her eyes against the tide of nausea rising up her throat. "Fuck," she muttered before clambering up to her knees and leaning over the toilet bowl. Her stomach clenched and the dry heaves started up again.

This time she was well aware of Blake behind her. He pulled her hair away from her face once more and held it with one hand at her neck. His other hand rested on her belly and supported her, as every muscle in her body tightened as she tried to throw up.

Alexis had never been so embarrassed as she was right that moment. Not even when she'd been in the tenth grade, and she'd dropped her tray in the middle of the lunchroom, and every single person had turned to stare at her. Not even when she figured out she'd only been asked to the prom by a boy she'd had a crush on to pay for the limo and dinner for three other couples. Not even when she'd thought a guy in college liked her, and she'd leaned in to kiss him, and he'd pulled back, horrified.

Nope. This was the most embarrassing moment in her entire life. And if she could sink into a hole in the ground, she would've welcomed it.

"I've got you, Lex," Blake murmured into her ear as she knelt in front of her toilet, panting in exertion. "It'll stop in a minute."

An hour later, Alexis lay on her side in her bed, finally feeling as if she might actually live. She'd been able to move back into the bedroom after three more bouts of dry heaving and had only had to run back into the bathroom once since then. It had been twenty minutes since the last urge to puke had come over her, and she hoped like hell she was done.

But now that the nausea had passed, other aches and pains were making themselves known in her body. Her head was pounding, her stomach muscles hurt, which wasn't surprising, and she was freezing.

As soon as the thought entered her head, Blake was there, pulling her comforter up and over her shoulders, engulfing her in the warmth it provided.

"I know it doesn't feel like it, but now that you've gotten some of the alcohol out of your system, you'll start to feel better."

"How in the world do people do that all the time? I feel awful."

His lips quirked up in a smile as he looked down at her. "I think their bodies get used to it so they don't react as . . . strongly . . . as you do."

Alexis could feel herself blushing. "Well, it's horrible."

"Agreed. Think you'll be all right for a bit while I go and make you something?"

"I can't eat anything, Blake. No way," Alexis told him, groaning.

"Nothing big. Plain toast. A glass of water maybe," he told her soothingly. "It'll help."

"And I might end up throwing that up again as well," she retorted.

"True. But I don't think so."

Alexis looked up at Blake for a long moment. He was wearing the same clothes she remembered him having on that morning—jeans, black T-shirt—but he was in his socks now, his black military-style boots obviously having been discarded somewhere.

"What time is it?" Alexis asked, not taking her eyes away from Blake.

He looked down at his watch on his wrist and then back to her. "Around six."

"At night?"

"Yeah."

"Don't you have someplace you need to be?"

At her question, Blake leaned down, propping himself up with one hand on her bedside table and the other on the mattress in front of her. All she could see was his face, and when she inhaled, all she could smell was him. She had no idea what kind of soap he used, but she knew she'd never be able to smell it ever again without thinking of this moment.

"I'm exactly where I need to be, Lex. Close your eyes, relax. I'll be back in a bit with something for you to try to eat."

Then he leaned in closer—Alexis couldn't help but look down at the muscles in his arm as he did—and kissed her on the forehead. It was such a sweet move; she bit her lip to keep the tears from falling from her eyes.

Blake stood, brushed a lock of hair from her cheek to behind her ear, then strode out of her bedroom.

The second he left, she dashed to the bathroom to brush her teeth. She hadn't remembered doing it after she'd puked, and there was nothing she wanted more right this second than to wash away the lingering taste of vomit.

Thankful the taste of her toothpaste didn't start her up again, Alexis returned to her bedroom and got under the covers, once more getting comfortable. She turned her head into her pillow and took a deep breath, surprised when all she could smell was Blake. She lifted her head and stared down at the pillow. Had he lain beside her while she'd been sleeping? She racked her brain trying to remember what had happened after she left the bar, but it was all a blank. She vaguely remembered feeling safe, but that was about it. *Damn.* What had happened? Had she said something to Kelly and the others and ruined the undercover operation? Would Blake still be here with her if she had?

She had so many questions, and now that her body was finally easing its powerful rebellion against what she'd put into it, she could think more clearly. Alexis carefully eased up into a sitting position on the mattress, putting the pillows behind her back to support her, and looked around.

She didn't see the clothes she'd worn to the bar that morning anywhere, although she did see the mic and the pendant with the camera sitting on her dresser across the room. Reaching up to finger her ear, Alexis realized she wasn't wearing the earrings she'd had on earlier either.

She had on a tank top and her sleep shorts, which made her turn red with embarrassment all over again. Lord, she'd been bent over her toilet, practically naked, with Blake Anderson tucked up against her. He had to have seen, and felt, every inch of her. And while she showed more when she was wearing a bathing suit . . . she hadn't shown it to *Blake.*

She wasn't exactly Kate Moss . . . more like a short Marilyn Monroe. And while she knew some men preferred the look of the curvy actress, she was convinced, if asked, most would pick the svelte and slender Kate ten to one.

Wanting to put something on, to cover herself, Alexis swung her legs over the side of the bed once more, only to quickly pull them back up and under the covers when Blake appeared in her doorway.

"You need to go back to the bathroom?" he asked quickly, the lines in his face deepening with worry as he hurried to her side.

"No, I'm good. I was just going to put something else on," Alexis admitted, pulling the comforter up to her chest.

"Oh, good. I was afraid you were gonna start dry heaving again," Blake told her, sounding relieved.

Alexis closed her eyes in embarrassment once more. Just the words "dry heaving" on his lips were mortifying. She was never going to live this down.

As if he could read her mind, Blake said, "I already told you, Lex, don't be embarrassed. About anything that happens between us." Blake's voice was soft and tender and didn't hold an ounce of mirth or teasing. Which kind of surprised her. He loved to tease her and always called her on her mistakes . . . in a nice way, but called her on them nevertheless.

She opened her eyes and looked at him. He'd taken a seat on the mattress near her hip, and his eyes were glued to her own. He looked at her differently than he ever had before. She didn't know how, but she'd never seen him look at her like he was right now. As if he . . . cared.

"I don't remember you telling me not to be embarrassed, and it's not like you can simply order me not to be. Blake, you saw me throwing up. It's not exactly the best way to impress someone."

"You don't have to impress me, Lex. You already did that this morning during lunch."

Alexis bit her lip and broke eye contact, looking down at her hands.

"Do you remember anything?" Blake asked tenderly.

She shook her head. "Not really. Was I . . . did they say anything we can use?"

"Yeah, sweetheart. You were amazing. We learned a lot from today."

The use of the endearment threw her for a moment. He was acting extremely weird, and Alexis had no idea why. What had she said or done to make him act so . . . nice toward her?

"Good. I'm glad. Um . . . like what?"

Instead of answering, Blake reached over and picked up two pills he'd brought in from the other room and a glass of water. "First, take a little sip of water, let it settle, then try another. If it seems like it'll stay down, then you can take the pills. It'll help with your headache."

"Thanks." Alexis did as he suggested, relieved when it seemed like her body was going to accept the water. She wanted to chug it down but knew that would be stupid. She was able to swallow both pills, and she leaned back against her pillows in relief.

"I'll tell you what we learned, and I'm sure you can watch the video and listen to the audio as well, but I think that will have to wait. The video is pretty shaky and would probably make you even more nauseous, at the moment. Do you trust me to tell you what went down?"

"Of course," Alexis said immediately. "Why wouldn't I?"

The smile on his face made her toes curl under the covers. It said so much. He was obviously pleased at her response, and didn't bother hiding his reaction. The look in his eyes was tender and full of that something she couldn't place. "I'll try never to do anything that will make you lose that trust you have in me, Lex."

"Okay," she whispered, sensing he meant a lot more than what she was understanding at the moment.

"Here," Blake said, holding a piece of plain white toast to her mouth. "Nibble on that while I tell you what happened."

He spent the next twenty minutes recounting the lunch. How Kelly had seemed standoffish at first, then seemed to warm the more she drank. How Damian had bragged about his brother still being in charge of the gang even though he was behind bars, and how Chuck couldn't keep his hands off her.

Alexis noticed that Blake's jaw got tight and his voice clipped when he told her the last part about Chuck.

"He even bruised you," Blake told her, obviously pissed on her behalf.

"He did? Where?"

"Your thigh. You said that he had his hand on your leg most of the lunch. I couldn't see it in the video. When you got up to leave, you told me he grabbed you hard and squeezed. You said it hurt."

Alexis shoved the comforter down so she could see her leg for herself. Sure enough, there was a slight purple bruise, which she knew from experience would get darker and uglier as time passed, on her leg above her knee. It was odd to be looking at her leg, seeing that what Blake was saying really had happened to her, even though she couldn't remember any of it.

Before she could bring the covers back up, Blake's fingers were touching her leg. He ran them lightly over the mark, as if by his mere touch he could erase and soothe it. Alexis held her breath as goose bumps broke out on her arms at his touch. She couldn't stop the next question. It burst forth as if water from a dam. "Did something happen between us?"

"Yeah, Lex. Something happened," Blake told her, resting his warm palm on her leg over the bruise, as if by covering it up, it didn't exist.

Alexis's breaths came out faster. "Did we . . ." Her voice trailed off, unsure she really wanted to know. The thought that Blake might've made love to her was both a blessing and a curse. A blessing because she'd dreamed about having him in her bed and arms almost since the day she'd met him, and a curse because she couldn't remember a second of it.

Blake moved then. Shifting over her, putting one hand on the mattress on her left side and the other on her right side. She lay back, giving him room, but he leaned into her, erasing the space she'd put between then.

"We didn't make love, if that's what you were going to ask. We didn't even kiss. There's no way I would've taken advantage of you like that. I knew you were drunk, knew you most likely wouldn't remember anything."

"Then what happened?" Alexis was pleased that Blake was gentleman enough to not take anything she didn't freely and soberly give, but couldn't imagine what in the world he was talking about if he hadn't kissed or had sex with her.

"You told me that you wanted me. That no other man had ever touched you or seen you naked. We slept together, you holding on to me like you never wanted to let go. So what happened was me deciding to stop dicking around, sweetheart. When you're feeling one hundred percent, I'm going to continue to pursue you. We're going on that date I asked you on a week ago, and I'm going to show you how much better a real dick will feel inside you rather than the toys you've been using. You're mine, Lex. That's what happened."

Alexis could only stare up at Blake in horror. What the holy fuck had she said to him? She had no idea what to say in response. She'd told him she was a virgin? And that she wanted to have sex with him? And what was that about her vibrators and a real dick? She closed her eyes in mortification. She'd thought his holding back her hair while she puked was bad, but that had been nothing compared to this. She'd have to move. To Tahiti. Immediately. She couldn't ever look Blake Anderson in the eyes again.

She felt his warm palm curl around the back of her neck and his thumb lightly caress the skin below her ear. She vaguely remembered him doing this exact thing to her in a car, but not *when* he'd done it.

"Did you know when you blush you turn red from the tips of your ears all the way down to your chest?" Blake asked conversationally. Not giving her a chance to answer, he continued, "And every time I touch you, goose bumps break out on your arms? I gotta say, Lex, it feels fucking awesome to know my touch affects you that way."

"So you only want to be with me because I'm a virgin?" Alexis whispered, trying to understand.

"Look at me," Blake ordered in a firm voice.

Alexis shook her head, refusing to open her eyes, not wanting to see the smugness that was sure to be in Blake's.

"Open your eyes, Lex. Look at me," Blake repeated in a whisper.

She couldn't deny him. She cracked her eyelids open and gazed up at him. He was still crouched over her, closer now. His lips were hovering a few inches over her own, and the look on his face was tender and soft.

"I want to be with you because I admire you, Lex. You're tough and strong, but tender and vulnerable on the inside. You don't hesitate to do what's right simply *because* it's what's right. You don't think about the consequences your actions might have on you, physically or emotionally. You just do it. I can see how much hurt you hold inside from how you were treated in middle and high school, but you don't let it hold you back. I love that you want to do your part to make the world a better place.

"I want to be the first and, hopefully, the *only* man who will ever be inside you. I want to be the man who gives you your first orgasm. I want my body to be the first naked male body you see, and I want to be the man who sees your naked body for the first time. I want to worship your curves and show you how much fun it can be to use your toys as we make love. I want your smile to be the last thing I see before I fall asleep and have it be the first thing I see when I wake up in the morning. I want to fulfill every one of your arm-porn fantasies and be the man you snuggle up to every night." He paused for a moment, not looking away from her eyes for a second. "Does that answer your question?"

"I think I talk too much when I'm drunk," Alexis blurted without thought.

Blake chuckled and leaned down to rub his nose against hers. "Alcohol does seem to loosen your tongue, sweetheart, but apparently only with me. You said and did all the right things with Kelly and her asshole friends. I have no idea how or why you're still a virgin, but I thank my lucky stars that you are. It makes me nervous because I want your first time to be a memory you'll treasure, but I'd be lying if I didn't also say that it makes me horny as hell to know I'll be the first man to be inside you. I'll do everything in my power to make it good for you. I swear."

"I know you will," Alexis told him, moving her arms for the first time. She brought them up to his biceps and held on tight. She licked her lips and asked, "I told you all those things and you really didn't even kiss me?"

"No, sweetheart. Not even a peck. I want you to be perfectly aware of who you're kissing when we make out."

"I'm perfectly aware now," she stated unnecessarily, never as glad that she'd snuck out of bed and brushed her teeth as she was at this moment.

"You want me to kiss you, Lex?" Blake asked, a devious glint in his eye.

"Yeah, Blake. I want you to kiss me," Alexis returned immediately.

"Thank God," Blake breathed before shifting the few inches it took to bring their mouths together.

Neither of them moved their hands as they kissed, keeping a tight hold on each other. Alexis moaned deep in her throat as she thought about everything Blake had just told her. She thought for sure she was still dreaming, or still drunk. There was no way Blake Anderson had just told her he wanted to make love to her. That he was pleased as fuck to be the man who would take her virginity.

Blake turned his head so he could fuse his mouth to hers at a better angle, and Alexis knew nothing would ever feel better than the feel of Blake drinking from her mouth as if he couldn't get enough of her.

Their tongues tangled together; he licked the roof of her mouth, then inside her bottom lip; then he thrust his tongue in and out of her just like what she imagined his cock would do as he made love to her. Alexis squirmed under him but kept hold of his arms as tightly as she could.

With one last twist of his tongue against hers, Blake pulled back, giving her three or four kisses with just his lips before lifting his head. As he'd done before, his hand came up and he wiped the moisture from her bottom lip with his thumb. A caress Alexis was coming to crave.

"Sleep, Lex. Let your body heal. We'll continue this at a later date. I want you. More than I think I've ever wanted a woman before, but I want you to be sure. If you give yourself to me, it's not going to be for a quick fling. My heart couldn't take it. I know once I get inside you, once I feel your hot body around mine, I'm not going to want to let you go. So be sure, Lex. Be absolutely sure."

"I'm sure," she told him immediately.

Blake smiled, then said quietly, "Take a few days. Think about it when you're not exhausted and probably still feeling like shit."

Alexis nodded, then bit her bottom lip, tasting Blake's unique essence on her skin still. "Are you staying?"

He looked down at her for a long moment before asking, "Do you want me to?"

"Yeah. If you want to."

"Then I'll stay" was his immediate response.

"I think I have an extra toothbrush in one the drawers in my bathroom if you need it. And probably even a razor if you can bring yourself to use a pink one. I don't have anything you can wear, though. I—"

Blake leaned down and kissed her swiftly, before pulling back. "It's fine, Lex. Believe me, if I can survive the army, I can rough it for a night here. Don't worry about me. Just get some sleep. You'll feel better in the morning."

"Okay. Do you need me to come in to talk to Logan and Nathan about the meeting?"

Blake shook his head. "No. You don't remember it, and I've got the tapes. I can tell them what I heard. If we have questions, we'll call."

Alexis looked away from Blake for the first time. "Sounds good."

He put his fingers on her chin, lifting it, making her look at him. "If I had my choice, I'd glue myself to your side and never leave. But I'm thinking you need some time to process this. I'll give you some, but not too much. I can't. Okay?"

"Okay." It made sense. Alexis was feeling overwhelmed already, so it was probably smart of him to give them some space. She just hoped *he* wouldn't decide she wasn't what he wanted anymore. There was no way she was going to change *her* mind.

He leaned down and kissed her on the forehead once more, then sat up. "I'll be in the other room watching TV for a while if you need anything. If you get hungry, I'll make some sandwiches and keep them in the fridge, just in case."

"Will you sleep in here?"

Blake eyed her for a long moment before simply saying, "Yes." He didn't ask if she was sure. He didn't say it wouldn't be smart. He'd simply said yes.

Alexis fell asleep quickly, content that the man she loved seemed to be interested in being in a relationship with her. It was enough. For now.

Chapter Nine

Two days after they'd had lunch, Kelly sent Alexis a text, wanting to meet up again. This time for, in Kelly's words, a "small party" at her place.

Alexis called Blake, clearly panicked, not sure how to respond.

Blake immediately wanted to say hell no, but after discussing the situation with his brothers, he called Alexis back.

"What should I do?" she asked.

"The decision is yours, Lex. I don't want you anywhere near that bitch and her friends. If it was up to me, I'd say absolutely not, but it's not up to me. And I know how much you want to help. How much pressure you've put on yourself. You're not a victim anymore, not like you were back in high school, and you've come a long way. No matter your decision, know that I, and my brothers, will support it one hundred percent. If you want to say no, we won't be upset about it. If you decide you'll do it, we'll support you however we can . . . including having your back, front, and sides while you do it."

He heard her take a deep breath, before she said quietly, "I don't particularly want to do it, but the job feels unfinished. If I don't, I think I'll feel like I let myself down. That I did what was safe rather than what was right . . . just like I did back in high school. I know it's not the same thing, not at all, but as long as you'll be there, and will step in if I need you, I'll do it."

"Of course I'll be there, sweetheart."

"Good. Do you think . . . will I need to drink like that again?"

The thought of Lex being vulnerable and drunk in Kelly's house, where anyone might be there, and where she could easily be taken into a bedroom, made Blake's blood run cold, but he knew they were so close to taking down Donovan and his entire gang.

He and his brothers had discussed the potential danger for Lex, especially at a private party, but Logan pointed out the merits of the information she could get. Blake didn't like hearing it but knew his brother was playing devil's advocate . . . trying to make them see all sides of the issue, good and bad, before they made a decision.

"I don't think you need to. You can probably nurse a drink since you'll be in her place. I'm sure they'll try to get money out of you, but I have no idea what ruse or sob story they'll use to try to make you feel sorry for them."

"I expected that, and it doesn't really matter what they say. I'll make sure I have plenty of cash on hand and give them whatever they want."

"Whatever happens, I'll be there, Lex. Me and Logan both this time. And we've talked to the Denver PD's gang task force. They're aware of what we're doing. They aren't thrilled, but because of Logan's and my background in security and with the military, they've relented."

"But I don't have that background. Do they care about that?" she asked quietly.

"Of course they do. But you won't be alone. We've talked a lot about what you should and shouldn't do and what to be aware of when you're with them. You really held your own in that self-defense class with us last week. I believe in you, Lex. You're smart. Too smart to do anything crazy."

"Thanks for the vote of confidence," she said dryly. "I can't promise that I'll remember everything you guys jammed into my brain, but I can promise not to do anything stupid and to get the hell out of there one way or another if I get uneasy."

"Good. Besides, us sharing the tapes with the task force hasn't hurt either. If you do this, they'll know where you are and what time you'll be there. You'll be safe. I swear."

"Okay, Blake. I can do it. I'll text her back and send you the details."

She hung up and didn't ask when she might see him again, but then again, Blake hadn't brought it up either. It was driving him crazy not being able to see her. He knew Lex was scared, but as was typical of her, she was going full steam ahead, trying not to let on how nervous she actually was.

The next week was excruciating for Blake. Even though he missed Alexis, he purposely avoided one-on-one time with her, wanting her to really think about what he'd said the other week. Losing her virginity was a big deal, even more because she'd waited so long to have sex with someone. He wanted her to be completely sure of what she wanted.

Not only that, but they'd been dealing with Kelly and the situation with the Inca Boyz as well.

The "little party" Kelly had planned was going to happen that night, and she'd given Alexis an address. It turned out it wasn't at her place but at Damian's, which didn't make either Blake or Logan happy.

It was early in the day, and Blake was determined to talk with Lex before the party. He was done waiting for her to make a decision about the two of them. He'd almost driven up to Denver several times, the urge to see Alexis almost painful, but he'd given her the space he thought she'd needed. He'd told her not to come to the office, so she and Nathan had been communicating via e-mail and instant messaging as they continued to monitor chatter via the Internet as it had to do with the gang.

Blake had spoken to Alexis almost every night on the phone, however, and they'd exchanged many texts over the last seven days. But he hadn't seen her. Hadn't touched her. Hadn't kissed her. He'd planned on giving her more time before taking her on the date he'd promised her, but when he'd spoken to her last night, she'd demanded to know why he was dragging his feet.

"If you're having second thoughts, Blake, be man enough to tell me. You told me you liked to be the pursuer, but you're not pursuing, and I can't figure out why. I already told you I wanted to sleep with you. I don't know how much more clear I could've been. If you're hesitating because I'm a virgin and you're not into that, fine, just tell me. I'm not going to break or slit my wrists if you decide that it was just your protective feelings coming through or the heat of the moment. But I'm done waiting. You told me you wanted to take me on a date, and I want my date."

On the surface her words were forceful, but he could hear the pain beneath them. The last thing he wanted to do was make her doubt that he wanted her. Besides, her last sentence made him want to chuckle. "I want you, Lex. I'll be at your place in the morning. We need to talk before we head out to the party."

All she'd said was "Good. It's about time. I'll see you then."

Now he was standing in the lobby of her apartment. Osman called Alexis to make sure it was all right to send him upstairs. It should've irritated him, but since the man had last seen him when he'd been practically carrying a drunk Alexis upstairs, he didn't mind Osman's protectiveness. He liked that the man looked out for her.

Alexis answered her door after his two short knocks, and Blake had to remind himself that he'd promised himself not to make love with her until after the shit with the Inca Boyz was over. But it was definitely easier said than done. Especially seeing her standing in front of him looking as fuckable as she was.

She was wearing a pair of skinny jeans that hugged her curvy legs. Her feet were bare, which made him want to pick her up and carry her inside, if only so her toes didn't get chilled. The shirt she was wearing was bright purple, with a wide scoop neck. It dipped both modestly in the front and in an arc at her back. Not even a hint of cleavage was visible, but he was intrigued by the thought that if he tugged her shirt forward just a bit, it would fall below her beautiful tits, showcasing them perfectly.

His hands almost itched to do just that, but Blake jammed them into the front pockets of his jeans. It served to keep them to himself and to try to stretch the denim to give his cock more room.

"Hey, Lex."

"Blake. Come in." She held the door open, and the muscle in his jaw twitched as her shirt fell off one shoulder. Her bra strap matched her shirt, and Blake felt his cock twitch as he imagined how she'd look standing in front of him in nothing but a dark-purple bra and panties.

"Thanks." He took a deep breath as he walked past her, and almost stumbled. She'd recently showered, and whatever lotion she'd used afterward smelled absolutely incredible. It was some sort of flower. Not overpowering, but subtle enough to make him crazy. The words came out before he thought about what he was saying. "You smell amazing."

Alexis shut the door behind him and smiled. "Thanks. It's my lotion. Honeysuckle. I don't wear it very often but figured it would boost my self-esteem and make me feel better, since I have to go into the lion's den tonight."

Her words struck him wrong, and he moved before thinking. He put his hands on her bare shoulders, loving how soft her skin was, and brushed both thumbs along the sides of her neck. "Since we're being honest, I'd prefer you smell like dirty socks when you walk into that house."

Alexis's eyes met his, and he could see the humor shining in their depths. "I'm not sure that would help our cause tonight."

"Maybe not," he concurred, then leaned forward and buried his nose in the curve of her neck and inhaled deeply before pulling back and saying, "But I can't help but be pissed, jealous, and anxious all at the same time at the thought of you smelling this irresistible when you're around those assholes. And for the record, you can do whatever you need to in order to feel good about yourself, but you don't have to do one fucking thing to look more beautiful in my eyes. Okay?"

She looked up at him with wide eyes and shivered once. "Okay, Blake."

He forcibly took a step back, but not before he noticed the goose bumps that had arisen on her arms at his touch and words. Fuck, she was gonna be the death of him. He'd jacked off to the thought of her so much this week he figured he'd be safe being in her presence, but he'd been wrong. If nothing else, he seemed to want her more now than ever before.

"Let's talk about tonight. What's gonna happen," Blake said abruptly, trying to get his mind out of the gutter. Knowing her bedroom was just down the hall, that he had time to take her down there and teach her all there was to know about sex, was torture. But he wanted to start their relationship right. Wanted to take her out on a few dates before falling on her like a dog in heat.

"Sure. You hungry? Want something to eat?"

"I could eat. But we can go out if you want. You don't have to cook for me."

"I'm too nervous to go out . . . if that's okay. I can make us sandwiches or something here."

"Sounds great," Blake told her immediately. If she wanted to stay in, they'd stay in. As much as he wanted to take her out, if for nothing else than to get away from her bed, which he knew was just down the hall, he didn't want her uncomfortable.

They worked together to make a simple lunch of ham and cheese sandwiches. She had some chips, which he added to each of their plates, and they took their meals into the other room to the couch. They talked about the upcoming night as they ate.

"Kelly told me the party would start around ten," Alexis told him.

"Right. I know we've talked about safety and security with you, but I have a bad feeling about this party. I hate that you'll be putting yourself in danger . . . again . . . while I'm not by your side. So far you've done an excellent job in staying calm and getting out when things are getting out of control, but there are a lot more things that could go wrong tonight at a private party than there were in the bar, which was a public place."

"I know," Alexis said. "I am not going to take any chances. The second things seem to be weird, I'm out of there."

"Good. As to what you should look for . . . furtive looks between the men, as if they're talking or plotting something. If you see them pull out weapons, or they start insisting you drink more and more. And if they use any kind of force against you to make you do something you don't want to—drink, eat, sit, go with them into a back room, kiss, touch . . . *anything*, Alexis—you get out of there, or say the code word and me and Logan will cause a distraction and get you the fuck out of there."

She quickly nodded. "I will." She put her hand on Blake's arm. "Can we talk about something else? You're freaking me out."

"Yeah, sweetheart. In a second. It was important in the bar, but it's even more important at a party like this that you don't accept any drink from anyone that you don't open or pour yourself or you haven't seen opened or poured. It would be way too easy for one of those assholes to drug you and haul you into a back room. Maybe later we can practice some of the self-defense moves we taught you last week as well. I want you to be able to get out of a choke hold, and if someone grabs your arm, I want you to be able to get away from them quickly and easily, without starting a huge fight."

"Yeah, a gang fight breaking out around me is the last thing I'd want to be in the middle of," Alexis agreed.

Blake closed his eyes for a brief moment, as if the image scared the shit out of him and he needed a moment. Then he looked her in the eye and said, "Logan and I thought it'd be best if you showed up a bit early . . . maybe before too many people got there. So around nine thirty or so. You can chat with Kelly, see what she'll share without the others around. Then you could hang out, listen to as many conversations as possible, and if the mood of the room seems right, ask some easy questions, then get out of there around eleven. That should be before things get too crazy."

"All right. An hour and a half . . . I can do that," Alexis said more to herself than to him as she studied the sandwich between her fingers.

Blake reached over and put his hand on her knee. "You can do anything, sweetheart. And remember, me and Logan will be right outside. If nothing else, we'll cause a distraction outside and you can slip away."

"You mentioned that earlier. What kind of distraction?" Alexis asked.

"Whatever it takes to get you the hell out of there," Blake told her honestly. "If shit goes downhill, your only job is to get out of the house and get to the meeting spot. You need to be careful, though. Make sure you're not being followed. Don't go straight there, and backtrack a few times to be sure no one is behind you. Listen for sounds of someone following you—breathing, or walking, or stepping on things. If you can, take shortcuts through yards, keeping away from houses with dogs."

"Right. It's not like you can just pull up and pick me up outside the house," Alexis observed, mostly to herself. "Walk quietly, check behind me, listen. Check."

Blake put his now-empty plate on the side table and took Alexis's out of her hand and did the same. He reclined against the corner of the sofa and held out his arm. "Come here, Lex. I need to hold you."

With a relieved sigh, she moved into his embrace, snuggling into his side as if she'd been waiting for this moment. She brought her legs up and tucked them under her and leaned into Blake, giving him her weight at the same time she wrapped one arm around his front and held the other bent up close to her chest.

Blake kissed the top of her head and held her close to him. They stayed that way for several minutes, neither speaking, simply enjoying the closeness they were sharing.

Alexis broke the silence. "I like this," she observed quietly. "I've never really just hung out with a man before. It's comforting, and you make me feel safe. But sitting next to you with your arms around me makes me want you all the more."

"When we make love, Lex, I want you relaxed and completely focused on me, not worried about what will happen with the Inca Boyz. I'm going to take my time and worship you from your beautiful head to your adorable toes, and I want you to do the same."

She looked up at him at his words. Her eyes wide and curious . . . and full of so much desire it felt like a punch to his gut. "You want me to touch you too?"

God, she was so innocent in some ways, and way too jaded in others. "Yeah, sweetheart. I want your hands all over me. Every time I've jacked off this week I've imagined it was your hands on my cock instead of my own."

"You . . . masturbated thinking about me?"

"Shit yeah," Blake told her, not taking his eyes away from hers, wanting her to see how much he wanted her. "Every time I close my eyes, it's all I could think about. And knowing no man's ever seen the beauty that is you . . . I don't deserve it, but I'm more thankful than you'll ever know that it'll be me who introduces you to passion."

"I've had orgasms, Blake," she told him haughtily. "I know what passion is."

"You might've gotten yourself off, Lex, but there's a difference between the orgasms you give yourself and the ones I'll give you." He wasn't being cocky, merely truthful. "Just as I know without a doubt that when your body squeezes my cock so hard I can't hold on anymore, it'll be the most powerful, beautiful orgasm I'll have experienced in my life."

Alexis licked her lips sensually, and squirmed against him.

"Does that turn you on, sweetheart? Do you like hearing how much I can't wait to be between your thighs?"

"Oh yeah," she told him, almost panting with desire for him. "We have plenty of time before we need to go anywhere. Hours and hours."

"I know it, but this will be your first time. I don't want anything going on in that head of yours except for how my hands, and tongue, are making you feel. Not about where you have to be in a few hours, or what you have to do. When I make you mine, you'll be thinking about nothing but me and what you're giving me."

"Do you want to know why I haven't had sex yet?"

It wasn't what he thought she was going to say, but Blake was happy for the moment to think about something other than how tight and wet she'd be when he finally pushed inside her for the first time. "I want to know anything you feel comfortable telling me," he told her honestly.

Blake moved then, from a sitting position, to a reclining one, shifting Alexis with him. They lay together, his head on the arm of the couch, his left arm around her waist holding her tight to his body, his right hand roaming from brushing lightly against her hair, down her neck, to her side and ass, then back up.

Lex's head rested against his shoulder, her warm breath against his neck, her legs straddling one of his, her body weight heavy against his torso. He'd never felt so comfortable in his life . . . except when he'd spent a few hours wrapped around her in her bed, when she'd latched on to his arm so tightly as she slept.

"I wasn't trying to save myself for anyone. I fully expected to sleep with someone when I was still in high school. See what the fuss was about, get it out of the way," she told him in a soft voice, her fingers playing with the buttons of his dark-gray button-down shirt. "But I *did* want to do it with a boy who at least liked me. But I couldn't manage to find even one of those. I thought maybe in college, away from the kids who knew about my rich family, I'd be able to date a man who liked me for me. But I didn't find even one guy who even remotely turned me on."

She took a deep breath and tilted her head up so she could see Blake's face. "I didn't know what I was looking for back then. I only knew that the thought of getting naked with any of the guys I'd been on dates with made me nervous rather than turned on. Not one of them made me wet just by looking at him. No one made me wonder what his hands would feel like on my skin. I couldn't imagine taking any of them into my mouth and seeing if I could make them lose control with only my hands and tongue."

"Lex . . ."

She brought her hand up to Blake's face then, laying it flat on his cheek and running her thumb over the edge of his lips. "The first time I saw you, I wanted you. I wanted to know what your hands would feel like on my breasts, how your body would feel as I straddled your hips, what it would feel like to finally have a man, you, inside me. I couldn't help it. There was just something about you that called to me. You knew I was rich, but you didn't come on to me. You didn't want anything to do with me. Somehow that made me only like you more."

"Jesus, Alexis, stop," Blake begged, feeling turned on and heartbroken for her at the same time.

"No, I won't stop. I've wanted you from the second I saw you, Blake. Why do you think I offered to work with you? It was torture, but I couldn't keep away. I spent as much time as I could with you, torturing myself, telling myself that you'd never look twice at me. A virgin, for Pete's sake. What did I have that you'd ever want? I thought I'd find out you were a jerk, and that would be that. But you weren't. You *aren't*. We became friends. You know how I like my coffee, that I'm a bear in the mornings until I have my caffeine. You trusted me to have your back on jobs, and you treated me like I was normal."

"You *are* normal, Lex," Blake insisted.

"You know what I mean. You didn't give a shit about the money my family has. Then I thought all I'd ever have was your friendship. It hurt, but felt good at the same time . . . if that makes sense. And now . . . here we are. I have no idea how it happened. But I'm afraid if we don't go back to my room right now, before that damn party, that somehow it's going to slip through my fingers. That something'll happen tonight that'll make you decide you don't want me anymore. That you'll come to your senses and figure out I'm just a plump chick who isn't anywhere near good enough for you and that you have no patience to teach me how to make love. I'm afraid if we wait you'll decide you want nothing to do with me. With my family. With my virginity."

Instead of answering immediately, Blake shifted until she was under him. Her knees opened naturally, and he settled his hips into the notch between her legs and gave her his body weight, letting her feel how hard his cock was.

She squirmed under him, pushing her hips up into him, and he let more of his body weight press down on to her, making it impossible for her to move anymore. He took Alexis's face between his hands, put his weight on his elbows next to her shoulders, and stared down at her.

Lex gazed up at him with a look so full of fear, lust, and anticipation it made Blake want to forget waiting. Made him want to strip off the sexy-as-fuck shirt she was wearing and feast on her nipples until she came from his mouth on her alone. He wanted to see firsthand how she tasted, smell her, lose himself between her legs. He also wanted to fulfill every single one of her fantasies. Reward her for saving herself for him. Staying away had hurt her, made her question his intentions, and he hated that. Respecting the fact that she'd been completely honest and open with him, he returned the gesture.

"I want you, Alexis Grant. I'm so hard for you I could come with a mere touch of your hand on my cock. It took me a while to see the wonderful woman you are. I'm not saying I don't believe in love at first sight, and I fucking love that you took one look at me and wanted me all for yourself. But I'll tell you, working with you, seeing you every week and seeing how hard you worked and the intensity that you bring to everything, made me want you. You crept under my skin so sneakily that by the time I realized you were there, I was a goner.

"I want you. I see you, Lex, the *real* you, peeking out from that tough outer shell you surround yourself with to protect your heart from the cruel world. I'm not letting you go. Make no mistake, I'm gonna take your virginity and be proud as fuck that I did. *Nothing* that happens tonight will change my mind. This might not be the eighteenth century anymore, hanging bloody sheets from the window might be frowned upon, but make no mistake. I'm more than excited that mine will be the first cock to breach your tight pussy."

"Um, that's kinda cavemanish," Alexis said, scrunching up her nose at him, but still slightly smiling, letting him know she wasn't turned off by his blunt and dirty talk.

Blake leaned down and kissed her wrinkled nose, then pulled back up. "Yeah, it is. And I'm not gonna apologize for it. With that said, I've never taken anyone's virginity before. I'm nervous. And you might not have your hymen anymore but—"

"Wait, what? Why did you say that?" Alexis asked, her eyes wide in shock and a blush staining her cheeks pink.

Blake smiled. "Oh yeah, that's one more thing you told me last week when you were completely smashed. You told me about your toys and that you didn't think you'd bleed when I made love to you because you'd already taken care of that yourself. You said that your vibrators hurt and that you wished men had a clit so we could feel how good it feels when it's stroked."

"Oh my God. Kill me now," Alexis moaned, closing her eyes, refusing to look at him, and bringing one hand up to cover her eyes to make sure she didn't have to meet his eyes. "I'm gonna join a convent and never look at another man the rest of my life."

Blake chuckled at her dramatics and reached up to remove her hand from her face. He kissed the palm, then let go. Her eyes opened at the feel of his lips on her sensitive skin, and she immediately clutched his bicep as he continued to speak.

"I hate to break it to you, but I don't think you'd last a day as a nun. You might not have any physical barriers, but it's still gonna be a new experience for you. I want to make sure you feel nothing but arousal your first time."

"I'm on birth control," Alexis blurted, then bit her lip in embarrassment and pressed on. "So if you're clean, you don't have to worry about a condom. I want it to be good for you too."

"No matter what, sweetheart, it's gonna be good for me. I've dreamed about taking you for the last two weeks. But you should *always* insist on a guy wearing a condom, especially when you first enter a sexual relationship. Birth control or not. We haven't talked about my sexual history."

"But, I trust you," Alexis protested.

"And that means the world to me," Blake told her. He'd never made love with a woman without a condom. Not once. He selfishly wanted to immediately take her up on her offer, but he felt compelled to protest for her safety. "Nevertheless, you still should always insist on a condom."

"Blake, if I trust you with my life, why wouldn't I trust you with my body as well? If you say you're clean, I'll believe you. Now if you're protesting because you aren't, then that's a different thing altogether."

Blake inhaled sharply. He knew she trusted him, but he hadn't *known* it. Her words made it clear just how much she wanted him. Liked him. Needed him. Dare he even think *loved* him?

His cock was so hard against her belly he could feel his heart beat through it. His voice lowered, and he met her eyes without blinking. "I'm clean, sweetheart. I haven't been with anyone since I moved back to Castle Rock, and my sexual encounters were few and far between before that. I've also never once made love to a woman without wearing a condom."

"Then what's the problem?" Alexis asked, tilting her head in question.

Instead of answering, Blake informed her, "I'm gonna love you so well, Lex, you're never gonna want another man. Not ever. My hands, my cock, and my tongue are gonna be the only ones you want anywhere near this delectable body of yours. I swear on the life of my brothers, I'm gonna make your first experience one you'll remember for the rest of your life."

"Good," she said with a satisfied grin. "I can't wait."

Not able to keep his hands, or lips, off her for a second longer, Blake moved his palms from her neck down her chest until he was cupping her tits for the first time ever. He gently squeezed them through her blouse as his mouth landed on her neck. She immediately lifted her chin, giving him room.

He licked and sucked her neck as he caressed her tits with his hands. He felt her nipples go hard under his palms, and she squirmed under him. Then her back arched, and she tilted her head back even more, exposing her vulnerable throat to his touch, and begged him to keep touching her chest. Blake moved his mouth up to her ear and took her lobe between his lips. He sucked on it hard, running his tongue over the fleshy skin. She moaned in response, moving her hand up to cover one of his on her breast.

After several minutes of him kissing and loving on her neck and earlobe, Blake finally pulled back. Her face was flushed, with arousal now instead of embarrassment. He reached up and tugged the scoop-neck shirt down toward her chest, smiling as it shifted just as he imagined it would. He stopped when both her tits in the amazing purple lace bra were visible.

"God, Lex, you are fucking beautiful."

He hadn't thought about what her reaction would be but was still surprised when she arched her back once more, pressing her chest toward him.

"Touch me," she begged in a tone he hadn't heard from her before. It was breathy and pleading at the same time. "I want to feel your hands on my skin."

Drawing out the anticipation, and knowing he couldn't take this too far without wanting to go all the way, Blake reverently flicked his thumbs over her peaked nipples. He knew the sensation would be dulled for her because of the lace bra, but he was still pleased when she inhaled sharply and whimpered.

"Blake. That feels so good," she croaked when he didn't say anything but continued his ministrations. "More," she demanded breathily.

"It's only gonna get better."

"I can't wait," she responded, opening her eyes and looking into his.

He wasn't sure what she saw in them, but she smiled, a wide genuine smile that he'd kill to keep on her face. Then her eyes darted to the side, and he saw her looking at his arms as he continued to play with her nipples.

"What is it about my forearms that gets to you, Lex? You told me that you'd been attracted to them from the start, but they're just arms. I don't get it."

She licked her lips before saying huskily, "I don't know. They're just so different from mine, from any guy's arms that I've seen before. They're muscular, but I can see the veins in them. Every time you flex, I imagine what they'd look like as you held yourself over me, kinda like you are now." She shrugged in embarrassment. "I can't explain it, but trust me, they're sexy as hell."

"I love that you love looking at me. Turning you on turns me on."

"Good. Because everything you do turns me on. Lately, it doesn't matter if I'm with you or if we're just talking on the phone. I usually have to get myself off before I can do anything else . . . then I have to change my panties because they're so wet."

Blake groaned at her words. God, he was so fucking turned on. He loved that Alexis wasn't afraid or ashamed to tell him what his presence did to her. Then, because he couldn't stop himself even if the room was on fire, he leaned over and gently kissed her left nipple. Then he moved to the other side and did the same to her other one. He so wanted to do more. Pinch them with his fingers, take them in his mouth and suck, learn what she liked—gentle licks or a more forceful suction—but as he'd told her, now wasn't the time or the place.

She made a high-pitched noise of frustration and protest when he leaned back and adjusted her shirt so it covered her again. "Blake, please, you can't stop now."

"I think we need some fresh air, sweetheart. How about if we head out for some ice cream? We can walk around downtown for a bit. You can ask me whatever you want, and I'll do the same. We'll get to know each other more. This can be our first unofficial date. I'm still taking you on a real date after tonight is over, but we can start with this. Then we'll meet Logan back here and go over the plan for tonight. Okay?"

Alexis huffed out a frustrated breath. "You're really stopping now?"

"Unfortunately, yeah. I was serious when I told you I wanted to wait."

"Damn. You're stronger than I am, that's for sure," Alexis told him. "I've always thought your stubborn side was sexy. Now I'm thinking not so much."

He chuckled, then bent down and gently kissed the tip of each of her breasts, now covered. "You still think I'm sexy," he deadpanned, his eyes twinkling. "Now, how about that ice cream?"

She shook her head at him playfully, but nodded and brought a hand up and rested it on the back of his head. "Sounds good."

Blake went to move off her to stand, but she stopped him.

"Blake?"

"Yeah, sweetheart?"

"Thank you."

"For what?"

"For being you. For being worth the wait."

Blake's decision to leave the apartment was seriously compromised by her words, but he gritted his teeth and held firm. "I promise you it'll so be worth the wait."

"I know it will. I have no doubts. So, thank you."

"You're welcome. Now come on, quit trying to seduce me."

She smiled happily. "*Could* I seduce you?"

"In a heartbeat, Lex. In a fucking heartbeat." He moved then, standing by the couch and holding out a hand to help her up. He pulled her into a long hug when she was upright, memorizing the feel of her smaller body against his own.

Finally, he pulled back. "Let's go."

"Okay. But Blake?"

"Yeah?"

"I need to change my panties first."

She said it with such a neutral tone it took a moment for it to register. When it did, all he could do was close his eyes and mutter, "Fuck me."

When he opened his eyes, she was grinning mischievously at him. He hoped when they were old and gray she could still manage to surprise him.

Chapter Ten

Alexis took a deep breath and knocked on the door of the ramshackle house, Blake's instructions and tips on staying safe running through her head. The house looked like she'd expected: run-down and creepy. Exactly the type of place she would assume Damian and the Inca Boyz lived in. The sooner she got this party out of the way, the sooner she could get Blake Anderson in her bed. He was her reward for getting through one more excruciating experience; at least that's how she was looking at it.

She and Blake had killed time that afternoon, getting ice cream and walking around downtown Denver, holding hands and sharing light romantic kisses. She'd learned a lot about him. He liked to read nonfiction books, mostly about military ships, and he hated green vegetables. She'd listed as many as she could think of, asking individually if he liked them. Asparagus, green beans, peas, broccoli, brussels sprouts, spinach, okra, kale, lima beans. He'd just laughed and told her no after each one. It was so . . . weird . . . it was cute.

She, in turn, told him things not many people, other than her family, knew about her. That while she loved the color pink, she wouldn't wear it. Also, that she was fascinated by anything that had to do with the Titanic and that she dreamed of someday going down in a submersible to the resting place of the infamous ship.

After their stroll, they'd met Logan back at her apartment, and he'd repeated many of the same things Blake had told her about being safe and what to be on the lookout for regarding the party atmosphere turning dangerous. They also discussed what the end goal was for the night: namely to gather as much intel as possible. The bottom line was that Alexis should mostly listen to find out how many jobs the gang had done, for whom and how they were contacted, and if the opportunity presented itself, which they all knew it would, to freely offer up money for whatever scheme they tried to trick her into.

She had two thousand dollars in various denominations in her purse, and another four hundred tucked into her back pocket . . . just in case. She'd kept on the skinny jeans she'd been wearing earlier. There was no way she was going to wear a skirt; it gave way too easy access to parts of her that she wanted to keep to herself, and Chuck had made his intentions abundantly clear at the bar. She had changed into a sequined spaghetti-strap top, and was wearing the wire tucked firmly between her breasts and the camera pendant around her neck.

Even though Blake and Logan were backing her up, and right out-side the house, Alexis was still scared out of her mind.

Kelly opened the door with a jerk, startling Alexis. She didn't look pleased as she jutted out a hip and declared snidely, "You're early."

Alexis might've been early, but Kelly was obviously dressed and ready to party. She was wearing another extremely short and tight mini-skirt and a low-cut blouse tied in a knot at her side. Alexis wasn't staring, but it was easy to see that the other woman wasn't wearing a bra. Her nipples were clearly outlined under the thin shirt, which was pulled tight in order to show them off more easily.

Alexis thought she should really get a medal for looking into Kelly's eyes, as her boobs were really hard to block from her sight. Alexis tittered, "I know. I'm so sorry! I was just so excited to see you again and hang out. I thought maybe we could chat a bit before everyone got here." She smiled broadly, tilting her head and opening her eyes wide in an obnoxiously friendly way.

"Whatever. You're here, so come in," Kelly said with an eye roll, backing away from the door.

"Thanks!" Alexis chirped. She entered the dilapidated house and glanced around. There was only one man in sight, which was good. Alexis would've been discomforted if there had been too many people there already. He was slouched on a brown couch that looked like it had seen better days. Stuffing was coming out of the seams in clumps. His feet were propped up on a low coffee table, which also looked like it was on its last leg. The top was gouged and stained with every color imaginable. The worn carpet in the room was also brown, which made its own plethora of stains somewhat blend in. There was a large older-model television on an entertainment center made out of planks of wood and milk crates, and a few uncomfortable and disgustingly dirty chairs, which probably were obtained from someone's front yard next to a "Free" sign.

There was an odd funk to the room, most likely the result of the now-legal pot—which could be smoked in Colorado—cigarette smoke, spilled liquor, body odor, and who knew what else. Alexis knew she'd get used to it, and that almost made her gag right then and there. The last thing she wanted was to leave the house smelling like the room she was currently standing in. She made a mental note to take a long, hot shower before letting Blake anywhere near her.

There were hallways on both sides of the room, leading to who knows where and a sliding glass door in the back that led out into a smallish backyard surrounded by a tall wooden privacy fence. From what Alexis could see, the weeds looked to be as tall as a small child. It definitely wasn't the kind of outdoor space anyone would go to, to feel rejuvenated or to commune with nature. She and Blake had scoped out the house via satellite, but experiencing it in person was way different.

They'd only gotten the outside view; the interior and smell were things that couldn't be experienced via technology.

All in all it was the dirtiest, nastiest, most disgusting place Alexis ever had the misfortune to step foot into, but she was careful not to let any of what she was thinking show on her face.

"Want a beer?" Kelly asked. "Don't have any of that froufrou shit you said you liked."

"A beer would be great," Alexis reassured her, secretly happy Kelly hadn't immediately started pushing shots of vodka, Everclear, or, God forbid, tequila, on her this early in the festivities. The memory of puking her guts out while Blake crouched behind her was still too vivid in her mind and wasn't something she wanted to repeat . . . ever.

Alexis followed Kelly past the man on the couch, who hadn't bothered to say a word to her, although his eyes bore into her back as if he could see right through her. He watched them walk through the room and down the hallway, to a small kitchen on the right. The linoleum on the floor was cracking in several places, and there were blotches of indeterminate origin on the floor. Alexis tried not to think about what could possibly have made the rust-colored stains and smiled at Kelly when she handed her a Natural Light beer.

Knowing from conversations she'd had with her brother how awful the beer was, Alexis steeled herself as she popped open the can and took a gulp. Yup, it was horrible. "Ah, that hits the spot," she told Kelly, barely controlling her natural reaction to curl her lip or to wrinkle her nose at the taste of the awful brew.

"It's cheap," Kelly told her, shrugging, then tipping her own can up and swallowing half the contents down.

"So who's coming tonight? Will Damian and Chuck be here?" Alexis asked, trying to get the conversation started.

"Of course. I told you this is Damian's damn house. Chuck heard you'd be here tonight and said he'd be around as soon as he took care of some shit."

"Great. Who else?" Alexis took another small sip of the beer and held back a shudder at having to see Chuck again. She didn't know what "shit" he had to take care of, but whatever it was couldn't be good if Chuck was involved.

"Well, everyone. It's Saturday night," Kelly said as if Alexis was stupid. She leaned against the cracked countertop and eyed Alexis over the edge of her beer.

"Cool. I can't wait to meet everyone," Alexis chirped, as if she didn't hear the censure in Kelly's tone. "Is everyone in your gang?"

"What the fuck do you know about it?" Kelly bit out. "You live in your fancy-as-fuck apartment downtown. You might go slumming at the bars, but you don't know shit about what it's like to actually live out here."

"You're right," Alexis agreed immediately, knowing she was treading a thin line and wanting to sound as if she understood but not wanting to go overboard. "I don't know much. But I *do* know that it pisses me off how hard some people have to work to get basic shit, and just because of who my family is, I don't have to work at all. I figure Damian must be doing pretty well for himself to have this house." Alexis waved her hand at the surroundings. "I don't know what you do, but I sure hope it's easy. I mean . . . I'm saying this badly, but I say, if you can get money easily, and I don't mean by selling drugs, because it has to be hard to stay ahead of the cops and crooked dealers, but by doing shit for people who have a ton of money, then good for you."

"What the fuck you talking about, bitch?" a voice said from the doorway.

Alexis jumped what seemed like ten feet at the loud, pissed-off voice and spun around to see the man who'd been lounging on the couch earlier, staring at her threateningly.

"Oh, you scared me," she said as cheerfully as she could, trying not to show how badly he'd frightened her, putting a hand on her chest.

"We didn't meet earlier. I'm Alexis." She held out her hand to the man as if they were at a thousand-dollar-a-plate fund-raiser.

He didn't reciprocate but leaned against the doorjamb and scowled at her. "I don't like to repeat myself, but I will. What. The fuck. You know. About what we do for money?"

"Alexis," Kelly drawled, smiling like a Cheshire cat, pleased as she could be that the man was obviously not impressed by her old classmate. "This is Dominic. Damian and Donovan's brother and second in command while Donovan's locked up."

Holy shit. They knew there was another brother, but they didn't have a lot of information on him and hadn't known exactly how much he was involved. Obviously, being second in command was a huge deal. Alexis's heartbeat increased, and she struggled to keep the surprise and shock from her face.

She made sure to face Dominic dead-on so the camera would pick up his face clearly. "Hi. It's so great to meet you," Alexis chirped. When the man scowled harder and made fists, she hurried on before he might decide that knocking her around was a good way to get her to answer his question.

"I didn't mean anything bad, promise. I was just tooling around on Facebook one day when I was bored at work and found your page. Cool banner picture, by the way. Anyway, I saw a comment on the page from a chick who said she wanted to hire you. I don't know what she was talking about, and it was gone the next day, but it got me to thinking. You guys are all strong and you know everyone around here. It just makes sense that you hire yourselves out."

She held up a hand when it looked like Dominic was going to beat the shit out of her, trying to keep up her ditzy persona even though she was scared out of her mind. She hoped the beating of her heart wasn't being picked up by the mic and drowning out the conversation. "I know you know who I am. That I'm the sister of the guy you guys were hired to take pictures of with that chick a few months ago. It was all over the papers. My brother is a big wuss, and it's not like he was hurt or anything, so whatever." Alexis rolled her eyes, as if Bradford irritated her, and took another sip of the beer, making it look like she drank more than she did. "I'm so sick of him looking down on me and telling me I'll never amount to anything just because I like to party. He's such a fucking nerd. Anyway, I got to thinking . . . it's pretty smart to charge people through the nose for things they don't want to dirty their hands with."

Alexis spoke faster, wanting to wrap this up. If Dominic really was related to Donovan and Damian, it'd get back to them what she'd said in no time. She had no doubt. "All I'm saying is good for you. It's American entrepreneurship at its finest. You have a service that others want. It's only fair that they pay you fair market value for it."

Dominic pushed off the doorjamb and stalked her way. Alexis wanted to be brave and stand her ground, but her feet moved without her even thinking about it. She took a step back, then another, until her butt pressed against the edge of the rickety table. *Shit.*

"You got a job you want done, bitch? That why you're slumming? A boyfriend you want to teach a lesson to? You want to take an Inca Boyz' cock down your throat to get back at him? Have us rock him to sleep early?"

Alexis's heart was beating way too hard, and she knew without a doubt Blake and Logan could hear it through the microphone now. She knew he was asking if she wanted him to murder someone. She did *not* want to go there. *Uh-uh.* She giggled—it sounded wimpy and scared to her—but that might work out better in her current situation.

"No, no, nothing like that. I just wanted you guys to know I had no hard feelings about what you did to my brother and that other chick. I don't care. I admire you for living the way you want, and doing what you want. Everyone has the right to make money, and you earning it by doing jobs for people is brilliant. That's all. I just wanted you to know I'm okay with it. That you don't have to keep it a secret while I'm hanging around."

Dominic leaned closer to her, and Alexis could smell a combination of the pot he'd smoked recently, rancid body odor that wafted up from his torso, and the cigarette smoke in his clothes. She held the beer can between them as if it was a shield, her fingers brushing against Dominic's black T-shirt as he pressed into her. He was trying to intimidate her—and it was working, dammit. The chain hanging from his back pocket, attaching his wallet to the jeans riding low on his hips, jingled as he moved into her space.

"For the record, A-lex-is"—he annunciated her name as obnoxiously as his brother had when she'd met him in Snake's Bar—"I don't mind you slumming around the Inca Boyz, but *no one* gets a free ride around here. You want to hang with us, drink our beer, take our men's cocks, you pay for it."

"Oh, I have money," Alexis chirped as if she wasn't a second away from either throwing up or fainting. "I can pay for my beer." She tried to make it clear that's all she wanted—and not to take a man's cock, as he so crudely put it.

Dominic took a step back—thank God—and held out his hand, palm up, wiggling his fingers at her obnoxiously.

Alexis put the disgusting beer on the table behind her and fumbled in the small, but expensive, crossbody leather purse she was wearing. She dug inside and pulled out her wallet, opening it and pulling out a hundred-dollar bill, making sure Dominic saw the other bills in there in the process, much as she'd done at the bar the other week. She closed the wallet and put it away at the same time she laid the benjamin in Dominic's outstretched hand.

"There ya go. I'm sure that'll pay for some of the drinks tonight." Alexis smiled big, hoping he'd take another step away from her now that he'd gotten some cash. "If you need more, just let me know!" She held her breath as Dominic looked from the bill in his hand to her and back again. Finally, he smirked, and the money disappeared into his back pocket.

"It's a start, princess. Later." And with that, he turned and went back down the hallway to the living area.

Alexis let out a covert, relieved breath and turned back to Kelly, who hadn't said a word throughout the exchange with Dominic.

"I didn't know Donovan and Damian had a brother." It was the first thing that came to mind, and Alexis mentally winced after she said it. In a weird way the three brothers reminded her of Blake, Logan, and Nathan. It was as if she were in an alternate world, where instead of the brothers being on the side of good, they were on the side of evil.

Kelly didn't seem to notice anything off about her tone of voice. "Yeah. They've always been close."

"Cool." Alexis wasn't sure what else to say, when they heard several voices from the other room.

"Looks like the party's starting," Kelly said, chugging the rest of her beer and throwing the now-empty can into the sink behind her.

"Yay," Alexis chirped, picking up her beer from the table behind her and following Kelly down the hall to the other room.

Two hours later, and thirty minutes longer than she'd wanted to be there, Alexis hadn't found a way to unobtrusively extricate herself. She stood by a wall and looked around in barely concealed disgust. The party was in full swing now, and she hadn't seen Kelly in at least half an hour. There were around fifteen men in the room, who were obviously a part of the Inca Boyz. They were all wearing the same thing: jeans that rode low on their hips, black boots, and black T-shirts, which Alexis could now see were inside out. She wasn't sure what the design on the other side was, but it looked like some sort of cartoon character wearing an odd-looking hat and holding up its hand, which only had two fingers, mimicking a gun. It was weird, and she wished she could get a clear picture of the image for the gang task force, but she wasn't going to ask anyone about it. No way. They'd have to deal with the still shots from the video to re-create it.

Along with the men were women . . . or girls. Most looked young enough to still be in high school; all wore skimpy clothes, like Kelly, that left nothing to the imagination. Alexis was definitely overdressed, but since she was being used as an ATM, no one was complaining.

Throughout her time at the party, several gang members had come up to her and asked for money. Each and every time, even though she hadn't even been introduced to most of the men, Alexis had acquiesced, handing over twenties and fifty-dollar bills without complaint and with an airhead smile as if the money were candy and the guys were trick-or-treating.

The seven or so girls in the room completely ignored her. Since the men outnumbered them two to one, their job seemed to be making out with, and disappearing with, whatever man demanded their time. She'd seen one girl, who couldn't have been a day over fourteen, go into a back room with three different men so far. And that was in the hour and a half since she'd arrived. The girl never complained, didn't even look surprised or pissed she was being used like a whore. She docilely followed whichever man took her hand and dragged her out of the room.

Another girl was pulled out of the room by four men at once. Even though Alexis didn't hear any screams or crying from the hallway they'd disappeared into, she shuddered to think about what was going on and what the poor girl was going through.

Kelly, somewhat surprisingly, hadn't hooked up with anyone, at least not that Alexis had observed. She'd stood next to Alexis for a while, arms crossed, a scowl on her face, as some of the gang members came up and demanded money. Chuck was the last to arrive, around thirty minutes earlier.

The second he saw Alexis, a wide, leering smile crossed his face, and he made a beeline for the wall she'd been holding up. He hadn't said a word in greeting, just reached out, put a hand behind her neck, and pulled her to him.

Alexis gasped in surprise at his actions, and it gave him the opening he needed. His tongue slid into her mouth and stroked against her own. It took everything she had not to gag at Chuck's rancid breath as he slobbered all over her. She plastered her tongue to the roof of her mouth and tried to block his access to the rest of her mouth. At her actions, he retreated and began to lick and nibble on her bottom lip instead, not even seeming put out that she'd blocked him.

Pulling away, and knowing it was only because Chuck allowed it, Alexis smiled weakly at him and said, "Hello again, Chuck."

"Alexis. Great to fucking see you. After the night I've had, you're just what I need." When she strained away from him, his hand tightened on the back of her neck, keeping her immobile in front of him. His grip was tight and scary, nothing like how Blake held her.

She put a hand up to his T-shirt and recoiled when she felt how damp it was. Alexis pulled her hand back and looked down, seeing a maroon smear on her palm.

Chuck laughed, and it once again took everything Alexis had not to gag at the foul stench coming from his mouth. The man needed a toothbrush and some mouthwash . . . badly.

"Sorry, doll. Work. I need to change and talk to my guys for a bit." His eyes flicked down to the bottle of beer she'd been nursing all night. "You look like you need a stronger drink." He turned to Kelly, never loosening the grip he had on the back of Alexis's neck. "Be a gem, Kel, and go get that bottle of vodka I know Damian is hiding in his freezer."

"Fuck off, Chuck. You don't own me." Kelly sneered, standing upright from her slouch against the wall, where she'd been for the last hour.

Chuck moved faster than Alexis had ever seen someone move before, his free hand wrapping around the front of Kelly's throat and squeezing. Kelly's hands immediately came up to his tattooed fingers and tugged, trying to get free with no luck.

"You might think you're hot shit, bitch, but Donovan's not fucking here. He can't protect you and wouldn't even if he *was* here. Shit, woman, he doesn't want you anymore. Everyone knows he's still got the hots for his ex. He only fucked you because you were easy and he was desperate when she ran off. When he gets out and we find her, you'll see you're nothing but yesterday's pussy. You're *nothing* to him. Hear me? Nothing. The only reason you're still around is . . ." Chuck paused for a moment, his eyes sliding over to Alexis, then back to Kelly. "You know why. Now go get the fucking bottle of vodka and start pouring shots. When I get back out here I want to show our new benefactor some Inca Boyz appreciation. Got it?"

Kelly nodded—at least Alexis thought she did (it was hard to tell since Chuck had such a firm grip on her throat)—and Chuck finally let go of her. She fell back against the wall and without another word, or even looking at either of them, slunk off toward the hallway on the right toward the kitchen.

Throughout the entire short, violent encounter, Chuck hadn't taken his hand from the back of Alexis's neck. She giggled nervously and said, "Wow, Chuck, you sure know how to get results."

He leaned into her again, tilting her head but applying pressure on her nape, then licked a path from the hollow of her throat up the side of her neck to her ear. Alexis shuddered in revulsion, which Chuck obviously mistook for arousal. He bit down on her earlobe, hard enough for Alexis to flinch in pain, then said, "Hold that thought, doll. I've got Inca business to attend to, and I need to change. Then I'll be back to show you a good time. I've had a bitch of a night, and you're just what I need to unwind. Trust me, these assholes have nothin' on me."

He thrust his hips against her while he spoke, his hard cock pressing against her belly, his intentions crystal clear. Chuck kissed her lips once more, and Alexis was careful to keep them closed this time, then pulled back. "Be back soon. Be here when I get back." It wasn't a question.

Alexis swallowed hard, wanting to rub the back of her hand over her skin to erase the feel of Chuck but knowing it wouldn't look good to the many people sitting around the small room unabashedly observing her. She knew Chuck meant his words as a sort of endearment, but they sounded like an obvious threat to her. As soon as he left her side, another man sauntered up to her and stated, "Kelly said we need more booze. Gotta make a liquor run. She said you liked the expensive shit. Need some cash."

Without protest, as she'd done throughout the night, Alexis took out her wallet and handed the man the last two hundred bucks she had. She still had the cash in her back pocket, but she'd only use that if she had to. If she ran out of money, she'd be expendable . . . she really didn't want that to happen. It was way past time for her to leave.

Thirty minutes later, she knew Chuck would be back any moment. Alexis had tried to get as many faces on the video camera as possible, and she'd hung as close as she dared around the pockets of men talking. It would have to be enough. She did *not* want to be there when Chuck got back from wherever he was.

She looked down at her hand and saw whatever the man's shirt had been wet with was still smeared on her palm. She wiped it surreptitiously on her pants, horrified to see it had dried and wasn't coming off. She needed a shower. A long one. Alexis wasn't sure she'd ever feel clean again.

She bent her head as if she was simply tired, and as softly as she could, in barely a breath of air, whispered, "Get me out of here."

One of the girls had unzipped a guy's pants and was giving him a hand job on the couch, not even trying to hide what she was doing and not bothering to go into the back rooms. Ignoring the way a group of gangbangers were ogling her, then laughing, Alexis breathed through her nose, trying desperately to keep herself together. The mood in the room had definitely shifted from jovial-party atmosphere to a darker, dangerous one. The men were drunk and obviously horny. As she watched, a man kneeled on the couch behind the woman giving the hand job and hauled her to her knees. He shoved her short skirt up over her ass, then reached for the button of his jeans.

She averted her gaze and eyed the sliding door, in yearning, that led to the backyard. If push came to shove, she'd go out that way and disappear before circling around to the meeting spot. She just had to hold on a little bit longer; then she could get out of this foul house with the terrible people and try to feel clean again.

Within minutes of her whispered plea to Blake, the sound of gunshots and a motor revving came from outside the small house. Everyone in the room froze. Then the men sprang into action, immediately heading for the front door, most pulling out handguns from wherever they'd stashed them on their bodies. The girls shrieked and ran for either of the two hallways to take cover before bullets started flying.

Alexis heard yelling from the front of the house where the men had disappeared, but she immediately slipped out through the sliding glass door. She ran for the gate she'd seen earlier and tugged. It didn't move. Not even an inch. She pulled again. Desperately this time. Nothing. *Dammit.* She had nothing on her to break the lock.

She looked frantically back into the house, no one was in the main room—for now—but soon the men would come back inside, or the women would get brave and want to see what was happening. If she got caught trying to slip away, it would look suspicious, which was the last thing she wanted. Escaping Chuck's amorous advances would be the least of her worries. And if anyone got her in a position where they could remove her shirt, they'd discover the wire, and she'd be as good as dead. She *had* to escape that yard. Now.

Desperate, Alexis looked around the small outdoor space. The gate had to be locked from the outside, which was insane. Who padlocked a gate from the outside? Wary criminals, that's who.

She spotted the stack of rotting wood that they'd seen on the satellite images, and Alexis expected to feel a hand on her shoulder any second. She could practically smell Chuck's rancid breath breathing down her neck. Blake had pointed out the debris pile absently, noting in passing that if she needed to, she could use a piece of wood as a weapon, but neither of them had thought about using it to escape the yard. But the second her eyes landed on it, Alexis had seen an exit point, not a stack of weapons.

Without stopping to think that she could be crawling out of the frying pan into the fire, Alexis climbed up on the unsteady stack of random wood and other trash lying forgotten and rotting at the back of the yard and reached for the top of the fence. Taking advantage of the adrenaline coursing through her veins, she jumped, managing to push her body up until the points of wooden fence slats were pressed against her belly. Seeing no one and, more important, no drooling, rabid, pissed-off dogs on the other side, she threw one leg up, then quickly, ignoring the pain of the wooden points sticking into her belly, brought her other leg up and dropped down to the other side.

It was quite a long drop, and Alexis landed hard. Her ankles buckled, and she fell back on her ass, wincing as she felt the jolt all the way up her spine. She could still hear yelling from the front of the house and crawled away as fast as she could from the fence, when she heard Kelly's voice faintly calling her name.

Turning and crab walking backward as fast as she could toward a group of overgrown bushes, Alexis kept her eyes on the top of the fence, fearing she'd see Kelly or one of the gang members looking over it any second. She probably could claim she was scared of the gunfire, but the last thing she wanted was to have to go back inside that house. She had a knife strapped to her ankle under her jeans, but she instinctively knew she'd only make a bad situation worse if she pulled it out. Blake might be outside ready and willing to do what he had to keep her safe, but even with Logan, they couldn't fight off over a dozen gangbangers.

Alexis heard the sliding door open and someone walk into the yard she'd just left. Whoever it was, was just on the other side of the fence, but she was too scared to move into the cover of the bushes. She didn't want to make any noise that might alert whoever it was to her presence.

"Goddammit, where'd she go?" Kelly asked someone.

"I didn't see her. We all ran. She must've gotten scared and gone outside with the guys," one of the girls who'd been at the party said.

"What a dumb bitch," Kelly spat venomously. "She was always so goddamn stupid."

"I heard we got two grand off her tonight, though. That's good, right?"

"It's fucking peanuts is what it is," Kelly told the other girl. "That bitch has tens of thousands of dollars at her disposal. Donovan wants that cash. He needs it."

Alexis held her breath.

"Well, you can text her later and act like you care. Then you can set up another meet. I know Chuck said he wants in her pants. So, while he's doing her, you can take her ATM card and go get some cash."

Alexis heard a smack, then Kelly said, "You're just as stupid as she is, bitch. You think she's gonna give me her pass code just like that? No, she won't. She likes to feel important by doling out the cash little by little and making us beg for it. Besides, we're done with this bullshit. I can't stand being around her anymore, and Donovan agrees. We're doing it *his* way now. He's ready to get the fuck outta that place."

Alexis had no idea what "Donovan's way" meant, but she didn't think she wanted to know.

"Chuck won't be happy."

Alexis was actually a little impressed at how the other girl stood her ground with Kelly.

"I don't give a shit. He'll get his piece of ass. Of course, Alexis probably won't like him as much when he offers her up to the rest of the gang."

Alexis stayed motionless on the ground, horrified.

The other girl laughed. "Better her than me."

Kelly's tone suddenly changed. She almost sounded motherly. "Very true. You just keep giving the guys what they want when they need it, and you'll be good. Sucking cock and letting them take you isn't so bad. You'll learn to enjoy it. The last thing you want is to be on the bad side of the Inca Boyz."

"No shit," the girl said. "Someday I'm gonna be an Inca Boyz old lady and get some respect. Come on, let's see what happened and if our guys shot up the fucker who took shots at our house."

Alexis heard the sliding door slam shut as the two women went back into the house. She let out the breath she'd been holding and turned over onto her hands and knees, ignoring the pain in her lower back and her ankles. She had to get to the meeting spot . . . and Blake. She'd crawl there if she had to. She wanted out of this yard, out of this neighborhood, and out of this part of Denver. She never even wanted to drive through it again. She was done.

Chapter Eleven

Blake fidgeted in the passenger seat next to Logan. "Where is she?"

It was somewhat of a rhetorical question as both men could see through the video camera she was wearing that she was still making her way to the rendezvous point. They could hear her heavy breathing and her mumbled words letting them know her progress.

"Keep it together, Blake," Logan warned in a low voice.

"If it was Grace out there, how would you feel?" Blake knew it was a low blow the second he'd uttered it, but didn't apologize.

"I'd feel exactly the same way you do," his brother said calmly. "And you know I've *been* where you are. Alexis was amazing tonight. She kept her cool, didn't panic when shit got real, was able to get some amazing intel, and she acted exactly how she was supposed to when we set up the distraction. She'll be here."

"That fucker Chuck had his hands on her," Blake bit out between clenched teeth.

"Just like Donovan had his hands on Grace," Logan reminded his brother gently. "Grace got through it, so will Alexis."

Blake didn't bother to point out that when Donovan touched Grace, she'd been unconscious and didn't even know it was happening. Alexis was more than aware of what Chuck wanted to do to her. "I love her," Blake told his brother. He turned to look at him. "I can't imagine anything happening to her. It makes me crazy. How do you stand it?"

Logan grinned. "It's a bitch for sure. Just wait until she's pregnant with your child. It gets a hundred times worse."

"Fuck," Blake grouched, but his lips quirked up in a half smile. Alexis pregnant. He could imagine her round with his child inside her. Damn, he hadn't even made love to her yet, and he already wanted to see her pregnant with his child. He certainly wasn't good enough for her, but he had a feeling she'd be a great mother. She naturally liked to take care of people and was always looking out for not only his but his brothers' best interests. He couldn't fucking wait.

"Here she comes," Logan stated quietly, pointing at the small screen they'd been watching through the camera lens around her neck all night.

It took a few moments, but finally Blake saw faint movement at the northeast edge of the deserted parking lot. "Turn off the tapes," he ordered his brother, not wanting anything Alexis said to him being videotaped, before he opened his door and walked as fast as he could across the parking lot. He wanted to run but didn't want to draw attention to either of them.

As he got closer, Blake could see Alexis was limping. He was in front of her within seconds. He wrapped one arm around her waist and pulled her into his body. He brought the other arm up and rested it on her cheek.

"You okay, Lex?"

"Yeah," she responded immediately, in a muted tone that sounded nothing like the spunky, give-'em-hell woman he'd come to know and love.

Blake leaned forward to touch his lips to hers, but she jerked her head backward, away from him, turning it aside at the same time, not letting him kiss her.

"No," she pleaded, shaking her head and pushing against his chest. "I need to shower. I need to wipe his touch off me. I don't want to taint you."

"Sweetheart—" Blake started, but Alexis cut him off.

"Get me out of here, Blake. Please? I need to get away from here."

He hated hearing the uneasiness and fright in her voice. He was moving back toward Logan's truck even before she'd finished speaking.

He turned, keeping his arm around her waist, taking a lot of her weight against his own larger body, and headed for the car. They didn't say a word, but Blake was happy for the moment to have her whole and relatively unscathed in his arms.

He opened the back door of the truck and helped Alexis sit. "Scoot over, Lex, I'm sitting back here with you."

She didn't protest and slid over, giving him room to get in next to her and shut the door.

Logan had them moving before he could fasten his seat belt. Blake clicked the belt over his lap and reached for Alexis. He wrapped his arms around her and pulled her to his side. One of her arms made its way behind his back against the seat and the other reached across his chest and clamped down tightly over his right shoulder. She buried her head into the side of his neck and shivered nonstop in his arms, as if it was thirty degrees inside the truck instead of a comfortable seventy-five.

"Where am I going?" Logan asked from the front seat.

The original plan had been for them to drop Alexis off at her downtown apartment, and to meet up with her at Ace Security the next day, but Logan could see as well as Blake that she was in no condition to be left alone.

Blake turned his head and kissed the top of Lex's head and murmured, "I'd like to take you to my place, sweetheart. If you can wait that long. I have a huge shower and tub. You can soak as long as you want."

She didn't say anything for a long moment, so Blake continued. "If you can't wait, that's okay. We can go to your apartment. But I'm staying with you either way."

"Your house," Alexis stated, her warm breath wafting over the sensitive skin below his ear.

Blake reached up, took hold of the hand that she had against his neck, kissed the palm, then put it back where it'd been. He put his hand over hers, holding her to him. "Thank you for letting me be with you tonight, sweetheart."

She nodded against him.

"Close your eyes, relax, we'll be there soon," he told her softly. "I'm so proud of you. I don't know any other woman who could've done what you did in there tonight. You're never doing it again, but I'm proud as fuck of you."

He thought he felt a small snort of laughter come from her.

"Seriously, Alexis," Logan piped up from the driver's seat. "You were able to get all of the men's faces on the camera, and I can't believe they didn't seem to be bothered with your presence when they talked about the jobs they had lined up. Murder for hire is a big fucking deal. I think there are at least four crimes that you being there tonight will prevent."

Logan's words caused Alexis to burrow herself even deeper into Blake's side. He tightened his hold on her and held on as Logan continued to speak.

"With that said, your role in taking down the Inca Boyz is finished. Tonight was too fucking close. I will not risk your well-being to take down the scum who tried to ruin my wife. Got it?"

Alexis spoke for the first time since getting in the car, but didn't lift her head. "Yeah. I get it. I have *no* desire to ever see or talk to any of those people again." She shuddered against Blake. "I'm glad I did what I did, but I'm afraid I don't have what it takes to do this for a living. It's a good thing we're on the same page, otherwise you would've had my resignation letter on your desk first thing in the morning."

Logan snorted from the front seat. "Freaked out and still throwing sass. I like her, Bro."

"Like I give a shit," Blake told his brother, relaxing a fraction when he heard Alexis's soft chuckle against him. He *did* care what his brother thought, but he was equally relieved that Lex was "throwing sass," as Logan called it.

"That doesn't mean I want to stop helping you with the surveillance at the courthouses and other tamer stuff," Alexis warned, her voice muffled by his shirt. "I'm pretty good at the social media stuff too—admit it."

"You are," Blake told her without quibbling. "You're way ahead of me in that department. I can write code and program shit, but searching for keywords and spending time on Facebook is akin to torture for me." He liked the fact Alexis was hinting about sticking around. He'd been half-afraid that she wouldn't want anything to do with Ace Security, or him, after the intense night she'd just had.

They continued down the interstate toward Castle Rock for several minutes with no one saying a word. Blake thought Alexis had fallen asleep, when she murmured, "I don't have an overnight bag with me."

"I'll make a quick stop at the twenty-four-hour drugstore," Logan said easily, overhearing her remark. "We can get you whatever toiletries you need to tide you over."

"And I've got a T-shirt you can wear," Blake told her. "We'll figure it out."

"Okay," Alexis said. "Sounds good. But I'm going to want my own stuff as soon as we can swing it. A girl can't live in her boyfriend's clothes forever."

"You could always eschew my clothes and walk around naked," Blake teased, wanting to get her mind off what had happened, and what could've happened, to her.

As he hoped, she laughed, a more natural laugh this time . . . less forced. "In your dreams."

"Fuck yeah," Blake whispered. "You've starred in my dreams every night for the last month or so."

Before their banter could go any further, Logan asked, "Do you think you'll be up to a sit-down with Nathan and the task force tomorrow afternoon?"

"It's too soon," Blake protested immediately, but Alexis shook her head against him and loosened her hold on him for the first time.

"No, it's fine, Blake. It's better if I get it over with. You'll both be there, though . . . right?" Alexis added, the uneasiness creeping back into her tone.

Blake answered for his brother. "Damn straight."

"Then it's fine. It'll be fresher in my mind."

"How about dinner afterward with Grace and Nathan?" Logan asked. "My wife has been bugging me to set something up with you. She's dying to get to know you better."

"She has? I thought she couldn't stand the sight of me," Alexis said absently. "After what happened with her and my brother, I figured I'd be the last person she wanted to hang out with, even if I was dating her brother-in-law."

"She doesn't have a lot of friends," Logan said, not sounding concerned, meeting her eyes briefly in the rearview mirror before turning his concentration back to the road. "Felicity and Cole, they own Rock Hard Gym in town, and that's about it. Her parents were assholes and didn't really let her cultivate any relationships. She was impressed with your tenaciousness and defense of your brother. That kind of loyalty doesn't go unnoticed."

"Then I'd love to," Alexis said quietly. "I don't have many friends myself. I'd be thrilled to get to know her better."

"Then it's settled," Logan stated easily. "I'll set it up."

"You hungry?" Blake asked.

Alexis shook her head against his shoulder. "God no. I don't think I could eat anything right about now. I just need to get clean. Then I'll see how I feel."

"Okay, sweetheart. We'll be home soon." Home. It had been a long time since Blake had actually looked forward to going back to the small house he'd lived in growing up. It held a lot of awful memories. Memories of his mom hitting not only him and his brothers but his father too. Ace Anderson had been abused by his wife his entire life, and his mom had eventually taken his life.

Thinking about the violence he'd experienced at home brought his thoughts back around to tonight. Alexis had been too close to danger. He'd seen through the hidden camera how the gangbangers had taken the other women to the back of the house. He'd heard the casual way they'd discussed the bedroom skills, or lack thereof, of the women they'd just screwed. He'd listened to the way Chuck had spoken to Alexis, had heard him kissing her . . . *his* Alexis. He couldn't see everything that had happened—the bastard had been standing too close to her for the camera to record what exactly he'd done—but he had no doubt it had been bad. Lex had sounded uncomfortable and freaked out.

He needed to erase that.

To make her feel clean again.

And he couldn't do that until she was safe in his house.

So he wanted to be home. Now.

Thirty minutes later Logan finally pulled up to the house. He and Nathan had only been inside twice since they'd returned to Castle Rock. The four walls held too many ghosts for them to ever feel comfortable again.

Blake knew it was odd for him to *want* to live there, but it had been cathartic in a way. He'd shown his mother that she couldn't control his emotions anymore. He'd thrown out all her clothes and belongings and was slowly going through the boxes and boxes of papers that had been left in the small office.

Tonight, he'd take another step in purging the negative energy Rose Anderson had left behind. Alexis would sleep in his bed, in the same room his mother had shared with his father. But this time there would be nothing but love and tenderness. Not the hate and aggression of the past.

"Will three o'clock work for tomorrow?" Logan asked before Blake exited the car.

He considered for a moment, then nodded. "Yeah, that'll let us sleep in, then decompress before the meeting. You want us there an hour early to discuss how we want the meeting to go with the task force guy?"

"Good idea, yes. I'll tell Grace to meet us there around five. We can go to dinner after we're done."

"Want me to call Nathan?" Blake asked.

"No. I'll do it. You take care of Alexis," Logan said.

"You guys do know I'm sitting right here, right? I can hear you. And I don't need taking care of," Alexis protested.

"Most days you don't, but tonight you do," Blake told her without hesitation, "and more importantly, I need to do it." He opened the door, not giving her a chance to utter whatever witty comeback she was sure to have, climbed out, then offered her a hand to help her out of the car.

"See you tomorrow," Logan called out to his brother. "And again, good job tonight, Alexis. I'm proud of you."

"Thanks," she murmured, holding on to Blake's hand firmly as she stood up next to the car.

Blake put his arm around Lex and held on to the plastic bag of items Logan had picked up for her from the pharmacy earlier on the way home. He again took most of her weight as they made their way to the front door. "How badly are you hurt?" Blake asked.

"I'm okay," Alexis told him. "I landed hard when I climbed over the fence. My ankles are throbbing and my lower back hurts, but I think after I take a hot shower and get some aspirin, I'll feel better."

"Mmmm," Blake murmured, pissed all over again. "I'll get some painkillers for after your shower. You can take them to hopefully stave off more pain in the morning."

She agreed, and he unlocked the door to the house, holding it open, allowing Alexis to walk inside in front of him. She looked around and whistled low. "Holy cow. It looks great, Blake. You've made a ton of changes since the last time I was here. I almost can't recognize it as the same house I stayed in a few months ago."

She'd last been there while Logan and Grace were holed up in her apartment, after Grace had been kidnapped by the Inca Boyz. Blake hadn't thought much of Alexis then; he was too suspicious of her because of everything that had happened with her brother. He'd been shocked when she'd shown an interest in working for Ace Security and even more surprised when she'd actually been good at it. Once he'd seen how hard she worked and how much she wanted to help others, he began to wonder what else he'd gotten wrong about her. It was then he'd slowly started to see her as more than a coworker and more as a beautiful woman he'd like to get to know better.

"Yeah, as you can see, I knocked out the wall between the living room and the kitchen to open it up. Then I had all the carpets ripped out. The hardwood floors are a bit chilly in the winter, but I love the way they look."

"The couches are new too, right?" Alexis asked, her eyes taking in the warm space.

"Yup. Come on. You're about to drop. You need to get clean. I think you'll really appreciate the bathroom remodel." Blake took her hand and headed down the short hallway toward the master bedroom. There were two more bedrooms on the other side of the house, a fact all of the brothers had been thankful for when they were growing up. The more space between them and their mother, the better they'd liked it.

It wasn't the first time he'd held Lex's hand, but it felt just as good this time as the last. He'd had her in his arms, and he'd kissed her, but it was almost just as intimate to feel the skin of her palms and her fingers intertwined with his own. It felt small and petite in his, and unfortunately was ice-cold. It wasn't that chilly in his house, so he knew her chilled skin had to be a result of her state of mind.

She'd gone out of her way to seem unaffected by everything that had happened tonight, but it was pretty obvious that her nonchalance had been an act. She was freaked out by everything that had happened that night, and he hated that. Hated that she felt as if she needed to build a wall between them and not let him see how she was truly feeling. She'd hidden behind a false front long enough.

Blake led her through his bedroom and straight into his bathroom. He hadn't been sure what he'd wanted when he'd first consulted with an interior designer, but the woman had done an amazing job. The room was light and airy. On the floor were light-brown slate tiles, which could be heated with a switch of a button. Along one wall stood a long counter, with two sinks that had cost an arm and a leg. They were brass and looked like raised bowls. The brown concrete countertop blended well with the color of the sinks. Behind the counter on the opposite wall was a huge shower, big enough for two people, with two showerheads and two controls.

The image of him and Lex showering together, facing each other while they soaped up, sprang into Blake's mind. His cock hardened, and he turned away so Alexis wouldn't notice. The last thing she needed right now was to deal with him not being able to control his body. He wanted her, there was no doubt, but somehow he knew she needed some space to regroup, and he'd do whatever it would take to help her get her equilibrium back.

In the corner of the room was a large triangular tub with jets strategically placed around the edges. Again, he could easily imagine Alexis relaxing in that tub. The image of her bending over while he took her from behind was as clear as if it was a memory rather than a fantasy. Rounding out the bathroom, across from the tub, was the door to a small alcove containing the toilet.

Blake dropped Alexis's hand reluctantly and went straight to the linen closet. He pulled out one of the outrageously expensive towels his designer insisted he *had* to have and brought it over to where Lex was still standing, staring at the room around her.

"My God, Blake. This is amazing. It looks nothing like what used to be here. It's like it went from a Motel 6 to the Ritz-Carlton."

Blake chuckled and shrugged. "Yeah, I had to give up some of the square footage from the bedroom, but I figured it was worth it."

"It was *totally* worth it," she agreed. Alexis's words were reverent, but she held herself stiff, her arms wrapped around her waist as if that was all that was holding her together.

Blake put the towel down on the counter between the sinks and reached for the necklace Lex was wearing. Without a word, he pulled it up and over her head, placing it gently next to the towel behind them.

Next he slowly moved his hands to the front of her jeans. He undid the top button, which gave him some slack, and he eased his fingertips under the band. She shivered under his hands but didn't change her defensive position.

"I'm going to remove the mic now, sweetheart. Is that all right?"

She looked up at him with wide eyes. So many emotions swam in her eyes. It would kill him to leave her like this, but he would if she needed the space. Blake knew she could take care of removing the mic herself, but he needed to take care of her.

Finally, after what seemed like an eternity, she nodded slightly.

Blake held her eyes as he moved his hands up the front of her body toward her bra. She dropped her arms from around her waist, giving him access. Without pulling her shirt up, Blake's fingers zeroed in on the small microphone nestled in the tight, warm space of her cleavage. The bra she was wearing pushed her breasts together so high and tight, where the mic was held snuggly, that the piece of adhesive tape holding it in place was almost unnecessary.

Lex was shivering, and he could feel the goose bumps spring up on her arms, which she routinely got when he touched her. It made him feel better that she could still react to him, even as vulnerable as she was, but he didn't do anything to prolong the moment, working quickly, but gently, to peel back the tape and remove the mic. Blake ran the fingertips of one hand over the irritated skin between her breasts, wishing it was his tongue instead.

Knowing that her feeling clean was more important at the moment than his sexual urges, Blake slid his hands back down her body and out from under her shirt.

Without taking his eyes from her, Blake placed the microphone next to the necklace, then leaned on the counter with his palms, caging her in his arms in the process. "You want a shower or bath?"

"Shower," she said immediately in a soft voice.

"Okay. Take your time. I'll make us something to snack on."

"I'm not hungry," Alexis reminded him, still speaking in that low voice. She hadn't moved to put her hands around him, but instead had moved them to hug herself again.

"I know you're not, but you might feel differently after you shower. I'll get something ready just in case. If you're still not hungry, it's not a big deal. Okay?"

"Okay, Blake."

Remembering how she'd pulled away from him in the parking lot, Blake was careful to keep his intentions clear, as he leaned toward her now. He aimed his lips to her forehead and kept them against her skin for a long moment. Finally, he pulled back and, still not touching her, he kept his hands on the counter behind her by sheer force of will. He said softly, "I don't know what's going on in that brain of yours, but know this. I think you're amazing. I've never been so proud, scared, and worried all at the same as I was tonight. I'm in awe of you. You're the most unselfish, amazing, passionate woman I've ever known. Nothing that happened tonight has changed my mind about wanting to make love to you until you know nothing but me . . . surrounding you, inside you." He moved his hands to frame her face and kissed the top of her head. "Shower, sweetheart. I'll put a T-shirt and a pair of my running shorts on the bed for you. I'll be in the kitchen; you can come out when you're done."

She nodded at him, and he ignored the tears that shone brightly in her eyes, figuring she needed the release. Blake grabbed the necklace and mic before taking a step backward. He kept eye contact with her until he reached the doorway. He reached out, grabbed the knob, and shut the door silently behind him, leaving Alexis to her thoughts.

Chapter Twelve

Alexis stripped off her top and jeans in a daze, leaving them in a heap on the tiled floor. She quickly removed her panties and bra and reached into the shower to turn it on. After only moments, the water heated and she turned it as hot as she thought she could stand before stepping into the large enclosure.

When her body got used to the temperature, she turned the knob a quarter of an inch, making it just this side of scalding. Then she scrubbed. If she wasn't so concerned about getting clean, she might've found it funny that Blake owned, and apparently used, a shower pouf, on which she poured a liberal amount of body wash and did her best to remove the feeling of Chuck's hands on her and the feeling of revulsion that had clung to her after watching the men in the house take the girls to the back room to screw.

She rubbed her body until it was pink from both the hot water and her harsh ablutions. The hand that she'd touched Chuck's damp T-shirt with had been scrubbed until it felt like she'd taken off the top layer of skin. Then Alexis simply stood under the blistering-hot water, letting it hammer against her head and face until she was forced to take a step back to breathe.

Then, finally, the tears she'd held back all night burst free, as if they were water released from a dam. She couldn't keep them in any longer, putting her back to the tile wall and sliding down until her butt hit the ground. She wrapped her arms around her knees and cried as the water rained down on her. Cried because of how scared she'd been, cried because she was sure she'd be called out as a snitch any second and brutally raped and killed, cried because Chuck had stuck his disgusting tongue in her mouth.

Alexis cried until she didn't think she had one ounce of water left in her body. She stood on shaky legs, bracing herself with a hand against the wall, and turned her back to the water, letting it cascade over her hair, and down her face, one more time. She swayed, not wanting to leave. Even after showering, she still felt dirty.

It felt as if the Inca Boyz' awfulness and evilness stuck to her like a death shroud. She couldn't shake it off, no matter how hard she scrubbed or how hot the water was. Feeling defeated, she finally turned off the water. She opened the shower door and grabbed a towel. She dried off robotically, not even caring if she was thorough, and headed out of the bathroom into Blake's room.

On his bed was a shirt and a pair of shorts, just as he'd said he'd leave for her. She quickly changed, pausing only to inhale Blake's masculine scent, which clung to the T-shirt, and headed back into the bathroom to brush her teeth with the stuff Logan had picked up for her at the pharmacy.

She brushed three times and swished with mouthwash four times, trying in vain to get the disgusting feel and taste of Chuck out of her mouth. When she was about to fall over with exhaustion, she finally shuffled out of the bathroom to make her way to the kitchen.

But Alexis stopped in her tracks when she left the steamy room. Blake was standing by his bed wearing nothing but a pair of flannel pants that had polar bears all over them. They seemed so out of place. Lex had no idea where he'd gotten them, but he didn't give her a chance to comment.

He held out a hand and said softly, "Come 'ere, Lex."

She walked over to him without hesitation and placed her hand in his, sighing in relief when he closed his fingers around her. How holding his hand could make her feel so grounded, Alexis had no clue. But she'd give every penny she had in the bank if he held on and never let go.

With his free hand, Blake pulled back the covers. "Climb in, sweetheart."

"I thought you were making something to eat," she said, her voice sounding rough and scratchy from her bout of crying.

"You need my arms around you more than you need food."

His answer was brief and to the point, and oh so true. Alexis reluctantly let go of Blake's hand and climbed into his bed.

"Scoot over. I'm coming in too."

Relieved that he'd read her mind, she did as he requested, moving over to give him some room. Alexis kept her eyes on Blake as he leaned over and clicked off the light on a table next to the bed.

Then he turned and gathered her into his arms. Her bare legs brushed against his flannel-clad ones, and she sighed in contentment. She laid her head on his bare chest, and her breath suddenly hitched when she felt his fingers rest on her hip just under the waistband of her shorts. He simply held her to him, his warm, strong fingers pressing into her, letting her know he was there.

She'd thought she was all cried out, but apparently she still had some tears. She tried to keep Blake from knowing she was upset, but she obviously didn't do a very good job of it.

"Let it out, Lex. I've got you."

"I'm f-f-fine."

"No, you're not, and I don't fucking blame you. It took everything I had to not bust into the middle of the party and carry you out of there. Not to mention how hard it was for me to not come into the shower when I heard you crying. It killed me, more so because I know that's not you."

"It's n-n-not. I never cry."

"I know, sweetheart. You're the toughest chick I know. Cry all you want. I won't tell a soul."

And Alexis knew he wouldn't. His understanding and sensitivity made her stop trying to hold back. She held on as tightly to him as he did to her and gave up trying to be stoic. She bawled. Huge, ugly sobs that she knew she should be embarrassed about, but Blake didn't speak, or do anything other than hold her tight.

Ten minutes later, when she was finally done, Blake produced a tissue from somewhere and held it up to her nose. "Blow."

She didn't hesitate and did as he ordered.

When he leaned away to put the tissue on the table, she brought a hand up and wiped the tears off her face, then snuggled back into Blake's warm chest.

"Feel better?" he asked quietly.

Alexis nodded. "I'm sorry I snotted all over you."

He chuckled but said, "I'm not. You needed that."

She nodded against him again. "I did. Thank you."

"You don't need to thank me, Lex. I'd be an asshole if I told you to suck it up or not to worry because it was all over. All I want is for you to be yourself with me. If that means being strong in front of everyone else, and crying on me in our bed, so be it."

She shivered at hearing "our bed." "That was nice," she told him.

"It's not nice," he retorted fiercely, squeezing her. "It's called taking care of the person you love. Being there for them when they need you. I'll always be your strength when you don't have it for yourself, your sounding board when you need one, or simply your supporter, cheering you on from the background. The fact of the matter is that I know you don't really need me, Lex. You've done a hell of a job standing on your own two feet and taking on the world on your own. I just feel lucky you're here with me right now."

All of that was wonderful. Amazing, in fact. But there was that one little word Alexis heard echoing in her brain. She was afraid to bring it up. Afraid he'd said it in the heat of the moment. But typically, she couldn't let it go. She needed to know.

Lifting her head, she stared through the dim light of the room into his eyes. She tried to read his thoughts through his facial expression but failed.

"Taking care of the person you love?" she asked quietly, her eyebrows lifting in question.

Blake didn't hesitate. Didn't make her wonder for a second longer if he meant what he'd said. "Yeah. I love you, Lex. You snuck under my radar, and I realized that every day I looked forward to talking to you. To seeing you. I knew I loved you before tonight, but you being in danger and me not being able to do a fucking thing about it solidified it for me. I love you. Not because you'll be giving me your body. Not because you're the only woman I've hung out with since I got back to Castle Rock. And not because you're doing an amazing thing for my family. I love you for *you*. The person you show to the outside world . . . the strong, take-no-shit-from-anyone daughter of a bazillionaire, as well as the one I get the privilege to see in private. The woman who is self-conscious, stubborn to a fault, and who is uncertain and scared to show her true self to the world because she's afraid of what they might think."

Alexis could only stare at Blake in amazement. He loved her. When he didn't say anything else, she shut her eyes and took a deep breath. She couldn't believe it. She never thought she'd ever be where she was now. In Blake's house, in his arms, in his *bed*. She brought her hand up to the side of his face and laid it on the slight stubble there, running her thumb back and forth over the scratchy skin. "I've loved you for months. From practically the first moment I saw you."

"Did you wash away the demons?" he asked, an intense look in his eyes.

"What?" It wasn't what she was expecting him to say at all.

"You didn't want me to touch you earlier. You needed to wash away that asshole's touch. I want to kiss you, I *need* to kiss you, but I want you to be sure."

"I'm sure," Alexis told Blake with no hesitation. "I need you."

Blake lowered his head until his lips hovered over hers. "You're mine," he whispered. "I can't imagine ever touching another woman. You're the only one I want to be with, to kiss, to love. You don't ever have to worry about me cheating on you, Lex. You're it for me. I know it down to the marrow of my bones."

"Kiss me. Please."

Without another word, Blake's mouth dropped to hers. But instead of taking her in a hard, passionate kiss, he savored her. Gently kissing her with close-mouthed pecks, then licking each of her lips; then, when she was panting with desire, his tongue finally eased into her mouth. Alexis sighed in relief and relished the feel of his mouth on hers. She was surrounded by Blake, his touch, his smell. She didn't think about Chuck at all. All that time in the shower and brushing her teeth had done nothing to dispel him from her thoughts, but all it took was one touch of Blake's lips to hers and—poof—he was gone, as if he'd never taken up residence in her brain.

Alexis and Blake took turns being the aggressor; first his tongue dueled with hers; then he retreated, letting her enter his mouth and take charge of their kiss.

When it felt like her lungs would burst, Alexis pulled back reluctantly. Blake immediately tucked her head back onto his chest and held her tightly against him. She could feel his cock hard and long against her. She'd thrown her leg over his hips and had been grinding herself on him as they'd kissed. Blake's hand was all the way under her shorts now, his hot, heavy palm resting on her bare ass.

She lay there on top of him panting for a moment, expecting him to make the first move toward sex. But when Blake did nothing but lie under her, his heart beating a fast tempo under her palm resting on his muscular, slightly furred, bare chest, Alexis tilted her head back and looked up at him.

"You're gonna have to help me here, Blake. I haven't done this before." She smiled, knowing she was telling him something he was more than aware of.

"It's one thirty in the morning, Lex. We've had a long night. I'm tired, you're exhausted. Not to mention that you've been put through the emotional wringer. Sleep. There's no rush. We'll make love—have no doubt about that. But it doesn't have to be right this second."

For a moment, Alexis was worried he didn't want her anymore, but then reality sunk in. That was her old, less confident self talking. He was right. She *was* exhausted. Between being scared out of her mind and disgusted with Chuck's hands on her, then her emotional crying jag and the euphoria of Blake telling her he loved her . . . she was done. Just the thought of sleeping made her eyes suddenly extremely heavy.

"Okay," she whispered, tucking her nose into his chest once more and letting her eyes drift closed. "But I'll be more myself after some sleep. Just sayin'."

"Noted," Blake said, the humor clear in that one word.

She could almost hear the wide smile that was sure to be on his face.

"You comfortable? Or can we change positions?" he asked after a moment.

"I could move," Alexis told him, prying her eyes open with effort and lifting her head.

"Turn on your side, facing away from me," Blake ordered gently.

She did, and asked, "Like this?"

"Exactly like that," he told her, crowding in behind her, spooning her body with his. He wrapped his arm around her, tucking his forearm between her breasts and putting his hand under her cheek. He pushed his other arm under her pillow, totally surrounding her with his heat. He buried his nose into the crease of her neck, and she could feel his hot deep breaths against her skin.

"You smell like me," he commented completely out of the blue.

"I used your shower gel," Alexis told him sleepily.

"As much as I loved you smelling like honeysuckle, I think I like this better," Blake stated firmly. "It's sexy as hell and makes me feel even closer to you."

Alexis made a mental note to use his soap every now and then. She probably wouldn't use it in the mornings, because it wasn't exactly feminine, but she had to admit that she loved smelling like him probably almost as much as he enjoyed it.

They lay wrapped around each other without saying a word for a while. It felt familiar to Alexis somehow, as if she'd slept with Blake like this before . . . which was impossible. Wasn't it?

He answered her unasked question as if he knew exactly what she was thinking. "We slept like this when you were drunk the other day. You snuggled my arm as if you'd never let it go. I slept better than I ever have before. Do you mind? Are you comfortable?"

"Yes, I'm comfortable. I fit against you as if I was made to be in your arms."

"Good. Because I love this. I feel as if I'm standing between you and the world . . . and there's no place else I'd rather be."

"I love you, Blake."

"And I love you too, Lex. Sleep. I've got you."

"Mmmm." Alexis shut her eyes, expecting her mind to continue to race with everything that happened, but instead she fell into a deep sleep almost as soon as she closed her eyes.

She never knew that Blake lay awake for over an hour, simply breathing her in, and enjoying the feel of her clutching his arm to her breast, as if she'd fight and kill anyone who tried to take him away from her.

Chapter Thirteen

Blake was dreaming that he was on vacation with Alexis in the Caribbean. He had no idea *what* island, only that it was warm and the sand felt soft beneath him. They were both naked, and he'd never had an erection as painful and hard as the one he did right then.

His eyes popped open when he realized that he *wasn't* dreaming. The room was warm, he was sweating, and Lex was kneeling at his side on his mattress, naked as the day she was born, her eyes glued to his erection, which she had in one hand.

Blake had no idea what time it was, except that it was obviously morning. Sunlight was showing through the slits in the blinds. All thoughts of the time flew from his mind when Alexis leaned down and timidly licked the head of his cock. He couldn't hold back the groan that crawled up the back of his throat at the sight of her tongue licking her lips as she looked up at him.

"It's salty and kinda bitter at the same time."

"Fuck, Lex. You're killing me," he said on a sharp exhale of breath. His hand came up to her neck, and he pulled her up toward his face. "Good morning, sweetheart. Come up here. Kiss me."

Without hesitation, and without taking her fingers off his erection, she braced herself with her free hand and lifted her head to his.

Blake took his time, finding the faint taste of him on her tongue a turn-on. He lazily explored her mouth when all he really wanted to do was spin her around and fuck her so hard she wouldn't be able to move for hours.

But her virginity kept him from moving. There'd be plenty of time later for him to take her like that, but this morning was her time . . . was *their* time. They'd never have another first time, and he planned to make it as unforgettable as he possibly could . . . for both of them.

Her small, soft hand lightly and tentatively caressing his cock was unbelievably erotic. She lifted her head and asked in a soft voice, full of love and lust and even a bit of uncertainty shining clear in her big brown eyes, "Make love to me?"

"It'd be my pleasure, sweetheart," Blake told her, reaching down and removing her hand from his cock. He rolled, moving so he was hovering over her. He pushed his flannel pants the rest of the way down his legs.

Blake braced himself on his elbows next to her shoulders, tangling his hands in her hair and holding her head still. Her naked body was warm and pliant under his, and he could feel her hard nipples brush against his chest. The trimmed hair between her legs brushed against his belly as she unconsciously undulated her hips under him. She wrapped one leg around him, and he felt the wetness on her inner thigh against his hip, while she pulled his weight down onto her body and dug her fingernails into his biceps.

She licked her lips, and Blake felt her shift her hips under him, as if merely thinking about what was coming was turning her on.

"It makes me a douche, I know it," Blake murmured, playing with her hair as he spoke, "but I can't help but be pleased as fuck that I'll be your first, Lex. I'll be the first to watch you come apart and the first to suck on your delicious tits and pussy. The first to touch your clit and then the first to stick my fingers inside you and feel how hot and wet you are as you come around them." His voice dipped, and he leaned down farther into her, letting his chest rub against her nipples, which were hard as rocks. "The first to be inside you. You have no idea what a gift this is. I swear you won't regret it."

"It doesn't make you a douche," Alexis told him, softly squeezing his arms with her hands, trying to reassure him. "A caveman maybe, but I think I can handle that. Now . . . think you can stop *talking* about doing all those things to me and get on with it?"

Blake chuckled and smiled. Leave it to Lex to make lovemaking fun as well as hot. "Yeah, sweetheart, I can stop talking. But you should know . . . this is a give-and-take thing. Don't be afraid to touch me however you want. I'm happy to let you explore too."

Her eyes lit up with interest. "Really?"

"Really. I want to find all the places to touch that turn you on, and I expect you want to do the same. I'm happy to be your guinea pig. We'll start here," he said, moving so his thumbs brushed over her nipples. "Nipples can be either extremely sensitive or not. It depends on the person. Now, I think yours are more on the sensitive side. Whether or not you can come just from me sucking on and playing with them has yet to be determined."

Blake ran his fingernails over her small nipples and smiled as she arched up into his hands and her fingernails dug even harder into his biceps. Her breasts weren't huge, but they were a nice size for his large hands. He took them and squeezed, careful not to apply too much pressure. He plumped them up, running the pads of his thumbs over them at the same time.

Alexis whimpered under him.

"Feel good?"

"Oh God, yes. How come it doesn't feel like that when I squeeze them?" she asked.

Blake felt his cock twitch. "You've done this to yourself?"

"Yeah, a couple of times," she breathed. "Sometimes right before I come, if I pinch one of my nipples, it makes my orgasm get there faster."

"Fuck me," Blake breathed. "That is so fucking hot. I can't wait to watch you touch yourself."

Alexis's eyes opened wide as she looked up at him. "You'd like that?"

"Oh yeah, I would. Men are visual creatures. The thought of you getting yourself off while I lay here next to you is definitely one of my fantasies."

She didn't respond but stared at him as she panted, a small smile on her face.

"Let's see what you think of having them sucked on." Blake shifted down her body, pressing his erection into the mattress between her legs, hoping like hell he could continue to go slow, to teach her all about the pleasure her body was capable of without losing self-control. It was both a blessing and a curse that women could come more than once in a short period of time. A blessing because it meant he could see her lose it over and over, and a curse because he instinctively knew seeing her come would put him close to the edge.

Her hands fluttered at his sides as if she wasn't sure where to put them. "Reach up and grab hold of the headboard," Blake suggested. "It might be easier than trying to hold on to the sheet."

The burst of pleasure he felt as she immediately obeyed him made Blake inhale sharply. He'd never been into ordering women around, especially not in bed, but there was something extremely hot about seeing Alexis, a woman who never took shit from anyone, do what he asked as soon as he asked it.

He immediately bent to take one of her pink nipples into his mouth. He flicked it with his tongue, loving the noises that were escaping her mouth. She arched her back and pushed herself into him as she begged without words for his continued touch.

As his lips and tongue were busy with one nipple, he lightly pinched the other one with his thumb and index finger. He rolled it as he bit down on the other one, being sure not to bite down too hard.

Lex's hips surged upward, and she did her best to rub her clit against him. "You need something, Lex?" Blake teased, his free hand taking up where his mouth left off on her nipple. He continued to torment both nipples at the same time as he licked his lips. She was absolutely magnificent.

"Please, Blake," she begged.

"Please what, sweetheart?" he asked.

"That feels so good," Alexis moaned, her eyes squeezed shut as his fingers continued their torment.

"You want to see if you can come with just my lips and hands on your tits, Lex?" Blake asked, using the coarse word to test if she liked things a bit dirty.

Her eyes opened, and she brought her hands down from over her head and used them to push her breasts up toward him from the sides of her body. She met his eyes with hers and stated, "I don't think that'll be a problem, Blake. Please, put your mouth back on me. Your teeth felt so good. Don't be afraid to be a bit rough. I think I like it."

"Goddamn, Lex," Blake swore. He licked his lips and told her in a stern voice, "If I do something you don't like, which *doesn't* feel good, don't be afraid to tell me. I'd hate myself if I did something to you that really hurt."

"I will," Alexis whispered. "Please . . . make me come. I need it so bad."

Without another word, and without breaking eye contact with her, Blake leaned back down to her breasts. He put his hands over hers, pushing the mounds up even more than she'd been doing, then put his entire mouth over her areola and nipple and sucked . . . hard.

She closed her eyes and let out a high-pitched moan, arching up into him even harder. Her legs instinctively tried to close, but Blake moved his hips between her thighs, forcing her to keep her legs open . . . and increasing her arousal.

He sucked on her, using her fingers, and his, to squeeze the fleshy globe. He moved his other hand to her other nipple and began to tug upward, pulling it until it was stretched out. She again writhed under him, moaning his name.

Then he switched sides, using his mouth on the nipple he'd been tweaking with his fingers, and pulling, tugging, and squeezing the other one this time. Blake went back and forth, never spending the same amount of time and changing up how he treated each nipple.

Finally, he let go of the tight bud he'd had in his mouth and used just his fingers on both nipples at the same time.

"You're sexy as fuck, Lex. Look at you, you're dripping. I've never seen so much cream before. My sheets are soaked, and you smell so fucking good, a mixture of soap and sex. I can't wait to bury my tongue inside you and lick up all that sweet honey. Your body wants me; it's crying for me to stick my cock inside. And your tits—Jesus, sweetheart. I can't believe how sensitive you are. It's amazing. Your nipples are so hard they could cut glass. Does it feel good when I do this?" Blake pulled both nipples as far up as he dared and watched her head tilt backward and her fingers go white with the pressure they were exerting to push her breasts up toward him.

He added a pinch to each tight bud and continued to tug upward on them. First both together, then one at a time, changing up the pattern he used, but never letting go. He looked down and saw her belly clenching and her legs shaking. "You gonna come, Lex? You gonna show me how much you like this? You like when I torture these pretty tits, don't you? I think we're going to have to try a pair of clamps. I'd love to take you out to eat while you're lightly clamped . . . with every move it'll feel like me pulling on your nipples . . ." He demonstrated with several short tugs and pinches on her now-super-sensitive peaks. "And I bet I could put my hand under your skirt right there at the table and make you come with only one brush over your clit."

"Blake, please . . . oh God . . . I'm so close."

He wanted to slam himself inside her tight sheath, which was tilting upward toward him rhythmically. But he wanted her to get there without a single physical touch of her clit or her pussy. And he knew just how to do it.

"Look down, Lex. Look at my forearms as I play with your tits. Watch me."

Her eyes popped open, and she immediately tilted her chin down, her eyes going to his right arm. Blake made sure to flex his muscles in that arm as he tugged and tweaked her nipple. Her eyes dilated and her breathing quickened.

He continued to not only pinch and torment her nipple but to flex as he did it. "That's it, Lex. Just wait until you see what happens when I'm fingering you. You can watch as I make you come, and you'll never be able to see my arm again without remembering how it looked with my fingers deep inside your pussy."

That did it. Blake could almost feel the orgasm move from her breasts, down her stomach, and through the tight bundle of nerves between her legs. Every muscle in her body clenched, her hips frantically thrust upward, and he saw her butt cheeks tighten as she threw her head back and wailed as she came apart. Her hips jerked with her orgasm, and she moved her hands from her own breasts to his arms.

Blake reveled in the slight sting from her fingernails as they bit into him. Not hard enough to break the skin, but he knew he'd have the half-moon marks from her fingernails for quite a while.

She didn't make a sound, but her mouth opened in an *O* as she shook under him, lost in the euphoria of her orgasm. Blake kept his hold tight on her nipples for a beat, then gently eased his touch until he was gently caressing her entire chest. He ran his hands from her collarbone, down and over her tightly beaded nipples, and over her slightly rounded stomach, then back up. Up and down he went, caressing her as she came down from her orgasm.

By the time her butt relaxed on the mattress under her, she was covered in a sheen of sweat, and she panted in the aftermath.

Feeling extremely proud of himself and proud of *her*, Blake scooted up her body until his hard cock rested on her soaking wet folds and asked softly, "What'd you think of your first orgasm given to you by a man, sweetheart?"

Alexis opened her eyes into slits, and she moved her hands up his arms and into his hair, gripping him tightly. She let out a shaky breath and asked, "You want me to *think* right now?"

Blake beamed down at her. "You're amazing, Lex. Just thought you should know."

"I think that's my line," she quipped with a loving smile.

"You want more, or are you good?" It might kill him, but he'd stop and let her bask in the glow of her orgasm if that's what she wanted. For the first time, he realized that she might think *he* was in charge here, but just the opposite was true. She had him wrapped around her little finger . . . and he wouldn't change it for the world.

"More," was her immediate response. She tilted her hips up, rubbing herself against his erection. "I want you inside me. Now."

"There's so much more I want to do. So much more I want to explore," Blake told her, not able to stop himself from slowly easing his dick back and forth along her slit, lubricating his length in her juices, loving how slick and hot she felt against him. He made sure to notch the head of his cock on her clit with every pass of his hips.

"Later. You said I could play too, and I definitely want to. But for now, I need you, Blake. I might've come, but I still feel empty. It's like my body knows what it wants, and that's you. Inside. Please. I've waited long enough."

Blake felt his dick clench and knew he had precome leaking out the head of his cock and dripping all over her lower belly and tight curls. He'd never been this turned on in his life. "Do you want me to get a condom?" he asked, his jaw tight. They'd had this conversation, but he wanted her to be sure. He braced himself over her, his fists closed on the mattress next to her chest. Even as he asked, he couldn't stop his hips from continuing to move up and down through her wet pussy lips. He slid easily, her orgasm and arousal, as well as his own, providing more than enough lubrication.

"No," Alexis told him, meeting his eyes directly. "We talked about this. I'm covered and I trust you. I want you, *just* you. Please, Blake. Fuck me."

"Damn," Blake breathed. "I can't resist. I've never been this turned on. Ever. Trust me on that, sweetheart."

Alexis didn't answer with words, but she spread her legs as far apart as she could and brought her feet up until they rested flat on the mattress on either side of his hips. She let her knees fall open until she was completely exposed under him. Hiding nothing, offering her virginity to him as if on a silver platter.

Blake looked down between their bodies and groaned. She was spread eagle, her hips tilted up, her pussy dripping. He could see the sheen of her excitement not only on his cock but on her inner thighs as well. He reached up and grabbed one of his pillows and shoved it under her hips, making it easier for her to hold her position. Then he reached down and took hold of the base of his cock and rubbed the mushroom head up and down her slit, harder now, pressing hard against her clit on each upstroke. Each time he did it, she shuddered under him.

Alexis took hold of the backs of her knees, pulling them up even farther, opening herself even more to him. "Do it, Blake," she ordered in a low, husky voice. "Make me yours."

Not able to hold back anymore, her words notching his arousal to a point of no return, Blake fit the head of his dripping cock to her opening. Her muscles sucked him in, and he inhaled at the erotic sight. "You are so fucking sexy," he bit out, scooting up into her and putting both hands under her ass to lift her even higher.

Alexis's inner muscles contracted against him, trying to draw him inside her body. Blake pulled his hips back a fraction of an inch and slowly pressed inside farther than he'd been before. He began to sweat, wanting nothing more than to shove his cock all the way inside her hot, slick tunnel. But he didn't want to hurt her. Shifting until he had her butt braced with one hand, he moved his other hand until his thumb was resting on her clit. He massaged it once, and they both groaned as she twitched around him in excitement.

Lex bore down hard, causing him to slide in another inch. Blake could literally see her dripping with excitement as he made his way inside her.

"More, Blake. More," Alexis begged, looking down to where they were joining.

Blake pulled back, then pushed into her again. He did it several times while at the same time caressing her clit gently, keeping her arousal high, but not wanting to push her over the edge yet.

"Does this hurt, Lex? At all?"

She shook her head frantically, her hair flying around her head. "No. I feel full, but it doesn't hurt. I love it. Keep going."

Her toes curled at his waist, and Blake went in deeper than he'd been before. A drop of sweat rolled down his temple. She felt amazing. Tight. Wet. Hot. He'd never felt anything like it.

"Yesssss," Alexis moaned, trying to shove her hips up to get all of him.

Blake moved them, hooking one arm under one of her legs, then doing the same to the other. Then he braced himself next to her hips. The move freed her hands, but, more important, it tilted her hips up all the way, giving him complete control over the speed and depth of his thrusts.

"Keep your eyes on us, sweetheart," Blake ordered, even though her eyes hadn't left his cock, where they were joined. "Move one of your hands down between us and feel me. Cup my balls."

She quickly shifted and leaned until she could get a hand under her, and Blake felt another spurt of precome leak out his dick when her small hand brushed his balls tentatively, then when he groaned with pleasure, she continued with more confidence. She ran her fingertips over the part of his shaft that wasn't inside her. "I can't believe you aren't all the way in yet."

"You ready for me, Lex? All of me?"

"God yes." Her eyes flicked up to his, and he almost came at the look of tenderness and love that shone out of them. "Make me yours, Blake."

He couldn't control his actions; he moved without thought and didn't stop until he felt his balls up against her ass, his cock trying to burrow its way into her womb.

They both groaned as he bottomed out and flexed inside her. Blake held himself still, his head bowed, staring at their pubic hair meshed together.

"You. This . . . ," Blake stammered. The words wouldn't come. She felt perfect. He didn't want to move, wanted to imprint this moment on his memory. The way she felt clenching around him, the way her fingers felt caressing his balls, the way her breath hitched every time he flexed his hips against hers. Jesus. He could die tomorrow and know he'd held perfection in his hands.

"I love you, Blake," Alexis breathed. "I love you so much."

"Lex," Blake groaned, feeling the urge to move. He was scared to shift even a centimeter; afraid he'd blow prematurely.

Then she moved under him and he was lost. He pulled back until he was barely inside her, then steadily pushed back in. He did it again, then again, moaning deep in his throat at the feeling. He was close, so incredibly close. And the thought of filling her with his come was only making his orgasm rush up from his balls faster.

"Touch yourself, Lex. Rub your clit and make yourself come."

Without any sign of hesitation or modesty, she moved her free hand between her legs, slipping her fingers along his cock when he pulled out, coating them with their combined juices, before bringing them up to her clit and rubbing. Hard and fast.

She didn't ease into it, but quickly began to stroke herself, knowing exactly what she liked.

Blake felt her twitch under him, and it only ratcheted up his excitement more. "Fuck, Lex. That's it. Get yourself off." Her hips began to move under his. "Fuck my dick, sweetheart. Take what you need."

"Jesus, Blake. This feels so . . . ungh . . . good. My toys don't feel like this. Not even close. God, I'm so full of you and you're so deep . . . I'm gonna come . . ." And without another word, she closed her eyes and broke for the second time that morning.

She squeezed his cock so hard Blake couldn't move for a moment. He felt every pulse and every twitch of her inner muscles as she exploded in orgasm around him.

Her hand fell away from her clit in ecstasy, and Blake shifted, dropping one of her legs and bringing his own hand to her slippery center. He continued to press against her hard pearl, now poking out from its protective hood, prolonging her orgasm. She shrieked, and both hands came up to grip his biceps again, leaving more half-moon gouges on his arms to match the ones she'd left earlier.

As she came, Blake thrust into her hard. His balls smacking against her ass with each thrust, grunts coming from his throat. He thought about nothing other than rushing for the euphoria that came with an orgasm. But he knew that this orgasm would be stronger and more intense than any he'd ever had before . . . simply because of Lex.

After the sixth thrust, Blake held himself as deep inside Alexis as he could get and came. And came and came. Filling her channel with more come than he could ever remember unloading in his life. He felt it leaking out around where they were joined but couldn't bring himself to care.

The sex was messy and dirty and the most unbelievable thing he'd ever experienced. If it had been this good with Alexis the virgin, he was doomed, or blessed, to be a broken man every time they made love.

Having emptied himself, Blake carefully dropped Lex's other leg, which she promptly wrapped around his hip, and lowered himself until he lay draped over her body. They were both slick with sweat, but he didn't care. Careful not to dislodge himself from her, he turned them until he was lying under her once more.

Alexis brought her legs up until they were bent at the knees next to his hips, and she buried her head into his neck. Her forearms lay against his chest, her palms flat against him.

Blake could feel her hot breath against his skin and her heart beating hard in her chest. He could feel his come dripping out from where they were still joined, wetting his balls and the sheet beneath him, but he didn't care. He was so replete with love for the woman lying on top of him he couldn't bring himself to move.

Running his fingertips up and down her spine in a gentle caress, he turned his head and kissed Lex's forehead before whispering, "That was hands down the absolute best orgasm of my life. Thank you, sweetheart. I'll never forget this moment for as long as I live."

She raised her head a fraction, looking up into his face. Tears shone in her eyes, and for a second Blake was afraid he'd hurt her.

"I'm so glad it was you. I love you, Blake Anderson."

"I love you too, Alexis." He lifted his chin and met her lips with his own. They lazily kissed as they came down from their elation.

When his softening cock finally slid from her slippery sheath, Alexis pouted. "I like you inside me."

"I like me inside you too, sweetheart, but you gotta give me a while to recover. You turned me inside out."

She giggled, then wrinkled her nose. "Uh . . . we're all sweaty . . . and . . ." She shifted over him, obviously feeling his come leaking out of her.

"Shower?" Blake asked.

She nodded quickly. "Yeah. I can't wait to try out that double shower of yours. It's wonderful by myself, but I have a feeling it'll be a whole new experience with you."

Blake grinned and amazingly felt his cock twitch at her words. He glanced over at the clock next to his bed. Satisfied, he noted that they had plenty of time to play before they had to leave for Castle Rock.

He sat up quickly, ignoring Alexis's shriek of surprise. He grabbed her hips and pulled her into him as he moved toward the side of the bed. He stood, with her still laughing, clinging to him, and made his way to the bathroom.

"One shower for two, coming right up," he quipped as Lex wrapped her arms around his shoulders and held on.

Chapter Fourteen

That morning, while in the shower, Alexis had told Blake that she'd never really seen a man's cock up close and personal. That had led to an anatomy lesson, complete with him showing her exactly how he liked to be touched and how to get him off . . . with her hands and with her mouth.

And *that* had led to Blake kneeling on the ground at her feet, showing her how wonderful it could feel when a man reciprocated. He'd brought her to another huge orgasm with his mouth and fingers, which would've brought her to her knees if he hadn't been holding on to her hips.

Alexis smiled when she remembered how natural the morning had been. She'd been afraid she'd feel weird around Blake now that they'd had sex, but, instead, she felt even more comfortable around him. He was the same man he'd been before: considerate, attentive, and still somewhat of a prankster.

They'd sat on the couch after eating and laughed and joked while waiting for her jeans to dry. She was wearing a pair of his boxers and his T-shirt. And they'd also talked. About the night before. About how scared she'd been, about the Inca Boyz gang, about Blake's parents, about his brothers, even about Grace and what had happened to her a couple of months ago.

All in all, it was relaxing and normal . . . something that felt good.

"You feel okay this morning?" Blake asked, rubbing a hand up and down her bare thigh. "Not too sore?"

Alexis knew she was blushing, but shook her head. "No. You didn't hurt me at all last night. I'm a little tender . . . you're bigger than my vibrator, but nothing bad. I know I said it last night, but I'm glad I waited. You made my first time really special, Blake. Thank you."

He brought her hand up to his mouth and grinned. "No, thank *you*, Lex. I've never made love to a virgin before, and I was nervous. I didn't realize how much it would mean to me. How intense it would be."

"It *was* intense, wasn't it?" Alexis asked. "Do you think it was because it was our first time?"

"Maybe. But I have a feeling every time with you will be that way," Blake said, the look of love and tenderness in his eyes clear, as he brushed a lock of hair behind her ear.

"I hope so," Alexis said honestly, tilting her head and trapping his hand against her shoulder playfully.

The dryer's bell went off, alerting them that the cycle had completed and her clothes were ready. "You all set to go?" Blake asked. "We can stop by that boutique downtown before the meeting, and you can get a new shirt if you want. I don't give a shit what you're wearing—you're beautiful in anything—but I know you might feel more comfortable at dinner if you're dressed in something that fits better than my T-shirt."

It had been extremely thoughtful of him to suggest it, and Alexis was more than happy to take him up on his offer. She didn't want to show up for a meeting with his brothers, the investigator from the task force, and later on with Grace in the shirt she'd had on last night, an army T-shirt that was two sizes too big and clearly suggested "I spent the night with Blake Anderson last night and had nothing to wear the next day."

On their way to the office, they'd stopped into the boutique, and she'd picked out a navy-blue shirt, which buttoned down the front and had three-quarter-length sleeves. It had a V-neck and was tapered at her waist.

They reached Ace Security around two o'clock.

Nathan and Logan were waiting for Blake and Alexis in the large back room as they entered. "Hey, Alexis," Logan greeted.

"Hey," she said back, amused that Nathan didn't look up from the computer screen when they came into the room. He wasn't a man to talk much if he didn't have anything to say. When Alexis first started working with Blake, she thought Nathan couldn't stand her, but she'd eventually learned it was just his way.

"You guys get a chance to review the tapes?" Blake asked.

"Yeah, we just finished about an hour ago," Logan said.

"I'm sorry I couldn't have been there last night," Nathan said to Alexis. "You handled everything that happened really well. You kept your cool and didn't puke all over that asshole Chuck."

Alexis couldn't help it, she burst out laughing. If asked, she would've said there was no way she would've ever been able to laugh about Chuck kissing her with his awful breath, but somehow Nathan was able to say exactly the right thing to make that happen. "Uh, thanks. I think."

The other guys chuckled as they walked toward a large table they used for meetings with clients and their lawyers and sometimes police. Blake held out a chair, and Alexis sank into it, not missing the way he pulled the chair next to hers closer before sitting down.

"You want to join us, Nathan?" Logan called out impatiently.

"Start without me," he retorted, still not looking up from whatever had him so enthralled on his computer.

Logan and Blake merely shook their heads, used to Nathan's quirks. When he had something on his mind, he never gave it up until he was good and ready.

"I started a list of all the gang members who were there last night, as well as the women. I tried to match up their physical descriptions from the video and added any accents or tattoos they had. I only had time to go through it twice before you guys got here, though, and Nathan got distracted by something, so if you can help, I'd appreciate it," Logan told both Alexis and Blake.

Alexis felt Blake's hand on hers in her lap. She'd unconsciously been clenching her hands together so tightly her fingers were white.

"Why don't you go sit with Nathan and see if he needs any help? I can go through this with Logan," Blake suggested with a look of concern etched on his face.

She really wanted to protest and tell him that she'd be happy to listen to and watch the tapes from last night, but she couldn't. She had absolutely *no* desire to see Chuck or Kelly or any of the gang members ever again.

"Okay, thanks. If that's okay, Logan?" she asked, her eyebrows raised in question.

Logan was definitely the hard-ass of the three brothers, but there was nothing but sympathy in his gaze when he said, "No problem. See if you can't get Nathan to open up on what's gotten under his skin, would ya? I'll let you know when we're done, and you can review our notes and add in anything you remember."

Alexis nodded, relieved, and went to get up, when Blake laid a hand on her upper arm and leaned into her. She reciprocated without thought, tilting her head back to meet his lips as they came down onto hers.

Neither man said a word, and Alexis followed their lead, smiling to herself as she ambled over to Nathan. She pulled up a chair and sat down next to him.

"Can I help?" Alexis wasn't sure he was going to respond, but surprisingly he did.

"Yeah. Tell me what you can remember about what Kelly and the others said about Donovan's ex-girlfriend," Nathan demanded, turning from his keyboard and resting his elbow on the table in front of him. His eyes bore into hers with an intensity Alexis hadn't seen from him before. Nathan was the laid-back one. The man who seemed not to care about things as deeply as his brothers. But it was obvious she'd been completely wrong about him. He might not care about some things, but when he did, ooh man, he was intense.

"Let's see . . . I got the impression that Kelly was dating him, but one of the other guys, I forget who, said something about how Donovan was still hung up on his ex and that when he got out of jail, he'd try to get her back. I could be wrong, but it seemed to me that nobody was happy she was gone. Like she snuck away from the gang or something."

"Did anyone say her name?"

Alexis thought for a moment, then shook her head. "No, I don't think so. Kelly wasn't happy. It was obvious she wanted to be with Donovan and was pissed he was still obsessed with this other woman."

"Kelly is quite a bit older than the other women who were there last night, right?" Nathan asked, still watching her with his piercing gaze.

Alexis forced herself not to fidget under Nathan's scrutiny. "Well, yeah. Obviously, I didn't ask to see their IDs, but they looked like girls in their early to mid teens. When I was hiding on the other side of the fence, Kelly was giving one of them advice about letting the guys do what they wanted with her sexually, so she could move up the ranks in the gang."

Nathan nodded and finally turned back to his computer. "That's what I thought. I can't find any mention of an ex-girlfriend anywhere. I'm running a few searches that I hope will pan out, but it's curious that someone who had been dating the leader of the gang just disappeared without a trace."

"Now that you mention it, that *is* a bit odd," Alexis agreed. "I mean, if you were dating the head honcho, wouldn't you still be hanging around? Even if they weren't together, she'd still probably have some power over the other girls. Do you think she's okay?"

Nathan nodded. "I do, because otherwise why would Donovan want her back?"

"True," Alexis mused, then fell silent as she watched Nathan's fingers fly over the keyboard. Then she asked, "Want me to help?"

"Yeah. If you could dig around on Facebook—I hate that fucking place—I'd appreciate it," Nathan said, still focused on his computer screen.

Happy to have something to do, Alexis pushed back her chair and went over to her desk. She fired up the computer and happily lost herself in trying to track down Donovan's elusive ex-girlfriend.

Thirty-five minutes later, she'd had no luck in tracing the woman, when Blake called her name from across the room. Finding it hard to believe so much time had passed, Alexis wandered over to the other two men. Nathan joined her this time.

"Okay," Logan said pushing an iPad over to her with a list of names and characteristics. "We've gone through the tapes and did our best. Anything you want to add or have questions about, feel free to notate it. We'll give a copy of this to Ross, the task force detective, when he gets here, and we'll keep one in our files just in case. And for the record, Alexis?"

She looked at Logan.

"You did fucking great. There were over a dozen gang members there last night, and we have descriptions of what they look like, illustrations of their visible tattoos, and we have their names. We even have a pretty good rendition of that asinine cartoon on their shirts. I have no idea what the deal with them wearing their shirts inside out is about, though. Idiots. Anyway, I'm not sure the task force will be able to do much about the girls who were there, but we have as much information on them as we could get as well. It's a fuck of a lot, and I hope it's a huge step toward shutting down their thug-for-hire business. What you did will keep a lot of innocent people, like my Grace, from being caught up in the middle of their assholedness in the future. Thank you."

It felt good that what she'd done hadn't been in vain, and knowing that Logan, Blake, and Nathan were satisfied went a long way toward making her feel better. "You're not upset that I don't want to do it any-more?" she asked tentatively.

"Fuck no," Blake bit out at the same time Logan said in a calmer tone, "Not at all."

Nathan sat down next to her and put his hand over hers on the table as he spoke. "We wouldn't let you meet with them again, Alexis. It's not safe, and you've done more than we should've asked you to do in the first place."

"You didn't ask," Alexis told him. "I volunteered."

"Nevertheless. It's done now," Nathan said firmly, obviously closing the subject.

Alexis nodded and pulled the tablet over in front of her and started reviewing the notes. They were extremely detailed, and Alexis found that she really wasn't able to add more to them. The fact that Chuck's breath smelled and tasted rancid probably wasn't something that the task force needed to know.

She made a few notations here and there, but for the most part didn't change a thing.

Ross Peterson, their contact from the Denver Gang Task Force, showed up, and they spent the next hour and a half going over the notes and talking about what the Denver police department might be able to do to shut down the illegal activity. Ross was a good man, who was trying as hard as he could to try to make Denver safer for its citizens and seemed extremely happy to receive a copy of both the audio and video files. He promised to follow up with them if he had any questions or concerns. Blake and his brothers made it very clear that Alexis was done going undercover with the gang and would not be making any more meets with them, no matter what the PD wanted her to do.

As Ross was leaving, Grace Anderson entered the office.

Alexis hadn't spent a lot of time with the other woman, even though she'd been working for Ace Security for months, and was thrilled she'd get a chance to know her better.

"Grace," Logan murmured, taking her into his arms. "Have a good day?"

She smiled up at him and nodded. "I spent the afternoon with Felicity talking about marketing options for Rock Hard Gym. I think we have a pretty good plan in place, and she and Cole should start seeing an increase in revenue hopefully in a month or so."

"Awesome," Logan said, the genuine happiness for his wife clear in both his tone and the way he held her. He leaned over and kissed her in a manner passionate and intense, much like Blake had kissed Alexis earlier.

"It's good to see you again," Alexis told Grace when Logan finally let her up for air.

Grace rested her hand on her slightly rounded belly, in the way that pregnant women did, and smiled at her. "You too. I'm so happy we finally get to know each other better. We should've done it way before now."

"I agree. And I know I've said it before, but I feel like I should reiterate . . . I'm so glad you're okay after what happened earlier this year."

Grace waved off Alexis's apology. "It's not your fault, so don't worry about it. How's Bradford doing? I haven't talked to him in a while."

"Actually, it's kinda crazy," Alexis said. "After everything that happened, he decided he wanted to do something different with his life. He quit the firm and applied to work on a cruise ship."

"What? Seriously?" Grace asked, her mouth hanging open.

"Yup."

"But, he was one of the best architects in Colorado . . . maybe even in the United States," Grace protested.

"I know. But he said his heart wasn't in it anymore and he wanted to do something different. His ultimate goal is to be a cruise director, and he's excited about the opportunity," Alexis told Grace and the others.

"Jeez, I feel like it's my fault," Grace said, wringing her hands in front of her.

"No! Please don't," Alexis begged, almost sorry she'd said anything. "I haven't seen him so excited about anything in a long time. It'll be good for him to do something different . . . besides, he's already told me he met someone . . . one of the dancers from the ship. Denver is so conservative; I think he gave up on finding the right guy for him around here who wasn't after him only for his money. I can totally relate to that."

"Will you give me his e-mail address so I can write him?" Grace asked.

"Of course," Alexis told her, nodding enthusiastically. "He'd like that."

"What *I'd* like is to get something to eat," Nathan cut in. "I'm starving."

Everyone laughed. "You're always hungry," Blake teased, hitting his brother in the arm lightly.

"I think we should try the new place that just opened up where my parents' business used to be," Grace said firmly, holding up a hand when Logan went to protest. "I know you think it's too fast, and I'll have some sort of flashback if I walk in there, but I'm fine. Seriously, Logan. I'll be there with my husband, his brothers, and my newest friend. Nothing's going to go wrong." She sounded like she'd had the conversation with Logan in the recent past.

Logan wrapped his arm around his wife and squeezed her waist, putting his other hand on her belly. "All right, but if you start to feel weird, let me know, and we'll go."

Grace rolled her eyes and put her hand over her husband's on her belly. "It'll be fine. Come on, let's feed your brother before he starts gnawing off his arm."

Everyone chuckled again, and they headed out of the office and started down the sidewalk to the new restaurant. It was the Italian place, which had already gotten rave reviews by the *Denver Chronicle*, called Scarpetti's.

Since it was a weekday, the place wasn't crowded, and they were able to be seated right away. The evening was filled with laughter and teasing and a comfort level Alexis hadn't felt in a long time. She felt as though she finally had a group of friends who were with her because of who she was, not because of who her parents were or what was in her bank account.

All had gone well with dinner, until after they'd had dessert and they were sitting around chatting, laughing, and drinking a final cup of coffee.

A group of men and women seated across the aisle a couple of tables down had obviously been enjoying a few glasses of wine with their dinner. Their voices had risen until they could easily be heard in the half-full restaurant.

"I can't believe she has the nerve to eat here, especially after what her family did."

"I have no idea why she's sitting with Alexis Grant after she was in those pictures with her brother."

"Right? It makes no sense. You'd think she wouldn't want anything to do with her."

"It looks like they both enjoy slumming it. The Anderson brothers must be good in bed; why else would they have anything do with those white-trash boys?"

"I don't care how unattractive the women are; I'd do 'em if it meant getting my hands on their money."

Alexis was about to turn around and let them know that Logan, Blake, and Nathan Anderson were ten times the people they were, but, surprisingly, it was Nathan who beat her to it. He pushed back his chair so hard it almost toppled behind him and stomped over to the other table.

Alexis looked at Blake in alarm. She hadn't ever seen the youngest Anderson brother look quite so angry.

"Maybe you should—"

Blake interrupted Alexis before she could finish her thought. "Don't worry. Nathan has this. I almost feel sorry for those people." Blake leaned back completely relaxed and put his arm on the back of Alexis's chair, not bothering to turn around and watch his brother lambast the patrons at the other table.

"You think Grace Anderson shouldn't step foot into the building her parents forced her to work at?" Nathan's voice rang out in the restaurant. The contempt easy to hear in his voice and easy to see in his stiff stance. "Grace and Alexis have more goodness in their little pinkies than you four have combined. You might look at them as if they're money signs, but they're beautiful women who I wish had found my brothers years ago. And you know what? If you must know, we *are* good in bed."

"Look, man, I don't think—" one of the men began, but Nathan cut him off.

"That's right, you're not thinking. You're in a public restaurant gossiping loudly about people you don't know. If you think we aren't the kinds of men who will stand up for our women, you're wrong. We're all fully aware of what people around here think about us, but we came back here to try to help our community anyway. If you'll excuse me, we've had all we can stomach of the atmosphere around here." And with that final word, Nathan stomped toward the door of the restaurant, pulling it open and disappearing into the night.

"Come on," Blake said, helping Alexis stand with a hand at her elbow.

Logan did the same with Grace, making a point to peel off a couple of hundred-dollar bills and drop them on the table before he left.

Alexis glared at the foursome as she walked by and was pretty sure Grace did the same. Logan had a word with the hostess, who nodded energetically and took the business card he held out to her.

When they exited the restaurant, Alexis was surprised when Grace giggled softly.

"Seriously, Logan, I love Nathan. I wish we could've gotten the looks on those people's faces on tape when he lit into them."

They slowly walked back toward Ace Security. "Does he do that a lot?" Alexis asked no one in particular.

"You have to understand something about my brother," Logan told her. "He couldn't care less if someone bad-mouths him. You could tease him all day long. Call him names, swear at him, whatever. It wouldn't faze him. Growing up, me and Blake were in awe with the way he could ignore our mom's rants against him. It was as if he didn't even hear her. But the second someone says something bad about a person he deems more vulnerable than him, he turns into a completely different kind of man."

Logan continued. "I remember one day at school he took on three fifth-grade boys, even though he was only in the second. They were taunting a third-grade girl, telling her she was stupid and ugly, and they'd knocked her books out of her hands. She was crying and trying to get around them, but they'd surrounded her and were poking at her. Nathan didn't even hesitate. He calmly walked up to them and started to wail on them."

"Holy crap, what happened?" Alexis asked, eyes wide.

Blake answered from her right side. "The girl ran away, perfectly unharmed. And Nathan got beat up pretty good . . . at least until we joined the fight."

Logan laughed. "Yeah, we might've been three years younger than the other boys were, and smaller, but we'd had plenty of practice avoiding my mom's fists by that time, so we were able to hold our own."

"Did you guys get in trouble?" Grace asked, clearly not having heard this story before.

"Nope. The other boys were too ashamed to admit they'd been beaten by a bunch of second graders."

"And the girl?" Alexis asked.

Blake shrugged. "She had a crush on Nathan until they were in high school, I think, but he didn't even seem to notice her. He hadn't done it because he liked her; he'd done it because it was the right thing to do." He brought the conversation back around to what had happened that night. "So he would've sat there all night and listened to those idiots talk smack about the three of us. He wouldn't have cared, but the second they started in on you two, he was done."

They'd reached the doors to Ace Security, and the lights were on inside. "Should we check on him?" Alexis asked.

Logan shook his head. "No, he's fine. I promise. If you brought it up, you'd only embarrass him. Besides, he's probably already neck-deep in whatever it was he was doing before dinner."

"He's trying to find Donovan's ex-girlfriend," Alexis told Logan and Blake. "He asked me to help because he's better with numbers than with online searches."

"I'll set up a Google alert in the next few days and see if I can't help him," Blake told the others. "I know him; it'll drive him crazy that he doesn't really know how to go about finding her." He then leaned over and brushed Alexis's hair behind her ear. "You ready to go home?"

She turned into him and pressed her belly against his hips, feeling his solid length against her. "Yes." Alexis looked over at Grace and Logan, but they weren't listening to anything they were saying as they walked arm in arm toward the parking lot. So she stood on her tiptoes, looked Blake in the eye, and whispered, "I want you to make love to me in my bed."

A huge smile burst forth across Blake's face, and she could feel his erection hardening against her as he asked, "You've still got that vibrator you like to use?"

Blushing now, Alexis nodded shyly.

"Good. I want to watch you get yourself off, then I'll show you how much better my cock can be."

"I already know it's better," Alexis protested. "There's no comparison."

"Damn straight," Blake said, turning her toward the parking lot. "The sooner we get out of here, the sooner we can get into your bed."

Feeling the dampness between her legs, Alexis knew it was going to be a long ride back up to Denver. But at least she wasn't going alone. Blake would be with her.

When they got to their cars, Alexis turned to Grace to say good-bye and was surprised when the other woman held out her arms and brought her into a hug. It was a bit awkward with Grace's pregnant belly between them, but it'd been a long time since Alexis had felt such honest emotion from another woman.

"We need to do this again, soon," Grace told her. "Maybe you'd like to come out with me and Felicity sometime?" Grace swung her hand in the air indicating the downtown area. "I know she'd love you."

"Sure, that sounds great," Alexis told her, smiling.

"Cool. I'll text you."

"I'll look forward to it."

They hugged once more briefly, and Logan helped Grace settle into the passenger side of his truck and waved at his brother and Alexis as he got into the driver's side and pulled out of the lot.

"You ready to go?" Blake asked.

Alexis nodded. They settled into his Mustang, and Alexis said, "I had a good time tonight. Thanks."

"You're welcome. For what it's worth, I love seeing you hang out with my family. It feels . . . comfortable."

Alexis knew exactly what he meant. "It does."

"That being said, it's been way too long since I've seen you naked."

Alexis burst out laughing. "Blake, it's only been like five hours."

"As I said, it's been too long."

She rolled her eyes at him. "I thought anticipation was good for the soul."

"Nope. Not at all. Whoever said that didn't have a woman he wanted more than he wanted to breathe," Blake retorted with a smile.

Alexis loved their banter. She totally hadn't pegged Blake as the kind of man who could so easily make her laugh, especially after how serious he'd been when they'd worked together for all those months, but she definitely liked this side of him.

"How are you feeling?" he asked seriously. "You okay after everything we went over today?"

"I'm okay, Blake. I won't see them again, so I'm good."

The sexy, flirty smile reappeared on his face. "And your pussy? Still tender?"

"Blake!" Alexis protested, punching him lightly in the arm.

"Well?" he returned, the glint of lust easy to see in his eyes. "I need to know how I'm gonna make love to you tonight. If you're still sore, I'll go nice and easy, like I did last night. But if you're not, then maybe I'll fuck you hard and fast, then make love to you tenderly and slowly."

His words made Alexis squirm in her seat. Good Lord, the man was lethal. "I'm not sore," she told him, knowing she was blushing but wanting to feel him lose control so badly.

"Good. Then a hard fucking before we make love it is."

She licked her lips and glanced down at Blake's crotch. Holy crap, it looked like he was as turned on as she was by their conversation.

"And if you keep licking your lips, we might not even make it to your apartment," Blake told her. "It's a mighty long elevator ride, after all."

She giggled then. "I had no idea sex could be fun," she told him seriously, but with the smile still on her face. "I like it."

"Me too, sweetheart. I have a feeling it'll be a long time before having you in my arms gets boring."

"I hope so."

"I know so," he confirmed. "Now, how about we change the subject so my cock can calm down before I have to present myself to your doorman?"

Alexis wasn't sure she really wanted to talk about something else, but took pity on Blake. She only had to worry about damp panties, so her arousal wasn't literally sticking out there for everyone to see.

Alexis changed the subject, talking about her brother's new job, what she'd found out about Donovan's ex-girlfriend—which was nothing—and her favorites foods.

By the time Blake pulled up to her apartment, she'd almost forgotten his plans for her that night . . . almost.

Many hours later, after she'd masturbated with her vibrator for Blake, and after he'd shown her the difference between making love and getting fucked, Alexis lay boneless and replete in his arms, listening to him breathing deeply. She was almost afraid to think it, but her life was absolutely perfect.

Chapter Fifteen

The next three weeks were the best of Alexis's life. She spent almost every waking hour with Blake, and they'd slept together every night. They didn't always make love, but cuddling up with Blake's arm holding her tight to his chest was almost just as good as having sex. Almost.

They spent most of their time in Castle Rock at his house, and working. She went with him to Colorado Springs for a few jobs, once again being the lookout for an abusive ex while Blake was inside the courthouse with the client.

She continued to do research for Ace Security. She managed to pop into the Rock Hard Gym and meet both Cole and Felicity. She liked them immediately. Felicity was outspoken, covered in tattoos, and obviously a staunch supporter of Grace's. Cole was taller than Blake, but his smile made her feel at ease immediately.

Alexis had also exchanged quite a few texts with Grace. It felt good to have someone she could shoot a note off to about nothing in particular without feeling as if Grace were reciprocating simply because she wanted something.

Alexis was happier than she'd been in a long time. She'd found a group of people who enjoyed being around her, and who didn't expect her to pay for everything. As much as it annoyed her that Blake and his bothers straight-up refused to let her pay her way, it secretly felt good.

Today she was headed back to her apartment. Blake was driving up later, after escorting a man to his attorney's office for a court-ordered mediation session. His wife, who he was in the process of divorcing, wasn't handling the separation well and had threatened him on more than one occasion.

Alexis was more than happy to let Blake handle that job on his own. Pissed-off men seemed less scary to her than out-of-control women. Maybe it was because she'd seen a side of Kelly that scared the hell out of her or because of stories Blake had told her about his mother and how she'd beat him when he was little. But whatever it was, Blake had obviously realized how she felt and hadn't even asked her to tag along.

She needed to do some laundry and pick up a few more clothes. She hadn't exactly moved into Blake's house, but it was close. She had a second set of toiletries in his bathroom, his kitchen was stocked with food she liked to eat, and Blake had cleared part of his closet and his drawers for her to put some clothes away. He had a few things at her apartment, but since they spent most of their time in Castle Rock, it made more sense for her to stay at his place.

Tomorrow they were going back down to Castle Rock early in the morning. Blake had an appointment with a lawn guy. He wanted to replace the dead and weed-filled grass that he hadn't had any luck in resurrecting with sod to try to start anew. His parents had never taken care of the lawn, and he'd admitted to her that he wanted his own kids to be able to play outside and not have to worry about noxious weeds.

Alexis was proud of herself that she hadn't even flinched at his mention of kids, but the lusty look in his eye told her that he was thinking of the *making* of babies . . . with her. Grace might've gotten pregnant right away, but Alexis wasn't anywhere near ready for that step. Eventually she wanted kids, but she was selfish enough to want to have Blake to herself for a long while. He'd have to be content with being an uncle for a few years.

Alexis drove her Mercedes up to the front of her apartment building and with a smile handed her keys over to the valet. She headed toward the revolving door, also smiling in greeting at Osman, but stopped in her tracks when she saw Kelly standing off to the side. She looked awful. She had a huge black eye and her blonde hair was in disarray. She wore a pair of black sweat pants and a T-shirt. It was a tight shirt, and Alexis could see that she still wasn't wearing a bra, but the outfit wasn't something she thought the other woman would be caught dead in.

The most alarming thing about her appearance, other than the fact that she was standing outside her apartment building when she'd never told her where she lived, were the bruises running up and down her arm, which was in a sling. Kelly winced as Alexis came toward her.

"Oh my God, Kelly, are you all right?" Alexis asked. She had no idea what Kelly was doing there. She wanted to ignore her altogether, but she couldn't. The memory of their childhood friendship and her work with battered women at Ace Security wouldn't let her turn away.

"I'm okay," Kelly croaked, her voice sounding even rougher than it had before, if that was even possible. "I need to talk to you."

"Okay, talk," Alexis said, her face open and concerned.

"Not here," Kelly insisted, looking around her fearfully. "It's not safe."

Alexis copied her mannerisms, her eyes scanning the immediate area but not seeing anything out of the ordinary. "Do you want to come in?" It probably wasn't the safest thing to do, but Kelly was moving stiffly and looked like she was in a lot of pain. They could stay in the lobby, and Alexis could find out what happened.

Kelly shook her head. "No, I don't want to be seen going into your building. Damian and Dominic are watching you. They're pissed that you haven't been around, and they called your parents' office and sweet-talked someone into telling them where you lived. They wanted me to tell them all I could about you, but I refused, so they beat me up. I know I wasn't all that nice to you back in school, but you're in danger.

I've got a place they don't know about. We can talk there." She reached out with her good hand and put it on Alexis's forearm.

"I'm sorry about what happened when we were kids. I'm also sorry that I got you involved with my friends. I was milking you for money because Dominic and Damian forced me to. I hated doing it to you, and I was hoping we could be friends again—that I could make up for being so horrible to you—but instead I got you sucked into more crap. I feel horrible about it, and I don't want you to end up like me." Kelly gestured to her arm in a sling. "I just want to tell you as much as I can about the guys so you can keep yourself safe."

Alexis was torn. She believed one hundred percent that Kelly had been beaten. The bruises on her face and arms, not to mention her injured arm, communicated that loud and clear. But getting involved deeper with Kelly and whatever was going on wasn't exactly high on her list of things to do. Not to mention it wasn't smart.

But on the other hand, she looked contrite. Really sorry for what happened in the past and the position she thought she'd put Alexis in. Kelly reminded her of the desperate and frightened women Ace Security helped every week. She wavered in indecision.

"When Chuck had his hand around my throat at the party, I was scared," Kelly told her in a soft voice, shaking with emotion. "I couldn't get any air in my lungs, and I thought he was going to kill me right there. I don't want that to be you."

It had *already* been her. When she was fourteen and the boys at school were beating her up, she'd actually thought at one point she was going to die. For the first time she felt a sort of kinship with Kelly.

"The gunshots scared me," Alexis told Kelly. "I might like some excitement in my life, but I think from here on out I'll stick with guys who are only a *little* on the wild side. The Inca Boyz are outside my comfort zone." It was mostly true.

"I'm not surprised," Kelly responded with only a small hint of hostility in her tone instead of the disgust Alexis had expected. "I didn't think you were the kind of chick who wanted to be a gang bitch. But seriously, you're not safe. Just hear me out. I'll tell you everything, and then you'll know what to be on the lookout for. We were friends once, right?"

Alexis's resolve wavered. They *had* been friends once. Best friends. Kelly pulling away from her and having her beaten up had hurt. Bad. But now she was as much a victim as anyone Ace Security helped . . . maybe more so. She gave in. "Okay, but I only have a little bit of time."

"This won't take long. Promise," Kelly said, smiling a bit lopsidedly at her.

Alexis waved at the doorman, who was now standing outside the door, his arms crossed, looking disapprovingly at Kelly. "I'll be back soon, Osman," she called out, letting him know she was all right.

He didn't respond and continued to look concerned as she turned the corner with Kelly.

Kelly didn't say much, but hurried down the street as if the hounds of hell were at her heels. Alexis thought how weird it looked for Kelly to be wearing sneakers. Not that high heels would go with her outfit, but she couldn't remember a day in high school when the other woman had worn anything other than the three-inch heels she loved.

They'd walked about three blocks, before Alexis asked, "Surely this is far enough?"

"We're almost there," Kelly reassured her. "I just wanted to make sure we weren't anywhere near your place. It wouldn't do either of us any good to be seen together."

Alexis silently agreed. She mentally reviewed the services she was going to tell Kelly about to help her get away from the gang, so she could start a new life.

They turned one more corner, and Alexis came to an abrupt halt. Standing in front of her were Chuck, Damian, and Dominic. Fucking hell.

Alexis immediately grabbed Kelly's good arm and pulled back the way they'd come, hissing, "Run!"

But Kelly didn't budge, only yanked her arm out of Alexis's grip and took a step back and away from her, smiling smugly.

Before Alexis could run, Chuck took hold of her bicep and hauled her toward an alley between two tall downtown buildings. She struggled and tried to twist herself away. She'd almost succeeded when Dominic took hold of her other arm. Now, between the two larger men, she was being dragged into the alley, her feet barely touching the ground.

"Let me go!" she exclaimed. "Kelly, what's going on?"

"Just doing my job, *friend.*" She sneered.

"But you said all that stuff about being scared and of being sorry about what you did to me. And you're all bruised up. I don't understand. You *let* them do that to you?" Alexis asked, cursing her short stature.

"Yeah, A-lex-is. It's called loyalty. Something you don't know dick about. You disappeared on us. We weren't done with you or your money. Not a smart thing to do," Kelly said with her eyes narrowed and her mouth tight. The hatred on her face was easy to read.

Alexis couldn't think straight. She didn't want to say anything that the Inca Boyz didn't already know, but she was in shock. It was hard to keep up with her own emotions, going from pity toward Kelly and wanting to help her to realizing that she'd just led her straight into a trap. One that could kill her. "Not done with me? I don't understand."

Obviously done with the back-and-forth, Dominic jerked her arm out of Chuck's grasp and slammed her hard against the brick wall next to him. Alexis felt her head bounce off the unforgiving surface, and she moaned in pain. She saw black spots in front of her eyes, but refused to pass out. There was no telling what would happen to her if she did. Especially with Chuck standing behind Dominic, licking his lips and looking pissed off and turned on at the same time.

"Money, bitch," Dominic growled, leaning into her. "My brother's been in jail long enough. He finally got a new attorney who has convinced a judge that he's not a threat to society. He's allowed out on bail, but we gots to get the money for him first. That's where you come in."

"I can get you whatever you need," Alexis said immediately, *more* than happy to give these assholes whatever they wanted, as long as they let her go. For once in her life she was glad she had money. She'd give it all over to the Inca Boyz if it meant she lived to see Blake again.

"Yeah, you will," Dominic confirmed in a scary growl. "But unfortunately for you, that's not where this is gonna end."

Alexis couldn't help the high-pitched whimper that came up her throat.

Dominic switched his grip from her arms to her neck. One hand wrapped around her throat much as Chuck had done to Kelly at the party and pushed upward until she was standing on her tiptoes trying to get away from him, to get air into her lungs, to no avail. He thrust his other hand under her tank top and squeezed her breast with an excruciating amount of force. His grip was so tight Alexis knew she'd be bruised. Her whimper turned into a choked cry.

"I don't know what the fuck you were doing with the Inca Boyz, but I'll find out before we're done with you. I have a feeling you were there under false pretenses, sugar. And I'll be needing to know what those were before we're done with you. We don't like snitches. Oh, and Chuck here says you're a cock tease. He gets first crack at that rich pussy before the rest of us get a shot. Then maybe, if we're satisfied, we'll see about letting you go on your merry way. Maybe."

Alexis tried to suck in a breath, but only got a sliver of air through the constriction around her throat. She felt someone cutting her purse off. She'd been wearing it across her body. She looked into the bottomless, unrelenting, and unsympathetic eyes of Dominic and knew without a doubt she'd be wishing she were dead before he was done with her.

Making the decision at that moment to do whatever she could to keep herself alive, Alexis went as limp as she could, making it seem as if the fight left her body. She'd learned a lot during her time with Ace Security. She'd pay attention, gather intel that she could share with Blake and Logan, and protect herself as much as she could.

Alexis stumbled as Dominic suddenly let go of her throat and marched her, with one arm twisted up painfully behind her back, toward a Cadillac parked nearby in the alley. Her arm felt like it was being ripped out of its socket, and she could do nothing but stumble alongside the man who held her life in his hands and pray she'd find a way out of this mess.

Damian popped open the trunk, and Chuck wrenched her from Dominic and threw her into the small space as if she was nothing but a sack of potatoes. She landed on something hard and cried out at the pain that radiated through her hip and down her leg. Before she could do anything, Damian slammed the trunk down, enclosing her in blackness.

Alexis lay still for a moment, trying to catch her breath and frantically trying to hear what was going on outside the car. She was happy she wasn't in the clutches of Chuck or Damian anymore and alone in the trunk. It gave her a chance to catch her breath and plan. Information was key to helping herself be rescued.

She heard the car doors opening and shutting, and could even hear the men and Kelly talking. Their voices were clear as they discussed which ATMs they could drag her to and how much money they needed.

Without hesitation, Alexis dug into her front pocket for her phone. She'd started carrying it in her pocket so she wouldn't miss a message or phone call from Blake. Thank God the phone hadn't been in her purse.

Knowing she couldn't say a word, as the gang members would hear her as easily as she could hear them, she prayed she'd get a signal inside the trunk and opened the text app. Her thumbs frantically flew over the keyboard, not sure how long she had. She ignored her typos, knowing it was more important to get as much information to Blake as possible.

She hit send as much as she could, hoping that the more dings he heard from the incoming texts, the sooner he'd realize something was wrong and would respond.

Alexis: im in trouble

Alexis: gang got me

Alexis: cant talk

Alexis: think theyre gonna kill me

Alexis: want $ for bail for Donovan

Alexis: kelly got me to follow her

Alexis: stupid

Alexis: sorry

Alexis: in trunk black cadillac

Alexis: going to atms

Blake: Where are you?

Alexis: not sure started about 3 blks from my apartmt

Blake: I'm on my way. I'm gonna find you

Alexis: im scared

Blake: I'm coming for you.

Alexis: Dominic said hed torture me

Alexis: wants to know why I was there

Alexis: should I tell him or no?

Blake: Play it by ear. If you think it'll help, do it. If you think he'll do something worse if you do, lie or string it out.

Alexis took a deep breath and tried to hold back her tears. God. She wasn't cut out for this. The car slowed.

Alexis: car slowing

Alexis: hiding phone in trunk

Alexis: dont text afraid they will hear

Blake: ok. ILY

Alexis's eyes filled with tears at Blake's last message. She used the light of the phone to look around the trunk, then shoved the phone deep into a pocket on one side that held a jack and something slimy.

The tears spilled over just as the trunk lifted. They were in another alley. Damian hauled her out and pulled her other arm up into the middle of her back, pulling on the tendons and muscles.

"Here's the deal. We're gonna walk around the corner and up to the ATM machine. You're gonna take out five hundred bucks without making a fuss. Don't signal to the camera, don't do anything but get the money. You hear me?"

Alexis nodded quickly. She hoped the more cooperative she was, the better they'd treat her. And the more stops they made, the more info she could give to Blake so he could hopefully find her.

"I'm serious, bitch. Don't do one thing wrong, or I'll put a bullet in your brain right here. Understand?"

"Yeah. I won't do anything. I swear," Alexis choked out between her tears.

"Let's go." Damian shoved her and she stumbled, trying to keep from falling. He handed her the ATM card he'd obviously gotten from inside her wallet and motioned for her to walk ahead of him. He walked two paces behind her as she hurried to the bank machine. He stood out of line of the camera, with one hand in his front pocket, the other behind him. Alexis knew he probably had a gun in his hand, ready to blow her head off if she did anything wrong. He didn't care that they were on a busy city street.

As calmly as she could, Alexis slid her ATM card into the slot and punched in her password. Why they didn't just get the code from her and use her card themselves, she didn't know, but she wasn't going to look a gift horse in the mouth. The more she was allowed out of the trunk and able to see where she was, the easier it would be for Blake and his brothers to find her. *Don't antagonize them. Do what they want as long as it doesn't get you hurt further.* Logan's words rang through her head. *Every situation is different. Sometimes it's better to fight, other times it's better to be compliant. It's up to you to read the situation and figure out the best course of action.*

The transaction was quick and painless, and within moments she had five hundred dollars in cash. She turned and walked right back to Damian and handed the money and the card over. He snatched them from her, grabbed her by the bicep again, and marched her back to the car, where the others were waiting. Once again, he shoved her into the trunk and slammed the lid. Before too much longer, they were once more on the move.

Alexis dug the phone out of the side pocket and clicked on the text app again.

Alexis: 5th and main atm

Blake: Good girl.

Blake: We're working on tracking your phone. How's the battery?

Alexis: half

Blake: Good. It should last awhile. Hang in there.

The car stopped again, and Alexis stuffed the phone back into its hiding spot. This time it was Chuck who opened the trunk. She flinched away from him as he reached for her. She much preferred one of the brothers. He grabbed the front of her tank top, his fingernails gouging four long furrows into her skin. Alexis shrieked as he yanked her out and shoved her to the ground. She landed on her hands and knees and flinched at the pain that tore through her as the cement scraped her skin. Her entire body hurt from the abuse it had received, but the adrenaline pumping through her body kept her from caring much.

"Get up, bitch. If you think that hurt, we're gonna have a whole heap of fun later." Chuck sneered, wrapping his hand around her wrist and hauling her upright until it felt like her bones would snap under the pressure.

He repeated the threats that Damian had said earlier and shoved her toward another ATM. She once again robotically removed five hundred dollars and handed it over as soon as she was out of camera range.

Chuck shoved her back into the trunk, but leaned down into her space when she was lying helplessly in front of him. He took her chin into his hand and squeezed her jaw so hard tears leaked out of Alexis's eyes. "No one fucks with an Inca Boy, sweet Alexis. Make no mistake, I'll be inside this sweet little body in every way I can be before the night is over. I'll take your cunt, your ass, and you'll take me down your throat. There's nothing I like better than seeing the panic in a slut's eyes as I cut off her air with my dick. I don't care what Donovan has ordered to be done with you. I'll come back when everyone else has gone and take what you owe me. You'll be *begging* for me to kill you by the time I'm done, but that would be too good for you. Dumb rich bitch." And with that he threw her head to the side and slammed the trunk.

Alexis sobbed once and bit her lip to keep the rest of her tears from escaping. For one, she didn't think she'd be able to stop if she got started, and for two, she didn't want to give Chuck and the others the satisfaction of hearing her lose it. As soon as she felt the car move again, she grabbed her phone.

Alexis: bank across from big sculpture

Blake: I know which one. You ok?

Alexis didn't answer. She wasn't okay. She was as far from okay as she could get. But telling Blake that wouldn't help her. She took a few big breaths and tried to regain control of her emotions.

She put the phone back into its hiding spot and waited for the next stop. She regretted the fact that she carried both of her debit cards, not to mention her credit cards. The gang could drive her from ATM to ATM for quite a while before she hit her maximum daily withdrawal amounts.

She refused to think she wasn't going to get out of this. Blake was trying to track her phone, and she was telling him where she was. She had to keep her mind on that rather than what was in store for her. Even if Blake and his brothers found her, what were they going to do against three gangbangers with guns? They'd kill the Andersons on sight.

The stop-and-go continued for four more stops. As expected, when she reached the daily limit for withdrawals on one card, they just moved to another. Between stops, Alexis reported her location as best she could to Blake, but the areas they took her to grew increasingly unfamiliar, until she had no idea where they were anymore. When she pulled out the phone after the last stop she was dismayed to see she only had one bar of service.

Alexis: one bar losing u

Alexis: stopped again

Alexis: dont know where we are

Blake: You hang on, Lex. Hear me?

Alexis: I love you

Blake: Don't do that. Don't you give up.

Blake: I mean it. I didn't find you to lose you now.

Blake: Logan is on his way. We're getting through the red tape to track you and I've got the entire Denver PD looking for you.

Blake: Lex?

Alexis: ok

Blake: Whatever happens, I love you. Nothing those assholes do matters to me. Stay strong.

Blake: I'm coming for you, sweetheart.

And that was it. Her phone moved out of range, and Alexis typed one last text, knowing it wouldn't be sent until they went somewhere that had service again. But since it seemed they were heading up into the mountains, she had no idea when that would be.

She once against shoved the phone deep into the side pocket, turned on her side, and tried to breathe deeply. Whatever Dominic and Chuck had in store for her wasn't going to be good. She read between the lines of Blake's text. He was saying that if she was raped, he wouldn't care. But *she* would. If she was violated, she wouldn't be the same person. The only thing she was thankful for was that Blake had shown her how beautiful making love could be. She wouldn't have rape as her first sexual experience.

When it came to that, though, she'd fight with everything she had. She wouldn't let those assholes do whatever they wanted with her. She was stronger than that. They might still violate her, but she wouldn't make it easy for them.

Chapter Sixteen

Blake swore as he combed the area where Lex had last said she'd been. It looked like they were taking her up into the mountains, as the second-to-last ATM had been in Golden. Alexis didn't recognize the last bank, and therefore couldn't tell him exactly where she was, which sucked. Blake drove around aimlessly, swearing when he couldn't find even one black Cadillac.

The thought of her being at the mercy of the Inca Boyz, especially Chuck, was eating at his soul. He could tell she was scared out of her mind, and Blake couldn't blame her. But she was hanging in there. Being strong as ever.

His phone rang, startling the shit out of him, but he clicked it on and heard Nathan's voice through the speakers in the car.

"Got her."

"Thank fuck," Blake breathed. "Where?"

"You're right—they headed up the mountain. They went up Route Six, headed for Clear Creek Canyon Park. How close are you?"

Blake swung a U-ey and went west so he could catch an exit. "How far?"

"Thirty miles or so," Nathan told him in a calm voice. "They're stopped. The signal is stationary."

"Dammit," Blake swore. "It's gonna take me too long to get there. Where's Logan?"

"He's about twenty minutes behind you, I think."

"The cops?" Blake asked more desperately.

"I called Ross, and he's getting a SWAT team together, but it could be more like an hour before they're on their way."

"Nathan," Blake choked out, clearing his throat and trying again. "Nathan, I can't lose her."

"You won't."

"They've got half an hour to torture her," Blake ground out.

"She knows you're on your way," Nathan said calmly. "She'll hang tough for you, Blake. Look, I don't pretend to understand what love is, but between Grace and now Alexis, I've gotten quite the education. I've had a front-row seat to your relationship for months now. She watches you under her lids as you work together, and anything you ask her to do she does. Not only because it's her job but because it's *you* who asks her. Because she loves you. Now that you've returned her affection? That woman is *not* going to give up now that she's finally got you. She's tough and I know she won't give up, so don't *you* give up on *her*. Don't you write her off. Hear me?"

Nathan's reprimand was just what Blake needed. His voice now firm and in control once more, he said, "Yeah, I hear you. Are there any shortcuts to get to where her phone is pinging?"

"No, but I'll tell the Denver PD that if anyone tries to pull you over, they'll have to chase you halfway up the mountain to do it."

"Thanks, Bro. I owe you."

"The fuck you do. Just keep me informed. Let me know when my future sister-in-law is safe."

Blake didn't even blink at his brother's words. He knew down to the marrow of his bones that he wanted to spend the rest of his life with Alexis. No matter what those assholes might do to her at the top of the mountain. He wanted her to wear his ring, wanted her to be his wife. With newfound determination to find her, he said, "Will do," before clicking off the phone and taking a deep breath. Then he concentrated on getting to Alexis. Nathan would take care of communicating with the cops and Logan. All *he* had to do was get to his woman.

Twenty-four minutes later, and after driving like a bat out of hell, Blake turned off Route 6 onto a dirt road. His stomach was rolling, not liking the fact that he was literally in the middle of nowhere. Glancing at his phone, he saw that he had no service. He couldn't even call Nathan and let him know he'd arrived.

Knowing every second counted, Blake parked his car in the middle of the dirt road, hoping it would slow down the gang if they tried to drive their way out of there. He grabbed the Glock on the seat next to him, made sure it was loaded, grabbed the two extra clips of ammunition he'd brought with him, and eased out of the vehicle. He closed the door quietly, and quickly walked toward the area where Nathan had said Alexis's phone last sent a signal.

Eight minutes later, Blake looked through the trees. He didn't want to chance getting too close to the group and alerting them to his presence. There were four people, Dominic, Damian, Chuck, and Kelly, staring at something on the ground.

They were talking, but he couldn't quite hear them. Blake frantically ran his eyes around the area, looking for Alexis. His heart nearly stopped when he didn't see her. Was she still in the trunk? Had they killed her and stashed her body somewhere? That didn't make sense, because why would they still be up in the mountains if they'd already killed her?

He crept closer until he could make out what the gang members were saying. It sounded like they were taunting someone.

"So you were trying to get information on the Inca Boyz to rat to the fucking Denver PD?" Damian scoffed. "That doesn't make sense."

"They already knew Margaret Mason hired us to take those pictures of her daughter and your brother. Their evidence against Donovan was weak. That's why he's getting out soon," Chuck added.

Dominic knelt down and stared at the small, dark shape on the ground in front of them. He shifted, blocking Blake's view of whatever was in front of him, and tipped the bottle he'd been holding in his hand for several seconds. "Keep drinking, slut," he ordered. "The drunker you get, the more you'll be willing to talk . . . at least if you know what's good for you.

"This is what happens to snitches, bitch," he continued in a low, controlled voice, which was scarier because it was so calm. "You'll sit out here and wish you were dead. I know Chuck here is dying to fuck you, but he'll wait two days or so. By the time he comes back, you'll beg to take his cock any way he wants to give it to you if he'll only give you a drink of water. Then he'll bury your fat ass again, and maybe, if you treat him real good, he'll tell the others where you are so they can come up here and fuck your face too."

Damian got down on his hands and knees and bent down until his face was only inches away from the dark spot on the ground. "You're nothing. Just a hole to fuck and a means to an end, just like every woman ever born. You'll die out here, a slow painful death, and you'll wish you never heard of the Inca Boyz."

Blake suddenly realized that the small dark blob on the ground was actually Alexis's head. The four gang members had somehow managed to bury her in the dirt up to her neck. Damian had been forcing her to drink vodka straight from the bottle, by pinching her nose shut until she gasped for air and had no choice but to swallow the alcohol he was pouring down her throat. Blake saw red, and everything around him seemed to slow down. He had no idea what they'd done to Lex before they'd buried her, but they'd regret ever laying one finger on her.

Whatever they'd done hadn't been easy. Damian had blood oozing out of his nose, Dominic was limping, and Chuck's lip was split. His Alexis had given them hell. She'd obviously fought back, and he was proud as he could be of her. She hadn't waited to be rescued and fought tooth and nail, against three men no less. He wouldn't let her down now.

Logan and the cops were coming, but they were too far away to be any help to Alexis and him, so Blake did what he had to do. He carefully took aim at Dominic's right leg and pulled the trigger. The shot hit true, and the man fell over with a yelp, holding his thigh.

"Mother*fucker*!" Chuck yelled, spinning in the direction the shot had come from and shooting wildly into the trees.

Using the techniques he'd learned in the army, Blake quickly and quietly moved twenty feet to his left and let another bullet fly, this time hitting Chuck in the shoulder, effectively cutting off his wild shots.

Damian, not being dumb, grabbed his brother off the ground and helped him to stand, then immediately made his way toward the Cadillac.

Chuck ran after the two men, holding his arm, swearing at the top of his lungs.

Kelly, apparently not as smart as the others, crouched down next to Alexis instead of trying to get away. She pulled a knife out and held it to Alexis's throat, looking around wildly for whoever had been shooting at them.

"Who's out there?" she yelled. "I'll fucking kill her if you don't get out here right this second."

"Come on, get your ass in the car, bitch," Chuck yelled to Kelly.

She ignored him, and Blake heard Dominic say, "Fuck her. She wants to stay up here, let her. Go."

The Cadillac's engine started up and within seconds was disappearing down the dirt road, leaving a cloud of dust in its wake. Blake didn't even flinch, but simply used the dust in the air to switch position among the trees, getting closer to Alexis and Kelly without breaking cover.

He had no concern about the men getting away. Nathan would track the car, because Alexis's phone was likely still inside where she'd hidden it, and his brother would let Logan and the cops know exactly where the gang members were. They wouldn't get far . . . not with two of them bleeding heavily from his bullets and not with his vehicle blocking the entrance to the highway. Both would at least slow them down.

All of his attention was focused on Kelly and Alexis right now.

Kelly grabbed a handful of Alexis's hair and yanked her head back, her knife pressed against her very vulnerable throat. Alexis was as defenseless as a newborn babe. Blake inched closer as Kelly ranted.

"I'll do it. I'll cut her from ear to fucking ear. Don't think I won't. Show your ass, whoever you are. You think you can get her out of this? I don't fucking think so. She's nothing. She's *nobody*. Just another rich bitch who thinks she can buy her way out of everything. Not this time. Not. This. Time! Dominic and Damian will get their brother out of jail, and then he'll find fucking Bailey. No one leaves him. Not even her. If she thinks she can get out of the gang that easily, she's delusional."

Blake had no idea what Kelly was ranting about, but he didn't really care either. All he cared about was Alexis. She was the only thing that mattered right now. He took careful aim and let out a deep breath, centering himself.

Kelly pressed the knife deeper into Alexis's skin until a trickle of blood fell from where the blade was cutting into her throat. Blake could barely see the blood with the mud caked on her body the way it was. "The Inca Boyz will rule Denver. Rich bitch and ex-girlfriends won't screw that up. No way, no how. We won't let them. We'll—"

Whatever she was going to say was lost forever as the .45-caliber bullet from Blake's pistol entered her forehead and came out the other side, splattering her brain matter across the dirt behind her. She fell backward with the force of the bullet, the arm holding the knife limp at her side, the blade safely away from Alexis's throat.

Blake was on the move before the echo had dissipated in the air around them. He fell on his knees beside Alexis's head and frantically started digging with his bare hands. It was a surreal experience to be able to see only her head . . . sitting on the ground as if it weren't attached to the rest of her body.

She blinked up at him as if she wasn't sure who he was.

"I'll have you out of there in just a minute, sweetheart. Hang in there."

"Blake?"

"Yeah, Lex. It's me."

"You're finally here?" It was more of a question than a statement.

Blake paused a moment in his frantic digging to run his dirty hand over her head and kiss her on the forehead. Both her eyes were almost swollen shut, and she had bruises on her face as well. There was a hunk of her hair lying next to where she was held captive in the ground, and there was a trickle of blood oozing down her neck from where Kelly had held the knife to her throat. He'd never been happier to see anyone in all his life. "Yeah, love, I'm finally here, and you're safe."

Her eyes closed—at least he thought they did—then they opened into slits again. "It's about time," she joked in a hoarse tone.

"Jesus, Lex," Blake breathed. "I love you so much. Only you would make a joke at a moment like this."

"I think I'm drunk again," she commented dryly. "Although this time I didn't do it to myself."

"Are you in pain?" Blake asked her, then said, "Shit, don't answer that, of course you are. Look at you."

"Surprisingly, I'm not really. Damian did me a favor. The vodka helped it not hurt as much when they hit me." Her words were extremely slurred, and Blake was worried the alcohol was masking more serious pains than he could see. "But I got in a few licks too. I did what you and Blake taught me. Went for their eyes and joints. I tried to run, but Chuck, that asshole, grabbed me before I could get too far."

Her head turned from side to side as if looking for someone. "Where's Kelly? You got her, right? She's dead? She's not faking it?" Alexis asked, not letting him comment on her previous statement.

"Kelly? Fuck yeah. She's dead."

"Good. Bitch. She totally sucked up to me. Made me feel sorry for her. And I stupidly fell for it."

Blake resumed his digging without comment. At that moment, he wanted to free her more than he wanted to get all the facts about what had happened to her. "Are you standing? Lying down? How far down do I need to dig? Can you move at all? Help me get you out?"

She audibly swallowed, then informed him, "I'm sitting. They handcuffed my wrists to my ankles so I wouldn't be able to dig myself out after they left. After I fought back, they weren't going to take any chances I'd be able to escape."

"Fuckers," Blake murmured under his breath in a hate-filled tone. "I should've shot them all in the head when I had a chance."

"Where'd you shoot them?" Alexis asked in a conversational tone, as if she was asking him what he wanted for breakfast or what time it was.

"Leg and shoulder. I didn't have time to get Damian, though." Blake grunted with exertion as he tried to move as much dirt as possible at a time. It flew behind him in clumps as he said, "Fucker ran like the coward he was."

"Are they getting away?" Alexis asked curiously, turning her head to look down the dirt road where the Cadillac had disappeared.

"No."

"It looks like they are to me. There's only one of you and there were four of them."

Blake stopped digging for a moment and looked Alexis in the eyes. "First, you were and will *always* be my first concern. I don't give a flying fuck about anything or anyone else. Second, I would do everything in my power to make sure those assholes go down so they couldn't ever hurt you again. And I'm not just talking a few years in the slammer for assault and kidnapping. Third, I told you we were tracking your phone, and it led me straight here. Nathan knows where they are because you left your phone in their car. Not only that, but Logan was right behind me, along with Denver PD SWAT. They'll be on those assholes before they can get five miles from here."

"Okay then," Alexis said calmly.

"Any other questions, or can I continue?" Blake asked, allowing a bit of humor to leak into his voice for the first time. He definitely wasn't happy with anything about this situation, but if Alexis needed him to lighten up, then he would. He'd follow her lead. Whatever she needed, she'd get. But first, he had to get her out of his damn hole so he could make sure she was in one piece.

"By all means, please continue," Alexis told him as if she was the Queen of England granting him a much-favored boon.

So he did. Digging for all he was worth, ignoring the dirt that caked under his fingernails and covered his clothes and not even feeling the twinges of discomfort in his arms as he worked. Just as Blake had removed enough dirt to reach her waist, he heard a car coming extremely fast down the dirt road behind him.

Standing and spinning so quickly he would've easily won a shoot-out in the old west, Blake had his pistol out and pointed toward the road in seconds. He wouldn't let anyone get near Alexis again. No fucking way.

As soon as he recognized the truck, Blake relaxed, shoving his pistol back into the holster at the waistband of his jeans. Logan jumped out of his vehicle and ran toward Blake, not even bothering to cut the engine. "What the motherfucking hell?" he bit out as he got close enough to see exactly what Blake was doing.

"Hi, Logan," Alexis singsonged. "Good of you to join the party."

Without another word Logan immediately dropped to his knees and joined Blake in digging. He raised an eyebrow at his brother in question.

Blake gritted his teeth and nodded.

The silent communication between the brothers would've made no sense to anyone else, but because the two men had been around each other enough growing up, and also in the last few months, they had no problem understanding what the other was suggesting.

"SWAT team has the other three at the entrance to Route Six. Your car is fucked, though. They slammed right into it as they came around the corner."

"Oh, your poor Mustang," Alexis cried. "We didn't even get to make love in the backseat."

Logan looked surprised at both her words and the fact that she was slurring them . . . again. He turned toward Blake for an explanation.

"Fuckers forced her to drink," Blake said, motioning toward the now-empty bottle of vodka lying nearby.

Logan nodded. He continued with his explanation of what went down between the gangbangers and the cops. "Chuck's in bad shape.

Between the gunshot in his shoulder and the fact he flew out the front window into your windshield . . ." Logan shrugged.

"And the other two?" Blake asked.

"Damian decided he'd shoot his way out."

"And?" Blake demanded, still digging.

"It didn't work," Logan deadpanned. "He's not going to be a problem anymore. He has a couple dozen holes in his body, and his brother didn't fare much better as he was sitting right next to him when the bullets started flying. I take it Kelly threatened Alexis?" Logan asked, tilting his head toward the obviously dead woman on the ground.

"Yup," Blake answered, without elaborating.

"Well, that's four gangbangers we don't have to worry about anymore," Logan said, telling his brother something that he already knew.

"You got any handcuff keys on you?" Blake asked his brother, concentrating on removing the last of the dirt from Alexis's almost tomb.

He knew Logan was looking over at him sharply, but Blake didn't take his gaze from what he was doing.

"No, but SWAT'll be here before too long," Logan told him.

Blake nodded and scooped out a large bit of dirt, uncovering Alexis's ankles . . . and her hands, which were cuffed to them.

"I can't feel my hands or feet. Dominic tightened the cuffs as much as he could," Alexis told them, sounding sleepy. "Are they still there?"

Blake immediately took her head in his hands and looked into her eyes. "Don't pass out, Lex. Stay with me."

She nodded, moving her head only a fraction of an inch.

"Help will be here soon. Can you tell me what they did to you?"

She shook her head, and her eyes pleaded with his. "I will. But not here. Not now. Please, just get me home."

"I'll get you back to your apartment as soon as I can, sweetheart, but first we'll be stopping at the hospital so the doctors can make sure you're all right," Blake reassured her.

But she shook her head more forcefully now. "No. I want to go *home. Your* home. I don't want to be sick in a hospital's toilet. It's bad enough to barf in my own!"

Blake's heart filled with love for the amazing woman in front of him. She was coated in dirt and mud—it literally covered her from head to toe. She'd obviously been beaten and emotionally tortured and was plastered to boot. Blake had no idea what else she'd been through, but she hadn't given up. Had obviously fought her captors to the end, forcing them to immobilize her to get her into the damn hole. And now here she sat, joking about her rescue, hands numb, feet too, and all she asked for was to go *home.* With him.

"I'll get you to *our* house as soon as I can, sweetheart," Blake reassured her.

"'Kay. Logan?"

"Yeah, Alexis?" Logan asked absently, trying to figure out the best way to get her out of the hole. They'd uncovered her, but with her wrists attached to her ankles, it would be extremely awkward to move her. She couldn't exactly lie on her back once they got her out, and there wasn't anywhere for her to sit. As much as he hated it, she was probably better off staying right where she was until they could get the cuffs off.

"Do you think Grace will go shopping with me soon?"

"What?" Logan blinked down at Alexis, surprised at her totally out-of-the-blue question.

"She has great taste in clothes, and I thought it would be fun."

"I'm sure she'd love that," Logan told Alexis honestly. "Maybe when you're back on your feet and not drunk as a skunk."

"Okay. Oh, and will you do me a favor?"

"Anything," Logan said immediately, impressed more with each passing second that the woman his brother loved was so calm.

"Tell Nathan her name is Bailey."

"Whose name is Bailey?" Logan asked, confused, looking at Blake for clarification.

Blake answered for Alexis. "Donovan's ex-girlfriend. He and Alexis have been trying to find out more about her. Kelly lost her shit and ranted about a chick named Bailey and how Donovan wanted her back."

Logan turned back to Alexis and said, "I will. But, Alexis, you can tell him exactly what Kelly said when he comes to see you in the hospital."

Alexis wrinkled her nose, then moaned a small sound, as it hurt her. "I don't like hospitals."

"No one does, sweetheart," Blake reassured her, running his hand over her hair in a gentle caress. He probably should've refrained, as all he was doing was smearing more dirt on her poor hair, but he needed to touch her. Reassure her.

"Am I gonna wake up puking again? I didn't like it last time. I think I'll like it even less, now that every part of me hurts."

Blake rubbed his thumbs ever so lightly against her bruised cheeks and tried to reassure her. "They'll do what they can to help you through the worst of the hangover, sweetheart. Try not to worry."

"Blake?"

"Yeah, Lex?"

"Will you make sure my parents know I'm all right?"

"Of course I will."

"Blake?"

He bit back the chuckle. "I'm still right here, sweetheart."

"I knew you were coming. I did what you and Logan taught me. It would've worked too, if there weren't three of them."

Lord, she was killing him. He didn't even know what had happened to her, but he knew without a doubt that she'd done her absolute best to stall and give him the time he needed to get to her. "I know you did. I bet you shocked the shit out of them when you tried to claw their eyes out."

She smiled as if remembering, then said in a low, confident tone, "Yeah. They weren't expecting me to fight back."

Blake opened his mouth to respond, but the sound of vehicles coming up the road interrupted him.

"The cavalry arrives," Alexis murmured. "It's about time. I could use a cheeseburger."

The men chuckled but kept a wary eye on the road, just in case it wasn't the SWAT members arriving.

But it was. Within ten minutes, Alexis was uncuffed, removed from the hole, and on her way back to Denver. She finally lost her battle with unconsciousness when she was laid flat on a backboard.

Logan stayed on the mountain with the rest of the police team and said he'd make sure Blake's vehicle, what was left of it, got towed back to the city.

Blake sat beside Alexis, his hand on her forehead, not willing to lose his connection with her. They were both filthy, but he didn't even notice. He was glad she wasn't conscious, as the ride in the back of the SWAT Humvee wasn't exactly smooth.

Two of the SWAT members were paramedics, and they'd done their best to clean some of the dirt from her and had gotten an IV with fluids into her vein. Blake had told them why Alexis smelled like a distillery, and they'd been reluctant to give her any painkillers, as they didn't want them to react badly with the alcohol that had been forced into her body.

They mentioned that the doctors might want to pump her stomach to try to get rid of any alcohol before it made its way into her bloodstream. Blake winced, knowing the next few hours weren't going to be fun for his woman.

Halfway down the mountain, Blake's phone vibrated with an incoming text . . . surprisingly, from Alexis. It was the last text she'd sent after losing connection earlier. They'd driven back into cell-tower range, and the text finally went through.

Alexis: no matter what ill hold on until you get to me ily

Blake didn't even realize he was crying until one of the SWAT members handed him a tissue, without a word. The faith Alexis had in him was almost frightening, but he silently made a vow to never let her doubt his love and devotion to her. Not ever. He'd spend the rest of his life making sure she knew how much she meant to him.

Chapter Seventeen

Twenty-four hours later Blake sat next to Alexis, in a hospital bed, holding her hand, while she spoke quietly to her parents. Nathan had called Brian and Betty Grant to let them know what was happening to their daughter. They'd known she was working with Ace Security, but not that she'd been doing undercover work to try to shut down the gang that had been involved in their son's drugging and blackmail attempt. At first they'd been upset, but then, obviously knowing their daughter, had simply been relieved she was all right, if not a bit proud of her role in taking down part of the gang.

Blake tuned out their conversation, instead concentrating on the feel of Lex's warm hand in his hand and the way she clung to him, even as she insisted her parents tell Bradford not to take a trip back to Colorado, that she was fine.

She'd had her stomach pumped, preventing her from experiencing the harsh aftereffects of too much alcohol. She still had a headache, but that was the least of her injuries.

She had bruises all over her, and she complained that just about every muscle in her body hurt. Her shoulders from having her arms wrenched up behind her, her head from smacking the brick wall when she'd first been taken, her ribs from where she'd been kicked, the muscles in her arms and legs from when she'd fought against the three men, and of course her wrists and ankles where the handcuffs had bitten into her skin.

Her face was puffy and swollen from the hits she'd taken, and she looked pretty horrifying, but she was alive. For Blake it was a gift, and as much as he wanted to hunt down Dominic, Damian, Chuck, and Kelly and kill them all over again for what they'd done to Alexis, he was content at the moment to have her back and relatively unscathed. He knew it could've been a lot worse.

The police, and Ross, were coming by so she could give her official statement. He and Logan had already told the cops what had happened from their perspective. At first they wanted to take Blake to the station for questioning because of Kelly's death, but luckily the SWAT officers had backed him up, explaining the cuts on Alexis's neck had come from the knife still in Kelly's cold grip. He'd still probably have to be questioned, but for now he was satisfied that his military reputation and the jobs Ace Security had done with the police department would work in his favor.

Alexis's pain was being managed by strong narcotics, and Blake was keeping an eye on her. He would be sure to press another round on her the second it seemed as if the other pills were wearing off. She'd experienced enough pain at the hands of the Inca Boyz; he'd be damned if she suffered needlessly now. No matter how tough she was trying to be. On the surface she seemed to be fine, but he could tell she was holding on by a thread. He didn't want her to have to relive what had happened to her, but he needed to know so he could help her get past it.

"Mom, Dad, I'm *fine*. Seriously. Blake is here and his brothers too. As soon as I'm released, I'm going back down to Castle Rock to stay with Blake for a while. He'll take care of me."

Mr. Grant eyed Blake for a long moment before commenting dryly, "So I guess you two are a couple then?"

Alexis rolled her eyes in exasperation. "Yeah, Dad. We're together."

The older man kept his intense gaze on Blake's for a long moment before he told him, "I don't expect to be woken up in the middle of the night again by a phone call telling us we need to get to the hospital to see our daughter."

Blake could more than read between the lines of the older man's words. In some ways, Lex's dad reminded him of his own. Ace Anderson had been gruff and not very demonstrative, but in his own way, he always let his sons know that he loved them.

"No, sir. Not if I have anything to say about it. Lex's brush with the gangs of Denver is over. I swear I'll keep her safe from here on out."

"Hey," Alexis protested. "What is this? Colonial America? Dad, I'm fine. Seriously."

Brian Grant held Blake's eyes for another moment, ignoring his daughter, then finally stuck out his hand. "Welcome to the family, son."

Blake shook Alexis's father's hand, without loosening his grip on Lex's own smaller hand, and nodded at the older man. Brian Grant's eyes flicked down to where Blake was still holding his daughter's hand, then back up. He nodded and finally smiled.

"Come on, Betty, we've been here long enough," he told his wife.

"But, Brian, we just got here."

He chuckled. "Honey, we've been here for over an hour. You need to call Bradford and tell him his sister is fine and not to make the trip back home, and I need to get into work."

"Okay, fine," Betty grumbled, standing up and leaning over Alexis. She kissed her on the cheek and stated, "Call me when you get to Castle Rock and get settled."

"I will, Mom. Thanks."

Blake heard Lex's huge sigh of relief when her parents finally left. She relaxed back onto the pillows and looked at him. "Thank you for not leaving when they got here. They can be a bit overwhelming, but it's just because they love me so much."

He leaned down and kissed her forehead and said, "I know, sweetheart. It's obvious how worried they were for you. You did good with them. Told them enough to let them know what happened, but not enough to worry them needlessly."

She nodded, then looked away from him toward the door and bit her lip nervously.

"You ready for this?" Blake asked quietly, running his thumb over the back of her hand.

"Honestly? No. But I know I need to get it done. The sooner I get it over with, the sooner I can get out of here and we can go home."

Blake loved that she so easily called his house *home*. "You don't mind Logan and Nathan being here when you give your statement to the cops?"

Alexis shook her head and looked back up at Blake and answered without hesitation. "No. Those assholes didn't do anything I'm embarrassed to talk about . . . per se. I'm not thrilled to relive it, but if anything that happened can help put the rest of the Inca Boyz down, I'm all for it. I'd rather only go through it all once, rather than have to tell the cops, then also tell your brothers. You know?"

"I do know," Blake reassured her with an easy smile. "Have I told you today how proud I am of you?"

Alexis smiled back at him. "Yeah, about three times already."

"How that I think you're amazing and beautiful and that I'm the luckiest man alive?"

She chuckled out loud at that. "Well, no, you haven't told me that today."

"Well, I think you're amazing and beautiful, and I'm the luckiest man alive."

"Whatever," she said with a small huff of laughter while rolling her eyes.

Blake was happy to see some of the pain recede from her eyes at his teasing. Miraculously, it seemed as if Damian and the others hadn't broken her spirit. Lex was still the innocent, passionate woman he'd come to know and love.

"Are you in any pain? Do you need a pain pill before the others get here?"

Alexis shook her head. "No, I think I'm okay. I'm just thankful I didn't wake up puking my guts out this time."

Blake didn't even smile. Lex knew the doctors had indeed pumped her stomach, but she'd been mostly out of it, so she didn't remember much of it. But Blake couldn't forget. He'd been able to stay by her side for most of her time in the emergency room, for everything but the physical exam she'd been given to make sure she hadn't been sexually assaulted. She'd been highly intoxicated, but luckily they'd been able to get enough liquor out of her so she didn't go into organ failure. They'd given her drugs to counter any nausea she might have when she finally awoke.

The amount of pain she'd been in when she had finally woken up had been hard to witness, but it had eased when the amount of alcohol in her blood was low enough for them to be able to safely give her pain medication.

"I'm glad too, sweetheart. As much as I didn't mind holding your hair back when you were sick before, I don't think I'd like to make a habit of it." Blake smiled down at her, teasingly, and was surprised at the serious look in her eyes.

"Thank you for staying with me, Blake. I know you probably have a ton of work to do at the office because of everything, not to mention dealing with the cops and all. I'm sorry you had to shoot Kelly. Not because I'm sad she's gone, but for *you*. It can't be an easy thing."

Blake moved so he was sitting on the mattress next to her. He braced his hands on either side of her shoulders and leaned in until his mouth hovered over hers, and he was staring into her blackened eyes. "I wish I could say that I feel remorse about taking another person's life, but I don't. You know why?" He didn't give her a chance to respond before he continued. "Because she was going to kill you. I didn't give a shit about anything but saving your life. Don't give it a second thought, Lex, because I'm not. Okay?"

"Thank you, Blake."

"You don't ever have to thank me for saving your life, sweetheart. I'd kill a hundred people fifty times over if it meant I could look into your beautiful brown eyes and kiss your pink lips."

She smiled, and he felt her small hands run up and down his forearms, but he didn't take his eyes from hers as she spoke. "I hope you don't ever have to even hurt anyone again for me, but if you do, thanks in advance for killing hundreds of people for me. I kinda like you, Blake Anderson, and you've spoiled me. I might not be up to fighting form yet, but I'll show you how thankful I am to be back in your bed later."

Blake leaned down and carefully and gently kissed her lips. The bottom one was split, and kissing had to be painful, but Alexis didn't even seem to notice. She opened her mouth under his, and her tongue came out to brush against his bottom lip. Blake pulled back before causing her any more pain.

He leaned back but didn't move his hands from caging her in. "If you need a break, just squeeze my hand, and I'll make sure the detective gives you some space. Okay?"

She nodded quickly. "Okay. But, I'm going to try to get through it as fast, and as thoroughly, as I can. To get it over with."

"Still. You need a break, just let me know and you've got it."

"Do you think I can sit in the chair?" Alexis asked. "I'd be more comfortable talking about it there."

"I don't see why not. As long as you're not in pain, I think it'd be fine."

Blake sat up and set about moving Lex from the bed to the large easy chair in the corner, the one he'd slept in the night before as he kept watch over the woman he loved.

Thirty minutes later, Alexis was telling the four men standing and sitting around her exactly what she'd been through at the hands of the Inca Boyz gang members. Logan was leaning against the far wall of the hospital room, his hands crossed over his chest, scowling as she spoke, obviously not happy with anything she was saying.

Nathan was sitting on the bed, taking notes as fast as she was speaking, even though there was a tape recorder sitting in front of her. He'd probably review every word she said several times just to make sure he didn't miss anything. Detective Ross was sitting in an uncomfortable hospital chair, jotting comments into a small notebook, and Alexis sat in Blake's lap in the big chair.

He wanted to be as close as he could get to her, and he hoped that maybe his warmth and caresses would make the entire thing easier.

"I wasn't going to make the mistake of getting into a car with Kelly," Alexis was saying, "But she said we could just go a little bit away from my apartment and talk. She sounded so sincere, and I actually felt sorry for her. She totally played on that. It was dumb of me, obviously. I know that now, but you weren't there. You didn't hear her."

It was Nathan who reassured her. "She somehow figured out the way to get to you was through your big heart. Don't ever apologize for that."

She smiled at him before continuing with her story. "But as soon as we turned that last corner, the others were there, and they stuffed me into the trunk before I could really say or do anything. Luckily, I had my phone in my pocket instead of my purse."

She shuddered, and it was all Blake could do to keep from cursing out loud himself. It *had* been very lucky. They all knew the situation could've turned out very differently if she hadn't been able to get in touch with Blake.

"We'll get the transcripts of your texts later, but you told Blake where you thought you were every time you stopped?" the detective asked. "How much money did you take out of your account?"

"Well, we stopped around six times, and I could only get five hundred out at each stop. But the last one didn't work for some reason. I'm not sure why. They wanted more, and I think they were going to keep me alive up there in the mountain until they had as much as they thought they could get."

The detective nodded. "What happened when you got to the burial site?"

Blake heard Alexis's loud swallow at the officer's terminology. It honestly *could've* been Lex's burial site if things had gone differently. They never would've found her grave if the gang had killed her and left her there. He ran his hands up and down Alexis's cold arms but didn't interrupt her as she began to speak.

"I could tell we were on a smaller road when we turned off. I was jostled around in the trunk, and I was scared that they would shoot me the second we stopped. Chuck opened the trunk and pulled me out. He wanted to rape me right there, but Damian stopped him."

"How'd he stop him?" the detective interrupted. "What exactly did they say?"

Alexis took a deep breath, then continued with her story. "Chuck shut the trunk and bent me over it. He shoved my head hard into the metal, and it hurt enough that he stunned me for a second. He stuck his hand up my shirt and was trying to undo my pants when Damian shoved him away from me. I fell sideways and landed on my hands and knees in the dirt, trying to get my bearings.

"I heard them yelling about the plan and Damian said something about how Chuck would have his turn when they were done with me. I wasn't going to hang around for that shit, so I took off. Chuck caught up to me and dragged me back. I managed to elbow him in the face, splitting his lip, but he didn't let go of me and hit me back. He was pissed that I'd made him bleed and thought when he'd hit me that he'd subdued me. He dragged me in front of Dominic, and before they could tie my ankles together or something, I did one of those side-kick things you guys showed me.

"I got Dominic's knee and—you were right—he immediately went down. Unfortunately, that only pissed his brother off. He grabbed me from Chuck and was shaking me like a rag doll, so I head butted him in the face. That really didn't please him, although I was happy I'd at least drawn blood. But he threw me to the ground, and they all kicked me a few times while Kelly cheered them on.

"Then Dominic pulled me upright by my hair, making sure to keep himself away from my feet and head, and Damian asked me what I was really doing hanging out with the Inca Boyz. I wasn't sure if I should tell the truth or not, so I tried to stick with the original story . . . that I just liked hanging out with bad boys."

She paused in her story for a moment, and Blake settled his hand on her thigh, squeezing her gently. She turned and gave him a small smile, trying to reassure him. Then she continued her heartbreaking story.

"Damian didn't believe me for a second and pulled out the bottle of vodka. He told me to drink it. I refused. He hit me a few times, and I still refused. He had Chuck kick my knees from behind, until I fell onto my hands and knees. Then he held the bottle to my mouth, while Chuck grabbed my hair and pinched my nose closed. They forced me to drink, until I was choking. Then Damian asked me again why I was so interested in their gang.

"They continued to force me to drink the vodka, until I was gagging. I knew they wouldn't stop until I told them *something*, so I relented and said that I was pissed at them for what they did to my brother. That seemed to amuse them, and they quit forcing the vodka on me and changed their game."

When she paused, the detective asked, "What'd they do next? How'd you get inside that hole?"

"I was pretty dizzy by that time. The alcohol went straight to my head. I don't know if it was because I was so scared and my heart was beating so quickly and it made it work faster or what, but they threw a shovel at me and told me to start digging. There was no way I was going to dig my own grave. I've seen way too many forensic shows to fall for that, so I pretended to be drunker than I really was and fell on the ground and made it seem like I couldn't get up. It pissed them off, Kelly especially. She came over and started kicking me and hitting me. I tried to use the shovel as a weapon, but my arms weren't working very well at that point, and the guys just laughed and let her do whatever she wanted while *they* started digging.

"I guess it was harder than they thought it would be, and they got tired pretty quickly. That's why it wasn't very deep. I think it was Dominic who got the idea to cuff my hands to my feet and to make me sit inside the hole. He figured with the way I'd fought them that if they didn't do something, I'd just dig my way out . . . which was smart, because I totally would've. I was getting worried that no one had shown up yet to help me, and the last thing I wanted was to be buried alive, so I made another run for it, but I tripped and Chuck easily caught me . . . again. He dragged me back to the hole by my hair and held me still and let Kelly take a few more shots at me. Then Dominic and Damian started in again. They kicked and punched me. My stomach, my face, my back. Chuck even took my breasts in his hands and twisted them as hard as he could. They wanted to know exactly who I was working with and what information I'd given them."

Alexis turned to Blake, and he almost cried at the look of shame in her eyes. "I told them everything, Blake. That I was working for Ace Security, and we were trying to get information about the gang to give to the task force so they could shut down their thug-for-hire business. I even gave them my PIN numbers and told them they could go back tomorrow and the next day and the next and take money from my accounts until they were empty. I'm sorry. I tried to be tough, but it hurt so bad. I didn't want them to bury me, and I was so scared."

"Shhhh, Lex. It's okay. You didn't tell them any big secrets."

Big tears welled up in her eyes and spilled over her bruised cheeks. "It hurt, Blake. It hurt so bad, and I just wanted it to stop."

Logan moved then and came over to where Alexis was sitting on his brother's lap. He turned her head with a big hand on the side of her face and looked into her tear-filled eyes. "You did nothing wrong, Alexis. When I was in the army, I was once captured by a group of Taliban soldiers. They were as surprised as my squad was to have been caught unaware. They didn't really know what they were doing, but they took great pleasure in beating us. I can tell you without a doubt that you held on longer with those assholes than some of the trained soldiers I was with. A few of them broke after only a few minutes at the hands of the terrorists. Do *not* feel bad. Not for a second. You hear me?"

"You were captured?" Alexis choked out, bringing a hand up to cover Logan's resting on her cheek. "Were you hurt?"

The fierce look on Logan's face gentled. "You remind me of Grace," he said softly. "More concerned about others than you are about your-self. Yeah, Alexis, I was hurt, but they didn't have us very long before a group of Delta Force soldiers came in under the cover of darkness and kicked some Taliban ass. Those guys killed every one of the terrorists without a sound. My point is you lasted longer under torture than some of the professional soldiers I served with. And you didn't have state secrets to blab like they did. I'm sure they already knew all about Ace Security because of Grace's connection to me. Cut yourself some slack . . . okay?"

Blake looked at his brother with narrowed eyes. He hadn't known Logan had been captured by terrorists and tortured. It wasn't something they'd ever talked about, but it looked like they'd be having a seri-ous conversation about how they'd spent the ten years apart after high school sooner rather than later. The three brothers hadn't been close, but he hated that he hadn't known that about his own brother.

Blake's eyes cut to Nathan, and he saw the same confusion and concern in his other brother's eyes. Yeah, the three of them definitely needed to have a heart-to-heart conversation.

Alexis nodded at Logan, and he leaned into her and kissed her forehead gently, before standing up and resuming his stance against the far wall.

She turned to Blake and looked tearfully into his eyes.

"You need a break, sweetheart?" Blake asked.

She shook her head, then said, "I do need a tissue, though."

Blake smiled and leaned over and took the tissue the detective was holding out. He tenderly wiped the tears from her bruised cheeks and under her eyes, before handing it to her so she could blow her nose. She crumpled the white tissue in her hand and took a deep breath before bravely continuing her harrowing story.

"Anyway, when I was crying so hard I couldn't talk anymore, they finally believed that I'd told them the truth. Damian and Chuck forced me to sit and held me still as Kelly and Dominic put on the cuffs. They squeezed them so tight I knew I wouldn't be able to slip out of them. Then they lifted me and dropped me into the hole. I swear I thought I'd broken my tail bone, it hurt so badly. But I refused to scream, not wanting them to see how freaked out I was. They shoved all the dirt back into the hole. Telling me all the while that they were going to leave me there. That animals would come and peck at me and try to eat me.

"Chuck wanted to fuck my mouth, but Dominic wouldn't let him, thank God. Of course he didn't care about me. They all knew Chuck was going to come back and do it anyway after they got back to the city. They kicked dirt in my face, and then they tried to get me to swallow more of the vodka. They were going to leave me there and come back in a few days, when I would be desperate for water, when you shot at them, Blake. I'd never been so glad to hear anything in my entire life."

"What'd they say about Bailey?" Nathan asked quietly from his seat on the bed.

Alexis bit the side of her lip that wasn't split and tried to remember.

"Kelly was really pissed off that Donovan still had a thing for this Bailey person. She ranted that when Donovan got out of jail, she thought he'd go looking for her. I got the impression that the woman ran away from the gang and that he was pissed she left him."

"Did she say what Bailey's last name was?" Nathan asked, looking intensely into her eyes.

Alexis shook her head. "I can't remember anyone saying her last name, sorry."

Blake spoke up then too. "She didn't say her last name, Bro. Sorry. But having her first name should make it easier to track her down, yeah?"

Nathan's nose was buried back in his notebook and he was scribbling things down. "Maybe, maybe not. If the woman was smart, and truly wanted to get away from Donovan, she got as far away from Denver as possible. She's probably long gone by now.

"Is there anything else you want to add about what happened or what was said?" the detective asked Alexis.

She shook her head slowly but stared the detective in the eye, her own eyes narrowing and her mouth tightening into a thin line. "Just that I know without a doubt that Blake and Logan and even the SWAT guys saved my life. If Blake hadn't shot Kelly, she wouldn't have hesitated to slit my throat. She hated me. I was pretty drunk from all the alcohol they made me drink, but if you're thinking about charging Blake or Logan with murder, I'll get my family involved and hire the best lawyer Denver has to fight the charges. He *saved* me."

Blake squeezed Lex's hand in support, touched that she was defending him so staunchly. It was unnecessary but made him love her all the more.

When the detective didn't protest or argue with her in any way, she continued in a less fierce tone. "All Damian and Dominic were interested in was getting cash for Donovan's bail and hurting me."

"We've got the money you took out of your accounts," the officer told her. "It was in Damian's pocket. We'll get it back to you, but it might be a while, as it's evidence."

Blake cut in and asked, "Will Donovan still be able to make bail?"

Now the officer looked anywhere but at Blake or the other men in the room. "It's possible. He didn't personally kidnap and hurt you. There's no evidence that he ordered anyone to kidnap Alexis either. His lawyer will claim that it was his brothers who acted on their own out of their love for their brother. So unfortunately, yeah, if his friends can get together enough money, he'll probably still be able to make bail."

"Fuck," Logan swore from against the wall. "So that means that not only will Alexis still have to look over her shoulder, but Grace will too. Just fucking great."

"Not necessarily," the detective said quickly. "Donovan's brothers are dead, and there's dissention in the ranks. He'll have his hands full trying to keep his gang together. He knows we're watching him carefully, and it's unlikely that he'll try to do anything against either Miss Grant or your wife. I think it's a better possibility that he'll go after this Bailey person, whoever she is."

"I'm not willing to take that chance," Logan growled. "From now on, you'll pass on any information about anything that has to do with the Inca Boyz. I will protect my family and my brothers' families from any threat. No matter how big or small."

"I understand," the officer said with a grim look on his face. "And I can't blame you. I'll talk to the chief and make sure he knows the seriousness of the situation. If and when Donovan gets out of jail, I'll make sure you're notified. We'll keep our eyes on what's left of the Inca Boyz and let you know if it looks like they're trying to regroup and come after your women."

"We'll keep our own feelers out as well," Logan told the man.

"No more undercover ops," the detective ordered.

"No, we're done with that," Logan assured him. "We'll use technology to get the information we need this time." And with that, Logan pushed away from the wall and held out his hand to the officer. "Thank you for coming to the hospital to interview Alexis. If you need to get a hold of her, she'll be staying with my brother. You can always contact any of us at Ace Security as well."

They shook hands and the detective turned to Alexis and said, "Thank you for your time, Miss Grant. I hope you feel better soon."

She nodded at him, but didn't say anything.

Blake was content to let his brother see the detective out. He felt Lex melt against his chest and heave a huge sigh. "Do you need another pain pill?" he asked her quietly.

"Yeah. I think so" was her quiet answer.

Blake carefully stood, making sure not to jostle Alexis in his arms, and brought her to the bed. Nathan moved, and Blake gently set her down.

"You'll stay?" she asked, grabbing onto his arm with a surprisingly firm grip.

"Of course. I'm not going anywhere," Blake reassured her. "Relax, sweetheart."

"Sorry . . . I just thought . . . never mind what I thought."

Blake kissed her lips softly and felt his muscles relax as she became less tense under him. "Nathan will stay here with you while I go find the doctor and see if she thinks you'll be able to be released today."

"Okay. Thanks, Blake. For being here today, for helping me, and for not thinking badly of me for what I did."

"I could never feel badly of you for surviving, sweetheart. Put it out of your mind. I'll be back soon."

Her eyes were closed even before he left the room. Blake wanted to get Lex home, where she could heal and be around people who loved her. The thing with the Inca Boyz might not be done, but *her* role in the entire situation certainly was.

Chapter Eighteen

Alexis lay in bed with Blake at his house and sighed. "You're being ridiculous."

"Lex, a week and a half ago you were in the hospital. We have the rest of our lives. There's no need to rush."

"But you're driving me crazy, Blake. I can't stand it anymore."

"You're not the only one suffering. But I won't hurt you. Not for anything. We can wait another week until you're not in any pain."

"If you think I'm waiting another week to have an orgasm, you're insane," Alexis stated bluntly. "I feel fine. Yeah, I still look like a poster child for an abused woman, but the bruises barely even hurt anymore. All I can think of is you. I need you, Blake. I need to know you still want me. That what I did and what I told those assholes hasn't changed anything about our relationship."

Blake immediately rolled until she was under him. He caged her body with his and held her head in his hands. The intense look in his eyes said more than he ever could with words. "I love you, Alexis. Nothing that has happened over the last week or so has changed that. No, wait, I think it's made me love you *more*. I just don't want to hurt you."

"You won't," Alexis said with confidence. "I'm not saying I'm up for any crazy bed gymnastics, but I need you to make love to me. Please. For a while I thought that I'd never see you again. I *need* this, Blake. I need your arms around me, to feel you so deep inside me I don't know where I end and you begin. I'm begging you."

"You'll tell me the second if anything I do hurts," Blake ordered gently, giving in.

Alexis relaxed under him, knowing she was finally going to get what she wanted. What they both *needed.* "Of course."

Without another word, Blake rolled over and removed his boxers and his shirt. He turned back to her and helped her push the boy shorts she'd been sleeping in off her legs and tenderly unbuttoned each of the six or so buttons down the front of the huge sleep shirt he'd bought her when she'd gotten out of the hospital. It had hurt for her to raise her arms over her head, so the button-up shirt was a must.

He eased it off her shoulders and leaned down to kiss each and every bruise on her battered body. They were mostly yellow and green by now, but he didn't miss a one. The sides of her breasts where Chuck's cruel hands had squeezed, the shoe print Damian's shoe had made on her side, the mark on her neck where Kelly's knife had nicked her.

By the time he made it back up to her mouth, Alexis was squirming under him with desire. The cut on her lip was mostly healed, and when Blake tried to be gentle, Alexis ignored his efforts and thrust her tongue into his mouth aggressively.

Loving that her actions made him lose a bit of his usual tightly held control, she reveled in the feel of his hard cock brushing against her belly as his hips thrust forward. She could feel his excitement against her skin, and she widened her legs and brought her knees up, bringing him closer to her body. Pulling her head back just enough to whisper against his lips, she said, "Now, Blake. I'm so ready for you." Alexis tilted her pelvis up toward him.

One of his hands feathered down her side and under him, searching for her center. He ran his fingers through her wet slit once, then twice, testing her readiness, before his hand came back up and planted itself next to her side.

"You're soaked, sweetheart," he commented unnecessarily before shifting his hips. He was so hard he didn't need to guide himself into her. The mushroom head of his cock found just where it needed to be, and he ever so slowly eased himself all the way inside her until their bodies were as close together as two people could be.

Then he made love to her. Slow and steady, without taking his eyes from hers.

Alexis knew he was looking for the slightest hint of discomfort from her, but he wouldn't find it. She was stiff and sore in places, but nothing would make his loving her uncomfortable. Their lovemaking was sweet and slow, and Blake took his time bringing them both right to the edge.

"Please, Blake. I need . . ." Her voice trailed off as his hand once more moved down her body between them. His hips pulled back just enough to give himself room, and he fingered her clit. Hard.

Her hips bucked up against him, and she moaned, exploding almost immediately at his familiar touch.

As soon as her muscles squeezed his cock, Blake groaned in return and planted himself as far inside her as he could and let himself go.

Alexis had barely recovered when Blake rolled them, putting her on top of him so he wouldn't put any of his weight on her still-recovering body. She lay boneless on top of him, feeling complete for the first time in almost two weeks.

"What are your thoughts about becoming a partner in Ace Security?" Blake asked in a low, tender voice once he'd recovered. "I talked to Logan and Nathan, and they agreed that we need more help in the office. I've been working more and more on jobs outside the office, and while Nathan is excellent at accounting, he's not as good at answering phones and e-mails. And none of us is good at making sure we don't run out of supplies. You've also really gotten good at digging into social media and researching abusers and finding out all the information about them they think they're hiding but really aren't."

Alexis's eyes popped open, and she lifted her head to look down at Blake. He was still semihard inside of her, and she'd just had the best orgasm she'd had since her ordeal, and he was talking work?

"You want me to buy into Ace Security?"

"Well, not buy. It'd be more of a gift. See, the way I figure it, as my wife you have access to everything I have anyway. But all of us have seen how much you love the research side of the business. We'd pay for you to take some classes if you wanted, and there's an excellent computer guy, who consults with the navy and army, who would probably be willing to train you . . . if you're interested."

"Uh," Alexis stammered, not sure she'd heard him correctly.

He took her statement to be one of uncertainty and hurried to keep talking. "I don't think you really want to be out in the field, and I know I really don't want to put you in any kind of position like you were in with the Inca Boyz, so this seemed like a good compromise. I love working with you, and we could see each other all the time, but you'd be safe."

"As your wife I'd have access to everything you have?" Alexis asked softly.

Blake smiled, and his face gentled. "Yeah, sweetheart. I know it's not much. Most of my money is sunk into this house and the business, but I'll work my ass off to give you everything your heart desires."

"I've got money, Blake."

"And I don't want a penny of it. I want to provide for you, not live off the money you got from your parents. Give it to charity, save it for our kids and for our nieces and nephews—give it all to charity—but I don't want or need it. In fact, I'm going to insist on signing a prenup that says I'll never get one penny of that money if you leave me."

"If I leave you?" Alexis asked, confused. Her head was spinning.

"Yeah, Lex. Because there's no way in hell I'll *ever* leave *you*. I hope you won't decide one day that you married a bum. I know you're so much more than I'll ever deserve, but I'm selfish enough to take you any way I can get you."

She smiled, her heart overflowing with love for the man under her. "You're stuck with me, Blake Anderson. You don't ever have to worry about me leaving or me deciding I want another man. And everything you said sounds wonderful except for one thing," she teased.

"What? Name it and it's yours," Blake told her seriously.

Alexis leaned down and put her lips next to his ear and whispered, "You haven't asked me to marry you."

She was flipped in an instant, noticing that Blake was still being very careful not to hurt her in any way. He'd slipped out of her while they'd been talking, but as she lay under him, she felt his cock harden against her once more. He shifted and eased himself back inside her body once more. Then he braced himself up on his hands, and she curled her fingers around the forearms she lusted over and gazed up at him, love in her eyes.

"Alexis Grant, will you marry me? Will you spend the rest of your life in my bed, in my heart, having my babies if we're so blessed, and working side by side with me to make the world a safer place?"

"Absolutely," she answered immediately, without a trace of doubt in her voice.

"I have a ring," Blake told her seriously. "It's in the other room. It was my grandmother's. My *dad's* mom," he clarified. "She never liked my mother and refused to let Ace give it to her when he proposed. My brothers said they didn't mind if one day I gave it to the woman I wanted to marry. It's old, so it might not be your thing, but I thought I'd propose with it and let you pick out what you wanted if you said yes."

"*If* I said yes?" Alexis asked in disbelief, furrowing her brow up at him. "Blake, I've loved you from the second I laid eyes on you. I'll love your grandmother's ring. Promise. But we have another problem now."

"We do?" Blake asked, looking both elated and stressed at the same time. "What?"

"We can't tell our children, your brothers, and my parents that you proposed to me when we were both naked and in bed. You're inside me and hard again for goodness' sake. We'll have to make something up."

He chuckled, and Alexis could feel him jerk inside her. She squirmed, rubbing her clit against him in the process. Then did it again after feeling how good it felt.

"How about this? I'll get down on one knee in the office tomorrow when Nathan and Logan are there, and maybe even Grace too. We'll pretend it's the first time I asked. Will that work?"

Alexis pushed on Blake's shoulder and said, "I want to be on top."

In an Olympics-worthy move, Blake rolled, keeping them connected until Alexis was on top of him once more.

"Yeah, that's perfect. God, you feel good," Alexis said, sitting up on top of him, noticing that Blake made sure to keep a strong grip on her waist to support her.

"What about Ace Security? You want to work there? Be our office manager and all-around social media expert?" Blake asked, holding her still against him.

"Yes. Of course. Please, Blake, let me move," she begged.

"Slowly, sweetheart. Don't hurt yourself," he ordered.

"I'm not feeling any pain, promise," Alexis told him, looking down at his muscular chest, then flicking them to his forearms. Her eyes dilated when she saw his muscles flexing as he held on to her.

"Alexis Anderson. I like the sound of that," Blake told her, licking his lips.

"Me too," she agreed.

"Make love to me, my beautiful fiancée."

"With pleasure," Alexis told him, losing herself in the love she saw in his eyes.

~

Nathan stared in frustration at the computer screen. He knew how to make numbers do whatever he asked them to, but he wasn't as good at finding information on the net. And for some reason, he needed to find the mysterious Bailey. He didn't know why—only knew with an increased urgency that she was in trouble.

She might be a hard-ass gang bitch, and might be hip-deep in another gang in some other city, but Nathan didn't think so. Except he couldn't find anything about her. Not her last name, not what she looked like, and not where she was or why she'd left the Inca Boyz.

It was frustrating as hell. After another thirty minutes, he finally turned off the computer and made his way out of the offices of Ace Security to his crappy Ford Focus. It was old, but he loved it . . . had even named it Marilyn, after the iconic movie star. Lately she'd been more and more finicky, and tonight, it took two tries, but the engine finally turned over, and he made his way toward his small apartment near the interstate.

Ace Security had other jobs they needed to concentrate on, now that the Inca Boyz investigation was over, but Bailey was always in the back of Nathan's mind. Hopefully once Alexis started taking some classes and working for the company, she'd be better at digging up information and could find her. If Donovan really was looking for his ex-girlfriend, she'd be much better off if Ace Security found her before he did.

Five miles away, on the far side of Castle Rock, in a small ramshackle house tucked into the mountainside, Bailey Hampton sat at a rickety table, trying to balance the spreadsheets in front of her. After another hour she closed her eyes in relief. She was making it. On her own. Without using money her gang-leader boyfriend had given her, which he'd gotten from who knows where. She definitely wasn't in the clear, but her job at the auto body shop was keeping a roof over her head and food on the table. For now it was enough.

Pushing back from the table, she padded into the other room and stood in the doorway, looking down at the small bundle on the bed against the wall. Joel slept, his face relaxed and open, with none of the stress he'd had because of her and choices she'd made in the past. He'd finally begun to look and act like a nine-year-old should, instead of being Donovan's personal slave. Rubbing her hands over the tattoos covering her arms, Bailey swore she'd do whatever it took to keep her little brother safe from the likes of Donovan and the Inca Boyz. She wouldn't allow him to be sucked into that world, not ever again. It had taken her quite a while, but she'd seen for herself how evil it was . . . and nearly lost her soul and her brother's in the process.

The night she'd walked in on Donovan showing Joel a disgusting porn movie on the computer while holding a joint up to her little brother's lips had been an eye-opener for her. She realized that if she didn't do something right then, she'd lose Joel to the Inca Boyz and Donovan, and he'd become as big of a loser and a thug, or bigger, than the men she'd spent a lifetime around.

She didn't want that for him. She was responsible for him, and she'd do whatever it took to allow him to grow up safe and happy, not surrounded by drugs, loose women, and guns.

She'd planned their escape for a few weeks, and it had been a close call. Bailey still didn't feel safe—she figured she never would again—but every day she spent away from Denver and the gang culture was a good day in her eyes. She'd never rely on or trust a man to care about her and her little brother ever again.

Men were nothing but trouble, and she'd never met a guy in her entire life who cared about anything other than pussy, money, and looking out for himself. She didn't think they even existed. Nope. She and Joel were doing just fine on their own.

Acknowledgments

Thank you to my readers. Without you, without your trust, there would be no stories. I appreciate your willingness to follow me into every new book with characters old and new.

Amy, you are the embodiment of the word *strong*. I admire you for your generosity, smarts, compassion, and stubbornness. I want to be you when I grow up.

Beth, thank you for reading my *really* rough drafts and telling me they're great, even when I know they need a lot of polishing.

Melody, thank you for taking my words and making my stories better. No writer gets where she is without an awesome editor standing behind her.

And to Maria and Anh, thank you for taking a chance on me. There are thousands of authors out there who would love a chance to write for Montlake, and you choosing me is humbling.

About the Author

Photo © 2015 A&C Photography

New York Times, USA Today, and *Wall Street Journal* bestselling author Susan Stoker debuted her first series in 2014, following shortly thereafter with her SEAL of Protection series. These tales of romantic suspense solidified her love of writing and of creating new stories for her readers to explore. She has a heart as big as her current home state of Texas, but this all-American girl has also lived in Missouri, California, Colorado, and Indiana. She's married to a retired army man who now gets to follow *her* around the country. Visit her at www.stokeraces.com.

Connect with Susan Online

Susan's Facebook Profile and Page

www.facebook.com/authorsstoker

www.facebook.com/authorsusanstoker

Follow Susan on Twitter

www.twitter.com/Susan_Stoker

Find Susan's Books on Goodreads

www.goodreads.com/SusanStoker

Email:

Susan@StokerAces.com

Website:

www.StokerAces.com